Harry Selwyn's

Last Race

Tony Bianchi

PARTHIAN

Parthian, Cardigan SA43 1ED
www.parthianbooks.com
First published in 2015
Adapted by the author from his Welsh-language novel,
Ras Olaf Harri Selwyn (Gomer Press, 2012)
© Tony Bianchi 2015
ISBN 978-1-910409-69-5
Editor: Susie Wild
Cover design by Dean Lewis
Typeset by Elaine Sharples
Printed and bound by Gomer Press, Llandysul, Wales
Published with the financial support of the Welsh Books Council
British Library Cataloguing in Publication Data
A cataloguing record for this book is available from the British Library.

'If we are going to sin, we must sin quietly.'
Eric Griffiths-Jones, Attorney General, Kenya 1957

1

Harry Selwyn v. The Mouse (1)

I saw a mouse yesterday. Little black smudge of a thing, skitting about on the kitchen floor. Just caught a wee flick of him through the corner of one eye as I was taking my new trousers out of the bag. Where did you come from? I thought. Because he was as quiet as a leaf. And not a hole in sight. Nothing. I got down on my knees, just in case. Ran a finger along the skirting. They say a mouse can squeeze through a wedding ring if he gets his head in first, because he's all hair and bone, your mouse. So I ran a finger right along from one end to the other. Lay down on my belly, too, to get my arm under the dresser. Not a crack. Couldn't slot a postcard through it. And a mouse is fatter than a postcard, whatever they say. I went and checked the other side. Pulled out the fridge. Shifted the bins. Not a crack there either. Black he was, the mouse. And quick as spit. Woosh! And he was gone.

And where did you go then, you little devil? Now there's a question. So I stood by the back door, holding my breath, waiting for the scritch-scratch, the nibble, the squeak. Five minutes I stood, stiller than a statue, until I almost believed I wasn't there myself, that I'd abandoned ship and left the mouse to it. But then I began thinking, damn and blast, the little devil's stood there doing the same as me. He's behind the cooker, twiddling his paws, saying to himself, Well, I'll hang on here for a bit, the old feller'll run out of patience soon, he'll have to go for a Jimmy Riddle. Because your mouse is as cute as a monkey even if he is just a bit of fluff on a twig.

He was right, too. No, I didn't run out of patience. I didn't have to go to the toilet, either. But I saw Bob and Brenda's

1

light go on next door and thought, best get these trousers on now, before they see me. Because that's what I was in the middle of doing, trying on my new trousers.

Beti came back from her sister's then and I told her, 'Beti, we've got a mouse. A little black devil. Just saw him running across the floor.' So she went to see for herself. Checked the skirting, same as me. Looked behind the fridge, too. 'I closed the cupboards,' I said, to show I was taking it seriously. But she looked there as well. She even looked in the plastic bag, even though it had had nothing in it but my new trousers, and it hadn't been in the kitchen a full ten minutes.

'No droppings,' she said.

And that was that. No droppings, no mouse. I had a mind to say, Well, he's only just come into the house, he's not had time to do his business yet. But Beti was looking at my trousers by then and shaking her head and asking me to turn around and shaking her head again. 'They're halfway up your arse, Harry!' So I let out the belt a bit and I thought it was just the job but Beti said she could still see my socks. Might have been true, too. Can't say otherwise. A man doesn't see himself, not properly, not when he's looking down. Which is why it's handy to have your wife there to keep you right. I shut up about the mouse then, because she'd got me vexing about the trousers.

'I'll take them back tomorrow,' I said. 'Get another pair. Longer in the leg.'

She was happy with that. Said she liked the style. The herringbone. 'Longer in the leg. That should do.'

But she was wrong. There was a mouse. There is a mouse. He's in the bedroom. I can see him now, up by the window. I'm lying in bed, the first light is leaking through the gaps in the curtains, and there he is, just a smudge caught in a sunbeam. Woosh! And he's gone. Which makes me think he's not a mouse after all, because how can a mouse get up there? He's a moth, that's what he is. Big bastard as well. Small for a mouse, but bloody big for a moth. Quiet, mind you. Quiet as a feather. None of your flip-flap against the window, like you normally get. And quick. Woosh! And he's away. Can they do that, moths? Can they keep as quiet as a feather? Can a mouse climb? If he gets his little claws into the curtain, into the hem, maybe, where there's stitches, can he pull himself up?

Beti would know. But I'm not going to wake her up now, am I? Not this time of the morning, not to ask her about a mouse. About a moth.

2

Friday 21 May 5.30am

When Harry Selwyn wakes at half past five in the morning and feels last night's beer pressing on his bladder and mistakes a floater in his eye for a moth, his wife, Beti, is already dead. Without warning, and quite silently, she has succumbed to what her death certificate will describe as acute myocardial infarction. He doesn't know this. Indeed, he has no inkling that anything is wrong. On the face of it, this might seem surprising. Beti, afflicted by asthma since childhood, is a restless sleeper. She has coughing bouts at irregular intervals throughout the night, is frequently short of breath and, when she finally settles, snores loudly. When her chest tightens really badly she will reach for her inhaler: its distinctive *Psh... Psh ...* tells Harry that the night is going to be a particularly bad one.

3

Today, no sound comes from her bed, no movement. You'd think that Harry might notice these absences, that he might be curious as to why this morning should be different from all the other mornings of their forty-three years together, that he might at least turn briefly to see whether his wife's eyes are open, and then whisper, 'Beti? Beti? You awake?' But he does nothing. He lies on his back, trying to focus on the strange moth that has just flown past the bedroom window. He hears a seagull bark outside. The moth returns. Just a brief flutter. He blinks. It disappears again. He thinks about last night.

Beti couldn't go to the Mason's Arms last night to have a drink with Joe, to wish his wife Nansi a happy birthday. When she said, 'I'm a bit short of breath, Harry, you'd best go without me,' he was disappointed. He'd have preferred her to be there with him, keeping the conversation alive: Harry isn't good at trading stories, even with his best friends. Nor does he feel comfortable trying to parry the banter which they invariably direct at him on such occasions. When your wife's there, he thought, people are more cautious. Especially when she's a little reticent herself, and on the fragile side, her chest wheezing, her inhaler at the ready. She would have deflected attention, lessened the embarrassment.

Beti was already in bed when he got back. This was his own fault: he'd stayed out longer than he'd intended, he'd had a lot more attention than he'd expected or would ever have sought. But Joe is his oldest friend and his wife was celebrating her seventieth birthday, so it would have been churlish to leave early. In addition, and perhaps more to the point, Sam Appleby of the *Gazette* turned up and Harry didn't have the arrogance to say 'No, can't answer any more questions tonight, sorry,' as though he were a footballer or a politician.

And who can tell, after the fourth pint, whether Harry hadn't actually begun to enjoy himself a little. When Sam Appleby came up to him, rested a hand on his shoulder and asked, 'What's it like being the oldest runner in Wales, Harry?' he shook his head but didn't protest. When Joe added, 'In the world, you mean. In the world!' Harry laughed with the rest of them. 'I haven't won a thing, boys,' he said. 'Nothing worth the telling, anyway ...' And then, when Sam asked whether he'd ever seen Emil Zatopek, he replied vehemently, 'Seen him? I shook his hand!'

Spurred on by his companions' curiosity – Sam now had a notepad and biro at the ready – Harry then seemed eager to reminisce about other celebrities he'd encountered during his long career. Although he had never beaten any of them, he had certainly run against more than one, had been in the company of several, had trod the same turf, the same tarmac, the same muddy pathways as most. And this is why, at eleven o'clock, when Harry was trying to remember when he first met Kip Keino – 'was it '64 or '65?' – he borrowed Joe's mobile phone, went out into the street, rang Beti and said, 'Don't wait up for me, *bach*. You get off to bed. By the way, Sam Appleby from the *Gazette* is calling by tomorrow afternoon to have a chat about the race, to look at a couple of photographs. You remember Sam Appleby ...?' Beti said she had an appointment with the hairdressers at twelve, perhaps more to remind herself than to inform her husband. Then he returned to the bar to continue his recollections, to enjoy his audience's incredulity when he told them he'd been out there himself, supping ale with Keino's uncle when Kip was just a nipper in short pants. 'Tusker, that's what they called the beer there.' He even spelled it out, with mock pedantry, to make sure Sam Appleby got it all down correctly. 'Tusker, Sam. Because of the tusks.'

And that was another reason to have his wife there by his side. If Beti had been present, she could have answered some of the journalist's more difficult questions. What was Harry's best result in the Wenallt Round? In what year did he run the Three Peaks for the first time? What was the name of that place in Scotland where he had to change his shoes half way through the race because one of the soles had come loose? That sort of question. It was Beti, after all, who had ferried him to most of these places, had taken care of his kit, had made sure he had appropriate food and drink. Despite her reserve she would have fielded Sam's probings soberly and thoroughly. Beti has a good head for facts, and a better memory than Harry has ever had. It would have been easier to return home at a reasonable time then, instead of maundering aimlessly and, as Harry now fears, somewhat imprudently, about the small adventures and mishaps of his remote past. But she wasn't there. He had to do his best without her.

Perhaps, after all, Harry does sense that this morning is somehow different; is surprised, between the gull's screeches, that he fails to hear Beti's usually insistent accompaniment. But it's all the same: if he is aware of these things, he clearly ascribes no significance to them. And that, if you put yourself in Harry's shoes, is only to be expected. Beti is a mere seventy-two years old: a good enough age, it is true, but she is still seven years her husband's junior and destined, surely, to be the one left at the end, waving him off into eternity. Not that he actually thinks such thoughts, but they are there in the substrata of his being, a basic presumption. Even her history of asthma, her coughing, her tight chest, do nothing to shake this belief; and they are certainly no reason for Harry to be on death watch this morning, this particular morning. She's having a better night of it, that's what he's thinking. Yes, and a better night than himself. Harry hears more gulls make their dawn procession downriver, barking, cackling. He bends his left knee, just a little, and feels the pressure on his bladder. He must go to the toilet.

Harry rises slowly, incrementally. First, he turns over onto his belly so that he can extend his legs more easily over the edge of the bed. He lowers each in turn, winces a little as the weight pulls on the tendons in his back and then, despite himself, emits a slight hiss through his lips. He leans on the bed, his hands taking the weight, until he feels the circulation return to his legs. If he were getting up properly, of course, to dress and have his breakfast and start on the day's chores, he would then push back his shoulders and draw himself up to his full height. But now, at five to six in the morning, he is getting up only to go to the bathroom and he can do that well enough as he is, hunched, half asleep.

He closes the door behind him so that Beti will not be disturbed.

You might expect, on Harry's return to the bedroom, that he would at last hear his wife's silence and think, Ah! She's awake. I've woken her. Because what else could that silence denote? However, having been on his feet for almost five minutes, his mind is now occupied by other matters. Tomorrow, Saturday, he will take part in the Bryn Coch Benefit Run (formerly the Bryn Coch Challenge) for the fiftieth time. This is not in itself cause for concern. A race of ten kilometres is still within his reach and the weather has been dry of late: there's no need for him to worry about muddy slopes, losing his footing, stumbling. Nor, in a race of this kind, does he fear his adversaries. On the contrary, Harry knows that he will be in better condition, both mentally and physically, than half of the likely participants, with their flimsy daps and fancy dress. Taking everything into consideration, of course. Making allowances for the age gap. Yes, for Harry, the Bryn Coch Benefit Run is scarcely a race at all.

But if Harry has little reason to worry about the race itself, he nevertheless approaches the occasion with a degree of apprehension. It is a milestone. No other member of the Taff Harriers has achieved the half century in this or any other competition. In addition, if he completes it, he will be the oldest to do so in the history of both the club and the race. The press will be there, and perhaps the television cameras. Most significantly, for Harry, a formal dinner will follow where he will be required to stand and make a show of himself. 'There's Harry Selwyn,' the wags will say. 'Look at him. It's a wonder he can run a bath, let alone run a race! How the hell does he do it?' And everybody expects a fellow of that stamp to be colourful and amusing.

Harry's hope, therefore, is that Beti will be well enough to come to the dinner tomorrow night, to share the burden of his exposure. He hopes, too, that she will be on hand today, to help answer Sam Appleby's questions and to correct him if he loses the thread. At the same time, he realises that Beti will not know all the answers. 'When was your first race, Harry?' Sam asked last night in the Mason's Arms. 'Have you run since you were little?' No, Beti couldn't be expected to know things of that sort and there'd be no point asking her. Harry scarcely knew himself. 'When? Well, let me see, now ...' That's all he could say, so that Sam started to laugh and Joe suggested, earnestly, that he might as well ask what Harry had done at Rorke's Drift, because it was all so long ago.

As he lies four feet from his wife's lifeless body and listens to the seagulls and, by now, the odd car and van making their way towards the city, these are the matters that Harry turns over in his mind. 'The first time, Harry ... When was the first time?' He draws a mental picture of his first sports day at school and tries to remember exactly when that was. He knows there's nothing in the box file where he keeps the press cuttings and result sheets, so how can he possibly find out? But then he thinks, No, if we're going back to school, it's got to be the first sports lesson. Surely we did running there, too. Then Harry shakes his head, because that couldn't have been the first time either. He knew what a race was long before he had any lessons. And he thinks, Well, bugger me, that's an odd question. The first time. How do I answer that one?

Suddenly aware of his heart's pounding, Harry begins to breathe more slowly and deeply. In ... two ... three ... Out ... two ... three ... four ... five ... In ... two ... three ... And since he's lying on his side, his head buried in the pillow, he hears the pulse in his ear, too. *Sh ... Sh ... Sh ... Sh ...* Like little cupfuls of water hitting the bottom of a bucket. It is almost as powerful as the heartbeat itself, and the heartbeat precedes the earbeat by the tiniest fraction, just enough to know that there is a gap. *Da-sh ... Da-sh ... Da-sh ...*

In this way, through breathing and counting and trying to measure the tiny interval between the pulse in the heart and the pulse in the ear, Harry manages to suppress Sam's insistent quizzing. His heart slowly regains its early morning composure. Then, between one beat and the next, he falls asleep. It is, however, a shallow and troubled sleep. You might guess, seeing his foot twitch under the blanket, hearing an occasional sudden intake of breath, that he is dreaming about the race tomorrow. Perhaps he is imagining himself climbing Allt y Big, because this is the steepest section on the whole Bryn Coch Benefit Run, and the most taxing, whatever your age. Or, on the other hand, you might assume that he's rehearsing the speech he will have to deliver after the dinner, to say thank you for the tributes, and to cast a few gentle jibes at those who have been pulling his leg throughout the year. But you would be wrong. By now, Harry's mind has drifted far from Allt y Big and the anxieties of public speaking. The cause of Harry's troubled repose is, rather, the image he holds in his mind of the trousers he bought yesterday at David Lewis's: the picture of himself, fastening the belt, feeling the light cotton against his skin and thinking, Well, that's a relief, after the heavy trousers he's been wearing, and especially this time of year, with the weather getting warmer. And then Beti's voice, saying, 'No, no, Harry *bach*. They're half way up your arse!' And although, in his dream, Harry loosens the belt and lets the trousers down a little, and then a little more, it's not enough. 'I can see your socks, Harry! Who wants to see your socks? Who wants to see an old man's socks?'

3

Harry Selwyn v. Sam Appleby (1)

I phoned Beti from the Mason's Arms and told her not to wait up. Then I asked her, 'Have you spoken to Sam Appleby? Did he ring you? Did he ask you any questions?' Or words to that effect. I said it all as casually as I could – not much more than a 'by the way' – but perhaps I spoke with too much urgency. I was using Joe's mobile phone and I know how much those devils cost to feed.

'Why's that?' she said. I could hear the wheeze in her chest. I explained how Sam had been quizzing me.

'Haven't spoken to Sam Appleby since the last business,' she said. And told me not to make such a fuss, people don't believe half what they read in the *Gazette*. Fair enough, too, I thought. But what about the other half? What about the half they *do* believe? Half a newspaper is still a lot of words, more than enough to garotte a man with and make his coffin afterwards, brass knobs and all. I didn't say that. She was wheezing, so I just said, 'Remember the *News of the World*, Bet? There's men been in jail for what they did there.'

'You think Sam Appleby's been tapping your phone, Harry?' she said. I think she was being facetious.

'Hacking,' I said. 'Hacking they call it now, Beti, not tapping.'

And that's where we left it. I went back to the bar and said, Sam, you don't know what old is. There's plenty out there older than me. I told him about the little Indian chap I'd read about in the paper the other day – not the *Gazette*, the proper paper – because he was a hundred. Ran the Marathon, and finished it, too. And what's Harry Selwyn compared with him? A youngster. A novice.

'Who was that, then?' he said.

But I couldn't remember his name and I didn't want to guess and get it wrong and have Sam look it up on his computer and come back with his 'No, Harry, I don't think that's right ... How do you spell it again?' So I said, 'He had a turban. He ran with a turban on his head.' I remembered the photo. The old man in his turban, smile from ear to ear. 'I'll look it up in the paper,' I said. Just to be on the safe side. After last time. Write it down so I wouldn't get caught out again. So the facts were there, for everybody to see.

11

4

Friday, 21 May 9.15am

When Harry wakes again he sees the trousers hanging on the wardrobe door, ready to be returned to the shop. Then, incredulous, he sees that his bedside clock says a quarter past nine. So unwilling is he to accept the evidence of his eyes that he reaches for the clock and puts it to his ear, to check that it is still going, that it is not merely regurgitating last night's quarter past nine. By now, indeed by over half an hour ago, the curtains should have been drawn, he should have been at the breakfast table eating his half bowl of porridge, drinking his single cup of tea. He should already be wearing his tracksuit.

'Beti?'

For the first time since her death, Harry speaks to his wife. He does so in a whisper. Although he knows she can't have meant to lie in so late, he is reluctant to bring her ease to an end. Such repose – after a particularly troubled night, perhaps, he can't be sure – is hard to come by and shouldn't be grudged. So just a whisper.

'Beti?'

His wife's silence tells Harry that she must, indeed, be enjoying a deep, tranquil sleep, a sleep on which it would be cruel to trespass. He sees only the back of her head, deeply impressed in the pillow, and a small segment of cheek and jaw, in shadow. The fingers of her left hand are still turned lightly around the top of the counterpane, as though she has just pulled it up to keep out the chill night air. And for Harry, that hand says all he needs to know: Beti wants to stay in her bed for a little while longer, to gather her strength, to help her face the day.

5

Harry Selwyn v. Sam Appleby (2)

Eight years ago he caught me out. And it's best I tell you about it now, while I remember. Eight years ago next month, it's all in the files. Just the once, mind you. But once is enough. You don't need to learn that lesson a second time, not with Sam Appleby. So, in case you hear different, this is what I said, no more, no less. I told him that Thomas Hicks used to take a swig of strychnine when he got tired. Won the Marathon in 1904, I said, and it was the strychnine made the difference. That's the word I used, too. Swig. It was an imprecise term. I should have been more circumspect. Nip would have been better. Less tabloid.

'What's the secret, Harry?' he asked. He was doing a piece on the Cardiff half marathon. It was the first year and lots of celebrities were taking part and he wanted to know, did I have any tips for Ranulph Fiennes, to help him through the race?

I said, 'Everyone's got his secret, Sam.' And told him about Thomas Hicks and the strychnine. No reason, just that's what came to mind. It's a fact, as well. Not a pleasant fact, but a fact nonetheless. Hit the wall at fifteen miles. Nip of strychnine. Legs shaking at twenty. Another nip. Round the bend for the last lap. Same again. 'St Louis Olympics, 1904,' I said. Not just strychnine, mind you. He mixed it in with a drop of brandy and a couple of eggs. But it was the strychnine made the difference.

Sam said, 'What do you think about that, Harry.'

'Think about what?' I said.

'Strychnine … Winning a race after you've taken strychnine … What's your opinion?'

'Everybody's got their secret.' That's what I said.

Reckless. But I was wet behind the ears and the *News of the World* business hadn't broken yet, to put us on our guard. 'Everybody's got their secret,' I said. Should have told him about Grandma and her Carters Liver Pills, her bread poultices. Or if I'd just said, Look, Sam, I've never swallowed anything stronger than Haliborange. I'd have been right then. But I didn't. The *Gazette* put two and two together, the strychnine and the secret. *What's Harry Selwyn's Secret?* That was the headline. Just the question. Crafty bastards. They were all at it then, with their winks and their nudges. 'What's your secret, Harry? Come on, you can tell me.' Expecting something worse than strychnine. Then the letter from the W.A.A. No wink there. But a lot more than a nudge. And what's a grudging excuse of an apology on the bottom of page six after you've had a letter like that?

Or maybe if I'd told him about the Kalenjin and their India Corn. He'd have had a good story there, too. Good enough for the *Gazette*. Would have got it out of the way, as well, the Kenya business. Shown I had nothing to hide. Saved a lot of trouble.

Anyway, that's why I asked him to write his questions down. 'Write it down?' he said, as if I'd told him to take his trousers off. He scribbled away then. Just to humour me, probably. Tore the sheet out of his book and gave it to me. I had a read through then, made sure it made sense. Put my glasses on, right there in the pub, and read it through. 'The first race ... The best race ... The worst race ...' That sort of thing. Humouring me. Buttering me up. But what choice did I have? So I said, 'Right you are then. I'll write the answers out as well.' To be on the safe side.

And come to think of it, it might be a good idea if you got your own piece of paper, too, so you can jot things down, in case you forget. There's no need to write everything. Don't bother with the mouse or the moth or Grandma and her Liver Pills. And I don't think I'll be saying much more about Thomas Hicks. The strychnine business was sorted in the end, even though it was a feeble squeak of an apology. But you might want to keep a record of the others. Sam Appleby. The Kalenjin too, because I'll be coming back to them. And you can never be sure when they're going to call on you, to give evidence. You know what I mean? To say, This is how it was. Just like this. Here are the facts.

6

Friday, 21 May 9.16am

Despite the heavy blankets, Beti's body is already cold. Her fingers, however, stiffening around the top of the counterpane, give the impression that she is still holding on to the last remnants of warmth. So, despite the unprecedented silence, Harry can be forgiven for thinking to himself, Well, I'll leave her be, then, and get about my business. In any case, by now, he can afford to wait no longer. He has scarcely half an hour to do his exercises, dress, eat his breakfast and make his way to the end of the road to catch the ten o'clock bus to town. And he daren't catch a later bus: Sam Appleby will be calling by at half past twelve and he doesn't want to come back late and test his patience even before they begin. Then, ticking off each task in his mind, Harry realises that he will have to forgo his breakfast. This is Beti's responsibility, and there simply isn't time to make it himself. He may also have to curtail his exercises, and that is a more serious matter. The last thing he wants to do a day before the race is pull a muscle.

Harry gets up slowly, following the same routine as before. It's a little easier this time: he has recently performed these same moves and his leg muscles have retained a residue of flexibility. Harry's back, although stiff, is a familiar adversary and he knows how to cajole it into submission. Standing with both feet on the floor, but still bent in the posture of sleep, he places his hands on his waist and kneads the muscles on either side of his spine. Little by little he raises himself to his full height. Then he rolls his shoulders and hips, back and forth. The stiffness in his torso has eased. He rests his chin on his chest and moves his head from side to side in slow, deliberate arcs, hears the vertebrae's clicks, the mash of neck gristle. He rolls his shoulders again, back and forth. Then stands still, breathes deeply. In through the nose ... two ... three ... Out through the mouth ... two ... three ... four ... five ...

He repeats the procedure.

Suddenly, as Harry works his thumbs into the muscles under his ribs, he feels a sharp stabbing pain and thinks, Jesus, where did that come from? He presses his fingers more deeply into the tissue and makes little circles around the area of discomfort, to measure its extent. He presses again and whispers, 'Push through the pain. Push through the pain.' Half a minute later he stabs his thumb into the centre of the muscle. Not too bad, he thinks. Not too bad at all. Maybe he's just got used to the pain, but that's alright. Harry knows from experience that pain always comes back, so you might as well learn to live with it. 'The only way out is through,' he whispers, and presses again. 'The only way out is through.' Then he goes over to the window and peers through the gap between the curtain and the wall. It is fine outside. Only a few feathery clouds ride high in the sky. He is glad that the weather, at least, is on his side.

Harry turns and takes the trousers down from the wardrobe door. He considers the label: *Taupe 'Charleston' Herringbone Flat Front Trousers*. He mouths the word 'Taupe'. He had intended to ask Beti about it yesterday but she told him the legs were too short and he forgot. It's probably French, he thinks, like *haute cuisine* or *mauve*. He turns the word on his tongue, sounds the 'p' with his lips. *Tope*. He looks again at the label and wonders, after all, whether it might be English. And if it were English, it would rhyme with … He tries to think of a word. Works his way through the alphabet. Gawp… Warp … Then, out of the blue: Thorpe … That's it. It would rhyme with Jeremy Thorpe. Torp. Tope. Torp. Tope … He will have to ask Beti. The herringbone's a queer customer, too. Not really what you want in a pair of trousers. Into the rubbish bag and tie it tight shut, that's what you do with a herring bone. Harry lifts up a leg, considers the weave and is forced to acknowledge that there is some resemblance. He isn't worried about the 'Charleston'. This word is in quotation marks: it's just the name of the model and names of models don't have to mean anything.

Harry decides to go to the bathroom to dress, so as not to risk waking Beti. He calculates, too, that he won't have to waste time chatting and explaining and answering questions, because that's what would happen, he's sure of it, if Beti woke. 'The legs, Harry … Remember the legs …' He will save a good five minutes through avoiding such exchanges. He looks at his watch. Yes, it's tight, but he should make it.

Harry lays the new trousers neatly over his left arm. Then, with his right hand, he picks up his tracksuit and underclothes and makes for the bedroom door. He takes hold of the doorknob and tries to turn it. This is difficult. His right hand is full, so he is compelled to use his left. In addition, he must perform the task with his fingers alone because, were he to use the whole hand, his arm would turn as well and the trousers would fall to the floor. But Harry Selwyn's strength lies in his legs, not in his fingers, and his efforts are in vain. At this stage he would probably be best advised to put the clothes down and start again. But time is short. He must open the door. He must go to town. This is why he grips the doorknob with his left hand and gives it a firm twist, in the hope that a combination of speed and will-power will be sufficient. The trousers fall. Instinctively, Harry tries to save them with his right hand. In so doing, he also drops his tracksuit and underclothes. They fall on top of the trousers. Holding his breath, Harry turns towards Beti's bed. The clothes made little noise when they fell. Nevertheless, he finds it hard to believe that his two mishaps have not, somehow, invaded his wife's consciousness, that his increasing anxiety, which is making such a clamour in his own head, is not audible to all. But her hand remains still, her eyes shut.

Harry turns the doorknob. It makes its customary click. He holds on for a while, knowing that another click will follow, as soon as it is released. It would be a pity, after going to such trouble, if that one small sound made the difference between sleeping and waking. A little pause, therefore, to allow the room's silence to restore itself, and then ... *Click*. Beti is still. Harry picks the clothes up from the floor and goes to the bathroom.

In the bathroom, Harry makes straight for the mirror. He draws the tips of his fingers across his chin and decides to defer his shave until later in the day. If Sam Appleby must endure the sight of his stubble, so be it: he is not minded to put himself out for a mere journalist. He prods at a hard little rod of hair that has begun to sprout under his nose. That can wait, too. Then, as he splashes cold water over his face, Sam

Appleby's voice returns. 'The first time, Harry ... When was the first time?' And for a minute, it is this question alone that occupies him, together with an uncomfortable feeling that another question lurks behind it somewhere, an altogether darker inquisition which he cannot yet put his finger on. 'The first time, Harry ... The first time.'

Harry takes off his pyjamas and puts on his vest, pants and tracksuit. This will save time later, when he goes for a jog in the park. He steals another glance in the mirror. He would like to tame the little tuft of hair – remnant of a youthful quiff – that pouts untidily above his brow, but he has left his comb in his jacket pocket. A little impatiently now, he wets his right hand under the tap and draws his fingers through his hair. The tuft divides into little spikes. He tries to pat his hair down with the palm of his hand. It springs up again, as if to mock his efforts.

Reasoning to himself that there's not much point tidying your hair if you haven't shaved, Harry picks up his trousers and goes downstairs. In the kitchen he fills the kettle to the lowest permissible level and drops a teabag into his London Marathon mug. 'The first time, Harry ... When was the first time?' While he waits, he rolls his shoulders, presses his thumbs and fingers beneath his ribs, gives the muscles a squeeze. He shakes his head. 'Is it running you mean, Sam? Or racing? Because there's a hell of a difference between running and racing.'

Harry makes his tea, then takes the big plastic David Lewis bag from the drawer by the sink and puts his new trousers into it. This is the original plastic bag in which the trousers were wrapped yesterday: a fact that affords him some comfort. He is following the correct procedure. On looking through the French windows and seeing an unexpected agitation in the upper branches of the ash tree, he decides, despite the sunshine, that it is probably not warm enough to venture out as he is, wearing only a tracksuit. He goes to the passage and puts on his blue anorak. Instinctively, he pats the left pocket, to make sure his wallet is still there; and then the right, where he keeps his spare reading glasses and his bus pass. Having satisfied himself that everything is in order, he returns to the kitchen, sits down by the table and sips his tea. Through the side window he sees his neighbour, Bob Isles, washing the dishes. When Bob catches sight of him, he raises a gloved hand and smiles. Harry waves back, lifts his mug in a gesture of easy *bonhomie*.

As he sips his tea, Harry decides reluctantly that he must go upstairs and tell Beti that he is about to leave. He should also ask her whether she needs anything from town besides the fish. He is reluctant to disturb her; on the other hand, he is certain that this is preferable to leaving without farewell. He is, in fact, already half way up the stairs when he looks at his watch again and changes his mind. No, best not, he thinks. Just in case. He returns to the kitchen, tears a sheet of paper from the pad by the telephone and goes in search of his glasses. Although his spare pair is readily to hand, in his anorak pocket, Harry knows it is wise to leave those be, lest he put them down somewhere and forget them, and what would he do then, in the clothes shop, without his glasses? He looks on the table, then on the dresser. Eventually he sees the glasses staring back at him on top of the fridge. Next to them is last night's *Gazette*, open at the crossword puzzle, which he is surprised to find barely half completed. He will return to it later. He takes a biro and writes his message in large, bold strokes.

Didn't want to wake you. Have gone to town. Back by 12. Will buy fish.

x H

Harry doesn't, in fact, need to refer to the fish. This is what he does every Friday: he buys fish because Raymond, his brother, will be coming over for supper. Beti knows this already and would be surprised if there were any departure from the usual routine. Nevertheless, Harry takes pleasure in assuring his wife that he is going about his business with due diligence. And anyway, the message is too abrupt as it stands. It needs amplifying, softening.

Remembering then that Beti has arranged to have her hair cut this morning, he adds:

P. S. Don't forget your hair!

Harry chuckles at the thought of Beti reading his little postscript, pictures her amused smile, imagines her own chuckle. It's a pity he won't be here to share the joke, but it can't be helped. He places the paper behind the wooden elephant on the dresser. He feels his anorak pockets again, stands for a moment and considers whether he's forgotten anything. He unzips the left pocket, removes his wallet and looks for the receipt. It is there, safe and sound, folded in two, next to his library card. He takes it out and reads. *Sales Receipt ... Store No ... Date ... Time ... £29.99.* He is soothed by its simplicity, its dedication to the facts.

Harry puts the wallet back in his pocket and pats the bulge with the palm of his hand. He stands on the spot for a while and rolls his shoulders; then he leans against the dresser and does a few stretches, the quads first, then the calves. These are merely gestures, a symbolic compensation for the fact that he hasn't had time for his proper exercises. He knows it is unwise to venture out into the cold, even to fetch the paper from the corner shop, without first warming his muscles, but he can do no more. He will have to take special care. A man can pull a muscle just stepping off the pavement, just getting on to the bus.

For all his haste, as he passes the study door, Harry thinks about Sam Appleby again. He wonders whether, having saved time on his exercises and his breakfast, he might have just five minutes to spare, to start getting things ready, to sort out a few cuttings and pictures, so there'll be less fuss later on. He looks at his watch. Two minutes, maybe? Yes, even two minutes should be enough to buy some peace of mind. He hangs his shopping bag on the front door-knob so that he won't forget it afterwards; then, a little agitated by now, he turns back and enters what was once the dining room but which has since become a repository for books, papers and unwanted ornaments.

'Now, then, let me see ...'

Harry stands in front of the fitted bookshelves that line the wall. He bends down and takes four photograph albums from the bottom shelf and carries them through to the kitchen. He lines them up on the table and stands back. Yes, he thinks, a fine little squadron, standing to attention for the coming inspection. He looks at his watch again, opens the first of the albums, the one with the grey cover and red tassel. This is an album from the old days, before spiral bindings were introduced, so Harry must use both hands to keep it open and cannot flick quickly through the pages as he had intended. He is made more anxious on discovering that many of the sticky labels that held the photographs in place have come loose. Several pictures are at a slant or have escaped their moorings altogether. He will have to stick them back later. Or perhaps, he considers, it will be easier to get a new album and start from scratch. But that, thinks Harry, as he closes the album, will be a task for tomorrow. Or perhaps the day after. Yes, on reflection, Sunday will be best. Sufficient unto the day.

Anxious now that he is not doing as well as he had hoped, Harry returns to the study, selects a large blue box-file from the bottom shelf and takes this, too, to the kitchen. By now he is moving with more urgency. The two minutes he allocated to himself for his preparations have long expired: these are borrowed seconds and they will have to be repaid.

'Now then ...'

The items in the box – press cuttings, result lists, programmes, letters, and so forth – are also in chronological order, the most recent on the top. Harry is surprised to find that the very latest item is the apology from the *Gazette*. He looks at the date and reads it out aloud.

'21st April 2003.' And again. '2003?'

Certain that something noteworthy must have happened during the last eight years, suspecting that some items have slipped out of order, he digs deeper. On finding only the programme for a school reunion in 2005, he shakes his head and returns to the apology. 'The Gazette regrets any offence or misunderstanding ...' Harry savours once more the righteous anger he felt at the time, the sense of vindication that followed. A little victory of sorts, despite the glibness of the formula. 'It was not the *Gazette*'s intention to suggest that Mr H Selwyn attempted to enhance ...' He will keep this up his sleeve and pluck it out should Sam Appleby get up to his old tricks again. 'Do you remember, Sam ...?'

Harry puts the apology to one side, goes straight to the bottom of the box and takes out the two oldest items. He is pleased that his records are in good order after all, are behaving better, more reliably, than his photographs. He thinks to himself, Yes, these are the things that count. The official documents. The proof. He fingers the gold lettering on his first membership card, *Taff Harriers 1947-8*. And beneath it, then, the results table for the Penwyllt 7 Mile Challenge 12 May 1947, his name underlined in red ink, misspelt.

```
17   Billy Curtis TH M50 36.32
18   Steve Bayley Worcester AC SM 36.34
19   Sam Worth Staffordshire Moorlands AC M50 36.40
20   Harry Sellwyn Taff Harriers JM 36.50
21   John Doe Telford AC JM 37.03
22   Clive Martin Swansea AC JM 37.10
23   David Felton Taff Harriers AC M40 36.54
```

'That's the first, Sam,' says Harry, under his breath. 'That's the start of the racing, right there. If it's racing you want.'

7

Harry Selwyn v. David Reynolds, November 1938

But running, now that's a different matter.

In the park, on the beach, on the football pitch. We all do it. Or at least the boys. Can't say I saw that many girls running, not in my day. Except on the school yard, when they were playing games, but that was playing, not running, not proper running. I had a watch later, from my Dad, so I could time myself. Christmas present. And you can call that racing if you like. Racing against the watch. But that doesn't alter things. Before the watch, there was just the running. It always begins with the running.

'See that, Sam?' I said, and put my finger on my forehead, just above the right eye.

'See what, Harry?'

I bent forward. 'By there, man, by there!' Because I'd had a pint or two and the old tongue was running away with itself. 'Put your finger there ...'

'There?'

'That's it ... Feel anything?'

It was November. Leaves still on the ground and I hadn't had my watch yet. Was I late for school? Is that why I was running faster? Or maybe I just had new shoes on. Not running too fast at all, just new shoes, a touch on the big side. 'So they'll last you.' That's what Mam said, back then. And bought them too big.

I opened the gate and crossed the road. Can't say why I crossed the road. It didn't make any difference, I went to school the same way whatever. But that's what I used to do,

25

so that's what I did. Liked crossing the road by myself, most likely. Just like I enjoyed running, getting the two feet up in the air, seeing the pavement slip by, as if somebody had got hold of it, pulled it out from under me.

But I didn't make it. Banged my toe on the kerb, tripped forwards and couldn't stop myself. Like somebody'd pulled the pavement, but pulled it too fast, with a jerk, when I wasn't looking. Didn't have time to put my hands out and went head-first into the brick wall. Robert Bramwell's, Number Four. A low wall, I know, only six bricks high. But that's not the point. A low wall was worse. Head first and straight down on the edge. Caught me by the eye. The scar's still there, you can feel it if you put your finger on the eyebrow. The bump under the hairs.

Went back home then and Mam said, 'Harry, Harry, Harry.' The blood was all over my face and she could see the bone through the cut. Wiped the red away and there it was, the white. Shining white. Spanking new. My head, inside out. 'Harry, Harry, Harry,' she said. I can believe it, too, about the bone, because there's not much to be had there, under the skin, not much meat. And she couldn't make out why I wasn't crying. 'Doesn't it hurt, Harry?' she said. 'No,' I said. 'Can't you feel it?' she said. 'No,' I said. 'What, nothing? You can't feel anything?' White as a sheet she was. Mouth hanging open. As though not feeling anything was worse than all that blood and bone.

We went down to the hospital then. The doctor put two stitches in the cut and the stitches were worse than the wall, because I knew they were coming, I'd seen the needle on the white cloth and the piece of curly thread. That's when I felt the tears, just inside. But the doctor said I could have a sweet if I didn't cry, so I held them back. And holding your tears back is a job and a half at six years of age. One tear and the rest want to follow, like they've all been queueing up, waiting their turn. But I found a place to put them by, somewhere behind the eyes, and I was chuffed then.

I didn't get the sweet. The doctor broke his promise. And even though Mam bought me a packet of Rolo's on the way home, it wasn't the same. It was the doctor's sweet I wanted. For holding back the tears.

We all run when we're little, I told Sam. Like the ground's got pins in it, and you've got to keep your feet in the air so you don't get spiked. I said, Put your finger there, Sam, just above the eye. There's a lump there still, where the cut used to be, where Mam saw the bone.

I remember why I crossed the road. David Reynolds lived the same side as me. Number Nine. David Reynolds with the fat neck and red cheeks. Smelled like potatoes. I was scared he'd jump out and give me a whipping around the legs. He had a piece of rope and he'd play at being Roy Rogers or John Wayne. *Night Riders*, he said. And then the whipping.

So there's another reason for running. Except, come to think of it, maybe that was a race, too. A race against David Reynolds. A race against the whip. Call that the first time, Sam, if you like. Makes no difference.

8

Friday, 21 May 9.17am

There are only two items on Harry's shopping list today: the trousers and the fish. He'll return the trousers first: he can catch the bus into town, go to David Lewis's, then walk back and buy the fish at Danny Irvine's, near the bottom of his own street. He knows there's something to be said for doing it the other way around. He wants to buy fillets of sole, mainly because he can't abide bones. He needs three of them, too, because Raymond, his brother, is expected to join them for supper. This has been the arrangement every Friday evening since Raymond lost his wife. And although that link has been forgotten, or at least is no longer referred to, a sense of obligation survives: to provide some familial warmth, to offer food tastier than he can surely be scraping together for himself, poor dab. Two fillets might well suffice, bearing in mind how little Beti eats these days, but that would seem miserly. It's a tricky business, too, dividing two fish between three. So three fillets it is. And if there's no lemon sole, then mackerel will do. You can take the bones out of mackerel easily enough. But more than likely both the lemon sole and the mackerel will have sold out. The shop opens at seven in the morning and Friday's still a big day for fish, and they're the first to go every time. There'll be plenty of cod, of course, and haddock too, but they are much more of a fuss and Harry hates it when the little bones get stuck between his teeth. Despite these misgivings, however, he sticks to his original plan. The trousers must come first. He'd hate carrying the fish through town and have their fishy smells waft everywhere, in the shop, on the bus afterwards, and the smells getting ranker and ranker all the while, no matter how much paper the fish is wrapped in.

Harry ascends the escalator to the third floor of David Lewis's department store and walks over to the Customer Service desk. There are four in the queue. Each carries a plastic bag bearing the Lewis name and logo. Although Harry feels a little uneasy – returning a pair of trousers implies a certain negligence on the part of the purchaser – he derives consolation from the fact that he, too, carries just such a bag: his own discreet badge of legitimacy.

He looks at his watch. It's half past ten, which means that he has twenty minutes, or thereabouts, to complete his task. He has placed the receipt in the bag, on top of the trousers, so that he won't need to hunt for it when his turn comes. Nothing remains to be done but wait for service, then observe the usual formalities. Everything is under control. He is not too put out, either, that the customer now standing at the counter, rummaging in her purse, is holding everyone up. She has already taken out a wadge of papers – Harry is too far away to see what they are – and gapes wide-mouthed as the sales assistant tells her how sorry she is, but the store can't exchange goods without a valid receipt. No, Harry is unruffled. Indeed, he indulges in a brief flush of *Schadenfreude* as he witnesses her discomfort, hears her stumbling apologies, and thinks, Good God, woman, you're only half my age. He turns to the man standing behind him, shakes his head and says, 'That's why you've got to keep them safe. All in the same place. Your receipts. Just in case.' He lifts up his bag, as testimony to his thoroughness, his good housekeeping. He looks at the woman again and thinks, Only half my age. If that.

Harry is glad, too, that he has opened his anorak. He has done so because he is uncomfortably warm, but as a result he has also inadvertently revealed his tracksuit top and its **T H** logo, the two letters set either side of the zip. Although a tracksuit is rather out-of-place in an old-fashioned, high quality department store such as David Lewis, it demonstrates to the other customers that Harry has more enterprising activities to turn to once he has completed his chores here, activities quite unrelated to plastic bags and trousers and the mid-morning round of the common pensioner. Unexpected activities, too, for a man of his age. But there it is. A man doesn't stop running when he grows old. He grows old when he stops running. That's the rule. And it's a rule the tracksuit announces eloquently to the world. 'Old? Me?' it says. 'No, my friend, only on the surface. And even then …'

As he stands in the queue, Harry thinks again about tomorrow's race. He hopes Beti will have regained her strength. More than anything, he hopes that she will be at home when Sam Appleby calls to look at the pictures, to ask his questions, to catch him out. He tries to remember when exactly Beti was to have her hair done. This morning, she said. But when? Did she say when? Harry considers the possibilities, recites them quietly to himself, the barest flutter on his lips … Ten o'clock … Half past ten … Eleven … None of them sounds familiar. And they're all in the wrong voice. His mind's ear needs to hear Beti. He hears only himself.

'Next please.'

When the girl behind the counter tells Harry that she needs to speak to the manager, he thinks she is referring to some other matter. He's surprised when she picks up the trousers, walks over to the crockery section and starts talking to a slight young man in a grey suit. And he's more than a little peeved that this idle chit-chat should be given precedence over his trousers. Only when the girl casts him a glance over her shoulder, and the youth does the same, then shakes his head, does Harry realise that this must be the manager of whom she spoke.

By now more people have joined the queue. Seeing that there is now no one serving behind the counter, some have become restless. The bearded man at the head of the queue looks at his watch, shakes his head, whispers something to the two women standing behind him – a mother and her daughter, judging by the way they nod and tut in unison. They, in turn, look across at the manager: they have been following the progress of the trousers and are now hanging on his deliberations. To their surprise – and to Harry's, too – they see him take the trousers from the sales assistant, raise them to his nose, lower them and raise them again, just as though he were smelling a flower and trying to remember where he last encountered that elusive scent. They see the girl do likewise, but more tentatively, holding the trousers at a more cautious distance from her face. She glances over her shoulder. He shakes his head with a firm finality and walks off towards the Electrical Goods.

'I'm sorry to keep you, sir. The Manager wants me to ask you whether you've worn these trousers.'

'Worn them?'

'Or someone else. Has someone else worn them, perhaps?'

'No, nobody's worn them. The wife said. When I took them home. They're too short in the leg, she said. Because I hadn't noticed. The legs, she said. They're much too short for you. You can't wear them like that.'

'So, then. When you took them home. That's where you wore them. In the house.'

'No, no. I tried them on, that's all. Trying on's different to wearing. And she told me straight. Beti, that is. The wife. She said, they're too short. The legs aren't long enough. She could see my socks.'

By now the sales assistant has unfolded the receipt and placed it on the counter.

'You see here, sir?'

'Mm?'

'Just by here, on the back.'

Harry unzips his anorak pocket, puts on his glasses and studies the receipt: 'Return the item within twenty-eight days ...'

'No, sir. Here.' The girl takes the receipt from Harry, points at the small print and reads slowly and clearly. 'Items of clothing must be returned in their original condition, undamaged and suitable for resale.'

'Yes, yes. I see.'

'May I ask you, Mr ... Mr ...'

'Selwyn.'

'Mr Selwyn. May I ask you where you wore the trousers?'

'But I haven't worn them. I told you. I just tried them on.'

'OK. Where did you try them on?'

'Where?'

'What part of the house?'

'Er ... I'm not sure ... In the ... In the ...'

'In the kitchen, perhaps?'

'In the kitchen?'

Suddenly Harry becomes aware of his own voice and the silence it has breached. He dislikes having to talk about his kitchen in this way: a kitchen is a private place, after all, and it is bad manners to parade it in front of strangers. He bends over the counter and whispers. 'Why would I want to try on my trousers in the kitchen?'

'I can't say, Mr Selwyn. But I can smell food on them.'

'You can smell what?'

'Food. They smell of food. Here. Have a smell.'

'What?'

'So you can see for yourself.'

'No ... I can't ... It's not ... '

'Sir?'

'It's not seemly ... Not in front of all these people.'

'I'm very sorry, Mr Selwyn, but I can smell it from here ... The Manager could smell it ...'

'Food, you say?'

'Curry. Something like that. Something with a strong smell ... You must have worn them when your wife was preparing ...'

'She can't abide curries.'

'Or a takeaway, perhaps ...'

'I said she can't stand them.'

'Pardon me?'

'My wife. She hates curries. Too much spice. Gives her heartburn.'

'But ...'

'Nor me. I can't be doing with them either.'

'I'm very sorry, Mr Selwyn.'

9

Friday, 21 May 10.50am

Harry Selwyn nurses the trousers in his lap, fingers the opening of the plastic bag, looks out through the bus window at the slow procession of cars.

'Busy today,' says the old woman sitting at his side. She also has a plastic bag in her lap. The top is rolled over, held tightly in both hands.

'Sorry?'

'In town. I said, it's busy in town today ... The shops.'

Harry smiles. 'The weather ... Brings them out.'

And this is enough. The woman nods her head towards the trousers.

'David Lewis?'

'Mm?'

'Your shopping ... You went to David Lewis?' She nods again, to remind Harry that the evidence is in his lap, displayed in full view, to make clear that she isn't prying but merely restating what is already public knowledge. She speaks more emphatically, too, no doubt suspecting that the elderly gentleman at her side is hard of hearing. Harry looks at his bag, then at the woman, her mouth half open in anticipation.

'David Lewis. Yes.' Then, seeing that her eyes crave more, he adds: 'Busy there, too ... Queues ... Long queues.'

This time, having been favoured with a fuller answer, she points her finger. 'But you got what you wanted ...?'

'Yes, yes. Just the thing.' Harry says this quite jauntily, in an effort to conceal his discomfort. Too jauntily, in fact, and he immediately regrets his lapse, because how else will she interpret such a response except as an invitation to probe further?

'And you?' he says, to divert her curiosity.

'I went to Mothercare.'

Harry is then pleased to discover that what the woman really wants to do is talk about her own shopping: her question is merely an opening gambit to make this possible within the bounds of courtesy. She takes two items out of her bag: a striped dress and a yellow blouse.

'For the granddaughter ... It's her birthday on Saturday. She'll be four.'

'Bright colours ... Is she having a party?'

Harry is content enough to hear about the coming celebrations. And this allows him, in turn, to talk about his own granddaughter and to avoid altogether the subject of the trousers.

'My youngest is almost five.'

'They grow fast ...'

'Likes school, too ... Likes ...'

'Ours hasn't started yet.'

'Oh.'

'In September ... She'll be starting in September.'

'Ah.'

The blouse and dress are put back into the bag and for a moment Harry thinks that's an end to it, that there'll be no more talk of shopping and clothes. However, seeing that the conversation has flagged, the old woman feels under an obligation to give it another nudge.

'For your little girl, is it?'

'I beg your pardon?'

'Got something for your little granddaughter?'

'You mean this?'

Harry looks at his David Lewis bag and then at the expectant eyes. 'No, no, this isn't for Cati, no ...' He shakes his head quite vehemently then because he can tell that the woman's eyes have already begun to tug at the opening of the bag, her tongue is preparing itself to pass comment on the contents. 'It's for the wife ... She's ... I got it ... Oh dear, I'm sorry, I must ...' Harry looks through the window, presses the red button on the seat in front of him and jumps to his feet. 'I'm so sorry ... Almost missed my stop ... I'm so sorry.'

As Harry has alighted from the bus a good half mile before his usual stop it is almost eleven o'clock when he reaches the corner of Blenheim Road. He needs to turn left here if he's to buy the fish. But he's already lost ten minutes and if he goes to Billy Irvine's he'll lose another twenty and he'll have no hope of catching Beti. And how can he hope to resolve the matter of the trousers without talking to Beti? No, he decides, he'll buy the fish later and if they're sold out, so be it. No fish won't be the end of the world, not even on a Friday. He can get something else. Chicken. Chops. Something.

So Harry doesn't turn at the corner of Blenheim Road. Taking quite long strides now, he crosses the road and carries straight on, past the chapel and the flower shop and the new cafe. He pretends not to see his neighbour, Brenda Isles, waving to him through the cafe window: she might want something and he'd have to go inside and find out what it was, and talking to Brenda would waste several more minutes. In any case, in his own mind, Harry has already embarked on the discussion he needs to have with his wife. 'Can you smell it, Beti? Can you smell the curry? That's what the girl said. Curry! Can you credit it?'

A hundred yards from his house, just as he approaches the telephone kiosk, these are the questions that tumble through Harry's mind. By now, however, Beti's voice has joined in, too, exclaiming, 'Good God, man, you mean to say you can't smell that?' Because this is also a possibility: that no one is at fault but Harry himself and Beti will tell him so. 'Where have they been, Harry? Where on earth did you take them?' And what will he say then? That's why Harry comes to an abrupt stop, enters the kiosk and does what he has been craving to do for the past half hour. First, to make good his cover, he picks up the phone and wedges it between his ear and his shoulder. Then he uses both hands to take the trousers out of the bag and place them on the little shelf in front of him. He glances through the window, on the off-chance that Beti might appear at the front door, but sees only another shopper, walking by. He takes the phone in his left hand and says 'Hello! Hello?', loudly and earnestly, to give his decoy credibility. Once the coast is clear he raises the trousers to his nose and sniffs. He looks over his shoulder. He sniffs again. Smells nothing.

When the woman's voice says, 'Please replace the handset ...' Harry obeys. On leaving the kiosk he takes a deep breath to see what else he can smell, thinking surely there'll be a difference between the stale, sour, confined air within and the fresh outside air of this fine May morning. This is no more than a presumption on Harry's part: he detected no alteration as he entered the kiosk and, despite his best efforts, he notices none on his exit. He is, nevertheless, surprised at this lack of contrast and wonders whether he might be nursing a cold, or perhaps the old sinus trouble has returned. The pollen doesn't help, either, this time of year. But the truth of the matter is this: Harry has never before had to smell with such attention and diligence and he is unprepared for these new demands.

Harry opens his front door and shouts, 'Beti!' He closes the door behind him and shouts again. 'Beti, come and have a look at this.' He stands for a moment, listens for an answer. When none comes he proceeds to the kitchen and looks through the French windows, thinking that perhaps his wife is pegging clothes on the line, or taking advantage of the good weather to do a little weeding. But she's nowhere to be seen. He looks at his watch. It's a quarter past eleven.

'Surely ...'

Harry turns and shouts 'Beti?' again, refusing to believe that she would have gone to town without giving him an opportunity to explain his predicament. Then, as he turns and walks back past the dresser, he notices a piece of paper half hidden behind the wooden elephant. He picks it up and is disappointed to see his own writing, saying he'll be back by twelve, promising to get the fish. He turns it over. Nothing.

So certain is Harry that Beti must have left some record of her departure, he sets about investigating alternatives. He checks through the pile of fliers and newsletters and other ephemera that have accumulated on the left side of the dresser. He turns then to the recipes that Beti has cut out of the Sunday papers and propped up behind the fruit bowl. He examines the corner of the counter under the wall-cupboards, where it's dark and things can easily elude the casual observer. He looks on the floor. And finds nothing.

'What the ...'

Harry returns to his own message and scrutinises it again, paying particular attention to the way one corner of the paper is bent over, considering whether this is evidence that it has been handled and read. He regrets picking it up in the first place: that, too – its precise disposition behind the elephant – might have held clues. Had it been moved a touch to the left? Was it just a tiny bit on the skewiff? Harry can't remember. But by now, that is the only explanation that Harry can think of: Beti didn't see his message.

'Damn.'

Harry sits down by the kitchen table and takes his trousers out of the plastic bag. This time, instead of raising them to his nose, he bends over, buries his face in the material and inhales deeply. He realises this is a futile act. He knows that it is the nose alone, its tiny olfactory bulb, that does all the smelling, that the lungs are quite irrelevant, and he might as well whistle at the moon. Nevertheless, for a few seconds, instinct usurps reason, and that instinct tells him that he must get to the root of the matter.

He smells nothing.

He bends over again. This time he takes only short little sniffs, shepherding his nose this way and that across the material, as though it were a mouse, or a dog tracking the scent of a bitch through the grass. He sniffs the waist, the crotch, the legs.

And smells nothing.

'Damnation.'

He has another go. He feeds the material through his fingers inch by inch, pulling it as tight as he can, so that his nose will not miss a single strand. This is a demanding task: there are so many inches, so many threads, even in this one pair of trousers. It is also a painful one. The arthritis in his fingers means that he must steel himself for each pull.

'Damn and blast.'

Beti gets the blame. Had she been here, Harry thinks, she could have adjudicated on the matter, one way or the other. 'Yes, Harry, that girl was right, there's a smell, just by here.' Or else, 'No, Harry, can't smell a thing. But they're still too short. I can still see your socks.' One way of the other. Then move on, without all this fuss and bother. So why isn't she here? And how can he move on without her?

Harry puts the trousers back in the bag. Then, fearing that the smell might escape and invalidate the experiment, he folds the bag in two. Beti must smell precisely what the sales assistant smelt, no more, no less. Anxious that folding might not be sufficient to contain all of the smell, he gets to his feet, takes three clothes pegs from one of the drawers under the counter and attaches them to the opening of the bag. Yes, he thinks, a tighter seal. He pats the bag approvingly with his fingers. So far, so good. He creates a mental picture of Beti opening the bag later on, delivering her verdict, taking his burden upon her. In this way he shifts his attention from the trousers to his wife. The trousers have caused him nothing but grief. He can trust in Beti. He must get hold of Beti.

Harry gets up again and goes to the phone. He has half an idea – inchoate but compelling – that Beti may have gone to see her sister, Amy. He vaguely recalls her mentioning such a possibility last night, on the phone. The hairdressers, then … then … It's worth a stab. He finds his sister-in-law's number in Beti's little red telephone book and begins to dial. *0 … 1 … 4 …* He pauses a moment, taps his fingers on the counter and looks back at the table, at the plastic bag. He makes a stuttering *p-p-p-p-p-p* sound with his lips, to fill the silence, to give vent to his agitation, and thinks, Bloody hell, what's the point of talking to Beti? She can't smell the trousers over the phone! But he carries on dialling anyway. Even if she can't smell the trousers, at least he can tell her the whys and the wherefores. She can advise him what needs to be done, in due course. She can tell him when she's likely to be home. That will put his mind at rest.

But there's no answer. And Harry doesn't have a message worth leaving.

Between the telephone and the wall stands a tall enamel bread bin. Under other circumstances Harry might have chosen something more appropriate for his little experiment, but it's the bread bin that's to hand. He removes the lid and places it on the counter. Then he reaches his hand to the bottom of the bin, takes out a small white loaf and holds it under his nose. He is unsure whether he can smell bread or not: perhaps that's what white bread smells like, thin and slightly damp, a smell that soon drifts off into the air, gets lost between the fingers. He puts his hand in again, finds a brown crust and thinks, Hell's bells, it's as hard as a rock. He puts this under his nose, too. Yes, he decides, that's how rock smells, more than likely. The smell of an old crust. That's what happens to things when they dry out and get hard, they all turn to rock.

Harry opens the cupboard above the bread bin and takes out a bottle of the Aspall Organic Balsamic Vinegar that Beti likes to put on her salads. Unfortunately this is a new bottle and the arthritis in Harry's fingers means that he struggles to open the top. He uses a towel to get a better purchase. After a minute or so of twisting, first with the right hand, then the left, and then the right again, the top yields. He raises the bottle, feels a sudden bite of acid in his nostrils. And he's glad. He does the same again, but more slowly and reflectively, so as fully to savour the sensation and its import.

Having restored his faith in his nose, Harry's other anxieties also abate. He no longer worries that his sister-in-law hasn't answered the phone. Quite the reverse: the lack of an answer confirms what he has, for some time, assumed to be the case, that she and Beti have gone to town. He begins to think that Beti might even have mentioned that this is what she had in mind, when he rang her last night. It would explain, too, why she set off so early this morning, so that she could have a good mooch around the shops. And her hair, of course. He mustn't forget about the hair. That takes time, too.

And everything is clear then. The evidence is incontrovertible.

Harry looks at his watch. It's a quarter to twelve. Does he have time to go for a jog? He's in the mood. And if he doesn't go now he won't get another chance until Sam Appleby has left, and God knows when that will be, between the questions and the pictures and the writing everything down. Harry ponders a moment. Would it be more prudent not to run at all today, given the demands that are shortly to be made on his body? That is the advice he would offer others. Don't drain the tank. Keep enough in reserve. Ration it out as and when ... But Harry runs every day. He has run every day since he was a boy; only illness has ever interrupted this routine, and that very rarely. He went running on the day his daughter was born: for sheer joy, he said. Even on Christmas Day, while Beti steals a nap in front of the fire, Harry will don his tracksuit and venture out into the empty dusk, to clear his head and shake off his torpor. But most of all, by now, Harry runs every day simply because he doesn't know how not to. And except for the obduracy of the girl in the shop that is what he would have done more than an hour ago.

So, finding himself in the mood, and adamant that he will not have his life further disrupted by a pair of trousers or the unfounded imputations of the David Lewis corporation, Harry realises that he must go for a run, come what may. He is pleased by his resolve. He has begun to restore order to his affairs: more than likely his other troubles will come to heel, too, in good time, with a little patience and application. This is how Harry feels. But he doesn't want to over-do it either, not the day before a race: once around the park will be enough, two miles at the most, and back home before he gets his second wind. That, he knows, is the most important consideration. There's only so much second wind to be had at his time of life and it mustn't be squandered.

Harry walks through the study and out to the old lean-to, where he keeps his running shoes. These stand in two rows on a wooden rack. Above are the cross-country shoes (with spikes of different lengths) and his old 'Walshes'. The 'Walshes' are worn, stiff and seldom used but Harry is reluctant to throw them out. He's fond of their distinctive blue and yellow: colours which, over the years, have become part of the livery of the dedicated mountain runner. On the lower shelf are four pairs of standard running shoes, including the New Balance RX Terrain. It is these that Harry has decided to wear today: they are best for the dry conditions, the hard ground. They are also well cushioned at the heel, which is important because he's had the odd twinge in his Achilles of late and he doesn't want that to flare up again.

Harry starts on his routine. He leans his hands against the kitchen doorframe and extends his right leg behind him. Keeping his heel flat on the ground, he counts to ten. One ... two ... three ... He feels the muscles tighten in the back of his leg. Then he raises his heel, bends his knee and counts again. One ... two ... three ... This time it is the Achilles that tightens. He must be careful. The weakness is still there, semi-dormant. So easy does it. Tighten, release. Tighten, release. No pushing through the pain now, not where the Achilles is concerned. He feels the blood, filling the capillaries, warming the tissue. Little by little, the tendon loosens. One ... two ... three ... Then the other leg. One ... two ... three ...

By now Harry has immersed himself entirely in the desire to run. He has forgotten the trousers and even the absence of a message from Beti is no more than a minor irritation, a little mystery that will no doubt be unravelled in due course. And that perhaps is why, on stepping out into the passage and taking a ten pound note from his wallet to pay for the fish, Harry fails to notice that Beti's coats – both the heavy wool winter coat and the lighter, blue raincoat – are still hanging on their pegs, that her shopping bag is there, too, with her purse and keys.

Harry shuts the front door behind him, puts his keys in his tracksuit pocket, and starts to run. The pattern of his breathing changes instantly, just as though there were some secret muscle connecting his feet and lungs. Breathe in for two. Left ... right ... Breathe out for three. Left ... right ... left. Although an awkward, asymmetrical rhythm to the uninitiated, for Harry it has become second nature. It is now as instinctive as running itself. Breathe in for two. Left ... right ... Breathe out for three. Left ... right ... left. He savours the little rush of euphoria as he settles into the old syncopation. Feet and lungs together, he thinks. That's the secret for you, Sam. If you must have a secret.

For the first hundred yards Harry is aware of a slight strain in his right heel, but this eases when he moves from the pavement to the grass and disappears altogether after another quarter of a mile. The pain in his side has gone, too. This, for Harry, means that the early morning twinges were that and no more: they belonged to the half-life of waking, getting up and coaxing the blood back to the extremities. For a while, his legs feel a little heavy, recalcitrant, but Harry knows from experience that they too will revive by and by, as the oxygen invigorates the muscles. Then his body will look after itself. His mind will be free to drift off amongst the wild garlic and the bluebells. To fly with the swallows.

10

1987 Harry Selwyn v. The Fox

Get your breathing right, Sam. It all falls into place then. That's what I told him last night, in the Mason's Arms. In for two. Out for three. Showed him then. Went out onto the floor, ran on the spot for a bit. Blew like an old bellows, so he'd get the rhythm. In for two. Out for three.

Midday's good for a jog, mind. It was tea-time for me, mainly, in the old days. No choice then, not during term. Had a head start on the way out, because teachers got home first. But a nightmare on the way back, park full of kids, bikes, dogs, what-have-you. And me wasting my breath on all the 'Scuse me's'. But it was like it or lump it, back then. Midday's better, if you get the chance. A bit of peace and quiet.

I ran to Pontypridd once. Left at eleven, arrived just in time to catch the 1.15 train back. Followed the river to Castell Coch, then up and along the side of the mountain. Had the path to myself almost, just the odd pensioner out with his dog, kids mitching. Had the view then as well, down into the valley – the fields, the trees, the sun on the river, a heron if you were lucky. But the cars and lorries, too, the coming and going. Close enough to see but far enough away not to be part of it. And you've got to see it to know you're not part of it.

And blow me, I get to Pontypridd, and I'm standing there in the middle of the traffic and the shoppers and their jabber, and what do I see, standing there right next to me? A fox. Not a dog. A fox. Just up by the roundabout he was, at the top of Sardis Road, minding his own business, waiting his turn to cross. And I'm thinking, Well I never. Is he catching the same train as me? Is he on his way back home, after a night out? Because maybe even a fox can have too much of the quiet life and he's been for a spin to town, to rummage through the bins, to hobnob with the shoppers. Which got me thinking, maybe the fox is really just the same as me, only the other way round. He comes to town for a break, I go out into the country. A fox in reverse. XOF. Never saw a fox on the path, mind you. Never. Or even in the fields. Just in the town. That once.

Get your breathing right. That's what I told Sam. It all comes together then. Stood up and ran on the spot for a bit so he'd see what I meant. Went out into the middle of the floor. Left, right, left, right, stamping my feet and blowing like an old bellows so he could hear the rhythm. Sucking the ins and blowing the outs, best I could, so he could tell it was 3-2 and not 2-2 or 3-3. And 3-2's a difficult one, if you're not used to it. Out, out, out. In, in. Out, out, out. Which means you've got to count more on the breathing out than the breathing in. But you won't get a stitch then, not if you breathe like that, the threes and the twos. And I did a bit more running then, a bit more stamping and blowing, to make sure he'd got it right, because it's a devil to explain, and I didn't want any more mistakes.

'But quiet,' I said, and got everybody to hush. 'When you do it for real,' I whispered, 'you've got to stay quiet as a mouse. Quieter. Hear your own breath, and you've had it. The only man you'll beat is yourself.'

So I did it again. Left, right, left, right, stamping my feet. But lips tight this time. Not a sound. 'That's how you do it,' I said. 'That's how you keep going.'

But they were all laughing by then. Joe was shouting out, 'It's Saturday the race is, Harry, not tonight!' And somebody else, then, 'Jesus wept, Harry, that's not running, that's an Irish jig!' So I started laughing myself, and I lost my rhythm. And it's not a good idea, running and drinking, so it was my own fault. I was sorry I'd ever started, ever opened my mouth. And got home much too late.

The shark. That's another one. A shark will die if he stays still. Suffocate. KRAHS. We'd get the kids to do that in the old days. Write little messages back to front. Helped them with their spelling. Wrote their words back to front so they'd have to think about the letters. Their shape. Their sound. What order they came.

11

Friday 21 May 12.47pm

When Harry returns from his jog, Sam Appleby is standing outside the house, smoking a cigarette. Harry apologises for being late and holds up the packet he is carrying.

'Had to go to Billy Irvine's.'

Sam looks at him blankly.

'Fish,' says Harry. 'Lemon sole.'

Sam nods. 'You've got to keep your strength up.'

'Three fillets ... I was lucky.'

'Having company?'

'No, no,' says Harry, a little brusquely, thinking such a question a touch intrusive. But then he adds, 'Just my brother.' The priority today is to get the facts straight, to leave nothing to chance or speculation. 'Raymond comes over every Friday.'

Harry opens the door and escorts Sam into the kitchen.

'Tea?'

'Milk, one sugar, please ... How's Beti?'

'Over with her sister today,' says Harry, because it's the first thing that comes to mind. 'Gone shopping ... Better, though, thanks. Yes, a lot better ... Sorry she missed last night.'

Harry would like to return the courtesy and ask about Sam's wife, but at the moment he can't bring her name to mind. He's pretty sure it begins with an 'F'. He considers Fiona and Fran, but these are other people's names, people he remembers well who have nothing at all to do with Sam Appleby or his

47

newspaper. This is why he says, 'All well with you, Sam?' Then, without waiting for an answer, he places the packet of fish in the fridge, puts the kettle on, gets some Welsh cakes from the cupboard and tips them out onto a plate. He turns back to the dresser and takes a banana from the fruit bowl.

'To keep up the blood sugar ...'

He bites off half, chews thoroughly and earnestly. Then he leans against the doorframe and starts his stretches.

'Be with you in a minute, Sam.'

'No worries, Harry. You take your time.'

Between exercises, Harry tells Sam about lactic acid and glycogen, that what a man does after he's been running is quite as important as what he does before. 'You don't want the muscles seizing up,' he says. He does some more stretches, then picks up the remaining portion of the banana. 'Half an hour you've got to eat this.' He takes a bite and chews briskly. 'Or you might as well chew your own thumb.'

He says all of these things with more zeal and more attention to detail than would be usual for a man describing his exercise regime. This is chiefly because he means to speak plain, without equivocation, to allow Sam no room for misunderstanding. But also, it must be said, he knows that once these preliminaries have concluded, the questioning will begin, and who's to say what will happen then? So the more he says the better, in a way, if he wants to keep a rein on the proceedings. These are his words and no one else's.

Harry puts the last piece of banana in his mouth.

'Be with you now, Sam.'

'Right you are.'

Seeing Harry and Sam standing side-by-side like this, one in his tracksuit, the other in his dark blue jacket and striped tie, it would be easy to assume that Sam is the elder of the two. In fact, while Harry is busy with his stretches, his face turned to the door, you would swear that he is only a young lad: his body is so lean, his legs so supple. You might speculate then, Well, if he's a young lad, who's the other one? Who's the affable-looking, chubby chap by his side? And come to the conclusion that he's the young lad's father, must be. He's come to wish his son well, to share in his success, even to claim some vicarious credit. And no doubt feeling a little pang of nostalgia for his own lost youth.

'You're not even sweating, Harry.'

'What would I be sweating for, Sam? I've only done two miles. And flat miles at that.'

'Two miles? Jesus. Wouldn't mind if I could run two miles.'

'Two miles?' Harry laughs. 'Who you kidding, Sam? You'd collapse if you ran two hundred yards!'

The journalist laughs, too. 'Fair enough, Harry. I'd best stop here, then.'

'Stephanie ...' Harry has remembered the name of Sam's wife. 'Is Stephanie well?' He realises with relief that he was right all along, that there is indeed an 'f' in her name, only that it has been buried deep down inside so that you've got to go and dig it out. Because of the suddenness of the recollection, he says the name with exaggerated urgency, as though Stephanie had been ailing of late and the subject of general concern.

'Stephanie? Yes, well enough ... Or she was when I saw her at breakfast, anyway.' He laughs again.

'Good ... Very good ... Glad to hear it ... And what's she doing with herself these days?'

Another five minutes pass.

* * *

49

'That's me ... By here.'

Harry and Sam are sitting in the kitchen, looking through the oldest of the four photo albums, the one with the red tassel and grey cover. Harry must press down on the cover to keep the album open. 'You see ...? Just by here ...'

The black and white photograph shows a group of young men in their running shirts and shorts. One stretches his left leg, another blows on his hands. The trees behind them have lost their leaves.

'Number eighty-nine. That's me.'

Unlike the others, this figure seems unaware of the cold. He stands motionless, looking at the camera, arms by his sides, an expression on his face that might be described as earnest if it were not also so detached.

'That was the first time. The first race. May 1947. Penwyllt. The first for the Harriers. That do you?'

Harry has resolved to follow the questions strictly in the order Sam has written them down, with as little deviation as possible. This will help him bring the session to a swifter conclusion. So, the first race first. Then he'll move on to the best race, which he's spent some time thinking about, and has one or two candidates in mind. And then, finally, the mishaps. 'Mishaps' is Sam's word, not Harry's, but he's not going to waste time arguing about semantics. It's Harry's choice, they're his mishaps, so Sam can use whatever word he likes.

Harry tells Sam to put a finger in the album to keep his place, then turns to the results table.

'Twentieth out of a hundred and eighteen ... Not bad for the first time ... Except they've spelt my name wrong.'

And that's the first race dealt with. Harry returns to the album and works his way systematically through the pages.

More young men in shorts and striped shirts stretch their legs and blow on their hands. In some, the leaves have returned to the trees and the sun shines brightly, so that several of the runners must shade their eyes with their hands. After ten minutes or so they come to a picture of the same severe-looking young man, together with two others. Each wears a medal around his neck. 'That's the first medal ... Here in Cardiff ... Just behind us, in the park.'

Harry pushes his glasses back on his nose and puts his finger under the caption. 'Lord Mayor's Cup. May 1949.' He flicks through the papers in the box and in a few seconds finds the results sheet. He places this on the table and points to his own name. 'There you are.' He looks Sam in the eye to make sure he's keeping up. 'That's the first medal ... Got my name right this time.' Then he gets up from his chair, walks over to the dresser and opens the left-hand door. After a little rummaging he takes out a small square display stand, covered in black velvet, with eight medals on it. 'There you are ... This one here.' He removes the medal, rubs it on his sleeve and places it next to the picture in the album. 'Lord Mayor's Cup. Ten miles. Came second.'

Harry never meant to spend so much time showing these things to Sam Appleby. He regrets not doing more preparation, more sifting, so that he could get straight to the things that matter and have it all over and done with. He hadn't even intended mentioning the medal: it was, in truth, a trophy of little worth, barely a curiosity. However, as they've been working their way through the album he has realised that there is more than one kind of 'first time'. The first medal is surely at least as important as the first race, so how can it be ignored? And having shown it to Sam, it behoves him to get the facts straight, lest he be misunderstood or misquoted. Which means he hasn't started on the best races yet, or the mishaps. He hasn't even opened the second album, let alone the third and the fourth. And he's already weary of the whole business.

Harry is relieved when he sees the journalist glance at his watch. At last, he thinks, he's had enough, he'll be gone soon, it'll all be over and no damage done. But Sam doesn't move. His watch tells him, in fact, that he has a good quarter of an hour to spare. He takes hold of his mug and asks, ingratiatingly, whether there's any chance of one last cuppa before he makes tracks. Harry groans inwardly but thinks, sooner done, sooner gone. So he puts on the kettle. Meanwhile, Sam leans back in his chair and lets his attention wander to a framed black-and-white photograph on the dresser. It shows a slight young man in army uniform. He's sitting on a wooden bench, his arm placed lightly around the shoulder of a serious-looking boy in short trousers and braces. The man smiles. The whiteness of his teeth accentuates his dark skin.

'Does it run in the family?'

'In the family?'

'Does running run in the family?'

Sam chuckles at his own joke and points at the picture. Harry, standing at the counter, waiting for the kettle to boil, must look over his shoulder to see his father. He pauses. This question doesn't appear on Sam's piece of paper and he's had no time to prepare an answer.

'No,' says Harry. 'Not so far, anyway.'

He says this, not out of conviction, but simply because it's the safest answer he can think of, and he doesn't want to risk a more nuanced response only to regret his candour afterwards. What Harry really thinks is this: a runner must choose his parents carefully. If you can taste the chicken in the soup then doesn't it follow that you can taste the soup in the chicken? And if so, who can say whether his father, given half a chance, wouldn't have turned out a champion runner himself? Had the war not intervened. Had Raymond not been born. And how can he possibly answer such a question?

Harry takes Sam's tea over to the table.

'Not having one for yourself, Harry?'

Harry shakes his head and attends to the medals. He replaces the one he's removed. Straightens the others. Carries them back to the dresser.

12

August 1942 Cefn Sidan Beach, Harry Selwyn v. His Dad

'You'll be giving old Wilson a run for his money soon,' Dad said.

He was back from the war. A couple of weeks' leave. Mam told him I'd won races at school. He said, 'Bet you can't beat me!'

Dad had been reading *The Wizard*. That's how he knew about Wilson, and that's why I think maybe it was a Tuesday. Tuesday *The Wizard* came out. *The Wizard* on Tuesday, *The Hotspur* on Thursday. Except it was every other Tuesday and every other Thursday in those days, because of the war, and not enough paper. So, Tuesday. Some Tuesday in summer. It was sunny and there were lots of people there, on the beach, in their bathers.

'Can't beat me,' said Dad.

He stood there, in his white shirt and flannels, his face all tanned after being out in Africa. But not with the lions, he said. There weren't any lions, not in the bit of Africa where he'd been. Plenty of Germans, but no lions. And I couldn't understand that, why the Germans had all gone to Africa. So I asked him, 'Was it the Germans killed the lions?' Very likely, he said. And no elephants, either. But he brought one home, anyway. A little wooden elephant. Black. He said, it's a real one, mind, just been shrunk so it would fit into the kitbag and I had to be careful because one of these days it'd grow back to like it was before it got shrunk and you wouldn't want to be about the place when it did its number twos. No, sirree. I knew it was a wooden elephant, and Dad knew I knew, but it made no difference. Every time he came home he asked me, 'Has he grown back yet? Has he done his number twos? Where are you keeping him now? Not in the kitchen, I hope!' He knew fine well that's where Mam kept it, on the dresser. That's where she put her letters and bills, behind the wooden elephant.

We were on the beach, just me and Mam and Dad. Sat down on the sand, facing the sea. What was Mam doing? Reading her magazine, more than likely. And trying to keep warm. I remember that. 'It's a sharp wind,' she said. And had to wear a cardigan over her frock, even though it was a summer's day and the sun high in the sky. Kept a hat on her head, too, for fear of burning. Mam burned easily and you could burn in the sun even when the wind was sharp. The same as Raymond. 'Fair skin,' Mam said. 'Burn easy.' But I didn't know that then because Raymond hadn't been born. Dark skin I've got. Same as Dad. Dark as boot polish, Mam said, when we got the sun. Just like an African.

'You'll be giving that Wilson a run for his money soon,' Dad said. Then looked over to the boat sheds. 'First to the sheds,' he said, and stood there, one arm in front, the other arm behind. His feet, too. Left foot flat on the sand, the other ready to kick. 'Starter's orders!'

Our eyes fixed on the sheds.

I beat him. Which wasn't right. And you might say, Well, you were young, Harry. Keen. Light. Light as a bird. And running on sand isn't like running on grass. Your feet slip back, and the harder you run the more they slip. The sand doesn't want you to go anywhere, it just wants to hold you down, suck all the strength out of your legs. So you've got to stay on your toes, best you can. Keep yourself up in the air. And that's easier when you're young. You're keen, you're light, you're not carrying so much baggage.

So, yes. It was an advantage, being young. But not enough. Not half enough. I beat my Dad. And how can a young lad beat his Dad, and him just come back from fighting the Germans?

'That's cheating, Dad,' I told him.

Dad was lying on the beach now, puffing and panting, kidding everybody he was out of breath.

'You weren't trying, Dad.'

I told Mam then, 'Dad cheated, Mam. Dad let me win. And that's cheating.'

But she was reading her magazine, saying the wind was sharp, wanting a cup of tea.

Dad said, 'You can have a packet of Rolos now. Prize for winning.'

But I didn't get any Rolos that day. Mam said a bomb had dropped on the factory where the Rolos were made. And I was glad I didn't get any because that would have made the cheating worse. And anyway, William Wilson was only a character in a comic.

13

Friday, 21 May 2011, 2.15pm

'Did he come back?'

'Eh?'

Harry stands by the dresser. To resume his seat would signal to Sam that he wished to continue the conversation. He puts his right hand in his tracksuit pocket and plays with the small change he finds there. He looks at his watch. He looks at the floor. The meeting has finished. That is what his body says. Their talking is at an end and he has other, more pressing matters to attend to.

'Your Dad. Did he come back from the war?'

'No, Sam, he didn't.'

'Oh ... Lost in action was he?'

'Yes. Lost in action.'

'Well ... I'm sorry about that, Harry.'

And when he shuts the front door Harry realises that he hasn't said a word about his best race.

14

January 1943 Harry Selwyn v. God

Father O'Keefe called by to see where Mam's soul had got to. It was a big thing, when the priest came into your house, and him just off the altar, breaking Jesus's body in half, drinking his blood. And I was glad enough, to begin with. Dad was away fighting the Germans and the house was empty without a man's voice in it, telling you how things ought to be. And Father O'Keefe wasn't just any man, he was a priest man, and

Dad's priest man at that. It was Dad's church, the church of priests. Mam only went to mass because she'd married Dad, and that's why she didn't cross herself when she walked past St Columba's. She didn't pray, either, not when Dad was gone. Food on the table and chocks away. Not a word about God or bounty or anything. Mam was chapel before that. But a church is bigger than a chapel. Our church was big enough to swallow two chapels.

'Put that away,' said Mam, when he came into the kitchen. Said it with a snap, as though I should have known I wasn't supposed to read *The Wizard* in front of a priest. I put it on the dresser. 'Haven't you got homework to do?' she said. I told her nobody had any homework. 'The snow,' I said, and pointed out through the window. She didn't like that either. But mainly she was cross because the priest had called by.

So it was a big thing, Father O'Keefe coming into our kitchen. But it was a little thing, too. Big and little at the same time. And the big got littler and the little got bigger. For one thing he was short, a lot shorter than he looked when he was up on the altar. And for another, he was all black. I knew it was only in church that he wore his capes and tassels and baubles and what-have-you. But all the same. And when he sat down his trousers crept up his legs so I could see the black socks. Black socks, black shoes, black trousers. Everything black. He had a cut under his chin, too, where the razor had slipped.

Chasubles. That's what they call them. Their capes.

Mam didn't know the priest was coming so we had to sit in the kitchen. There was always a fire going in the kitchen, that time of day, that time of year. Sat there, even though the ironing was piled high on the table, and making much more mess than *The Wizard*.

He said, 'Have you heard from Edward?'

I didn't like that. Dad was Dad to me and Ted to everyone else. I thought, that must be their name for him, that's what the men in the black socks call him.

Mam said this and that about Dad, then he turned to me. 'And how's this big lad getting on in school? Working hard?' But he didn't wait for an answer. Just said, 'Very good, very good.' With a little thread of saliva between his lips. Then, 'What about you, Mrs Selwyn? How are you keeping?' Because, he said, he'd noticed that she hadn't been to mass for a week or two. And smiled. Took a sip of tea. 'Will we be seeing you next week?' Smiled again.

Mam said, 'I'm not coming back to church.' And left it like that. Nobody smiling or drinking tea, just the fire crackling in the grate.

What next? I thought. Mam had never spoken like that before. And to Father O'Keefe, too. But all he said was, 'Yes, it's a hard enough time, Mrs Selwyn, a hard enough time for us all.' Just like he hadn't been listening.

'Harder for my sister,' Mam said.

It was a month before that, give or take. Saturday morning. A man knocked on the door and said, 'Telegram for Mrs Selwyn.' And Mam went white as a sheet, thinking it was about Dad, probably, telling her he'd been killed, lost in action, that kind of thing. And me thinking nothing, because I hadn't seen a telegram before. It was from Uncle Tom.

`Little Jennifer died this morning. Pulmonary`
`Atresia.`

She cried then. And I'm not trying to say she wasn't sad that her little niece had died, all I'm saying is that there was a drop of relief mixed in there somewhere with the tears, bound to be. Relief that she was crying for little Jennifer and not my Dad. I went and copied out the words on the back of *The Wizard* then so I could take them to school and show everybody I had a cousin who'd died of something Latin. I couldn't abide babies but I was proud of little Jennifer, that she'd been cut down by such a swanky disease.

'She was only two,' said Mam.

Father O'Keefe nodded. 'It's difficult to understand, right enough.'

But Mam had got her dander up by then. 'No, it's not,' she said, like she was spitting out pips. 'It's not difficult at all. Look. It says here.' And she went and fetched the telegram from the dresser and stabbed her finger at the Latin. 'Pulmonary Atresia. No might-bes, no maybes. Pulmonary Atresia. That's all there is to it.'

He looked at the telegram and gave another nod, to show he really was listening this time. Then he said something about keeping the faith and how faith was a light in the darkness and that we lived in dark times but if we kept every candle alight we'd see it out in the end, sure enough. Something like that. Which was beyond me. Mam only got the candles out when there was a power cut, and you got a poor light from them anyway, just half a step away from the darkness itself. 'She's in a better place now,' he said then. I didn't see much wrong with that, mind you, not at the time. Fair play to her, I thought, if she's found somewhere better than Uncle Tom and Auntie Dot's. But I reckon that's what got Mam cross. Not the candles. The better place business. Got her really upset.

'Better than where?' she said, spitting more pips. 'Better than at home with her Mam?'

'With God, Mrs Selwyn,' said Father O'Keefe. 'With her eternal father in heaven.' And said it softly softly, like it was a secret between the two of them. 'God loves little children.' He looked over at me then and raised his hand. 'We are all God's children ...' Because I was the only child there, probably, and I was a touch on the small side for my age. But I had a fright, seeing him point at me like that. I didn't want to be one of God's little children, not there in the kitchen, and I thought he might make me say something, just like you had to do in church, when the priest spoke in Latin. *Et cum spiritu tuo*. That sort of thing.

But Mam took no notice. She said, 'What does he do with them, then?' And left the question hanging in the air for a bit. No pips this time, just the words, light as fluff. And when she didn't get an answer she asked him again. 'Mm? What does God do with them?' Which put him off his stroke, because I don't think they're used to people talking like that. Priests, I mean. Even when they're not on the altar, in their chasubles.

'What does He do?'

'You say that God loves little children. So what does He do with them after changing His mind and deciding He doesn't want them to live with their mammies and daddies after all? Mm? Does He get the toys out of His toy box and say, Play with these? Little soldiers for the boys, little dollies for the girls? What does He say to Jennifer? Don't you fret, little girl, Mammy'll be back in a tick, she's just slipped out to bury her baby, you'll see her again in fifty years or so, less if you're lucky ... and sing 'Pop Goes the Weasel' to cheer her up? Mm? Is that what your God does with his little children? But how would you know? You don't have any children, do you?'

The priest wasn't looking at Mam anymore. He was looking at his tea, turning the cup around in its saucer, like he was making sure it was the right fit. He mumbled something then. 'I've got a m ...' Mam, probably. 'I've got a Mam.' No, he didn't have any children, but he'd been a child himself once, he'd been something other than a priest, of course he had. That would have been a reasonable thing to say. But he dropped his cup on the floor and the words got lost. Silly man, I thought. I'd had a bellyful of him by then, between his socks and his candles and his mumblings. But there wasn't much tea left in it, so no mess, and Mam didn't have to make him another.

He tried to say sorry. 'I'm so ... I'm so ...'

There was no faulting his manners. Whatever you say about the blacksocks, he was always polite. But he couldn't get it out, just mumbled again. That's when he followed his cup onto the floor. And I swear, for a second, I thought the man was going to say a little prayer, to say sorry to God for spilling his tea, because that's the way he went, down on his knees. But then he just crumpled into a heap, arse up in the air, nose sticking out sideways by Mam's feet. Eyes shut as well, so for a second he looked just like a big baby having a nap in his cot, like they do, head in the pillow, arse to attention. But babies are pink and this big baby's face was white, a big white balloon. Except for the cut under his chin. That had kept its colour. In fact it was standing out more than ever now, red raw, as though all his blood had rushed to that one spot. I could see the white of his legs, too, because his trousers had crept up again.

I asked Mam, 'Is he dead?' I'd never seen a man fall before. Children used to fall all the time, in the old days. But grown men didn't fall, not unless they'd been shot.

'Is he, Mam? Is he dead?'

She didn't answer. She just stared at his face. He looked

pretty ropey by now, fair play, white as an altar cloth and his lips opening and closing, like a goldfish in a bowl. Does that mean he's not dead? I thought. Or is that what dying does to you? Makes you go like a fish. There was another 'Mm' then, as if his soul was trying to get out through his mouth and fancied singing a little hymn or two on the way, by way of a ta-ta. Only trying, mind you. Trying and failing and then getting stuck in his teeth, flapping about against his lips. Is this what dying's like? I thought.

But Mam said 'Go ring the 999'. So off I go to put my shoes on, and Mam looks for change and I tell her, 'No, Mam, you don't need money.' I'd read about 999 in *The Hotspur* and Billy Reynolds at school had had to do the same thing when his sister put her hand through the window. So I was in charge then, and that felt good.

The best race, Sam? Well, you might say that was the best. Seeing Father O'Keefe on the floor, mumbling, knowing I had to get the ambulance quick as a blink or else his soul would creep out through his mouth, and once that feller gets out, there's no putting him back. And running fast then, running so fast my feet weren't touching the ground. Like flying on my own breath. Running so fast I didn't even think about running, just kept my eyes on the phone box at the bottom of the street, saw it getting closer, a voice in my head saying, Jesus, I can run like this for ever. And sorry then that it had to stop. Wanting the priest to come back for another chat so I could save him again.

Father O'Keefe was up on his feet within the month, but his mouth was all bent, his words higgledy-piggledy. I thought then maybe I hadn't run fast enough, that part of his soul had slipped through the lips after all and given them a bit of a twist. And maybe that was his punishment for failing to get Mam to go back to church.

'Does God punish priests as well, Mam,' I asked. 'Does He get cross with them when they don't do as they're told?'

Mam said not to talk such nonsense. So I tried to work it out for myself. If the priest really was dead on the kitchen floor, and I'd helped bring him back to life, did that mean I'd beaten God Himself? And what would God feel about that, seeing a twelve year old lad pass him on the final stretch, win by a nose? Would He go into a sulk? Would He start smiting, like in the old days? Or was it part of what He had in mind all along? Maybe he only ever wanted to give His priest a bit of a slap, a bit of a wake-up, and He knew to the last second how long a twelve-year-old lad would take to get to the kiosk, how long the ambulance would have to wait at the traffic lights on the corner, how long Father O'Keefe's soul would stay stuck between his lips. I had a hankering to ask, Is that what it is, Mam? Is it like a relay race? Sometimes you get the first lap, sometimes the second or the third, but you never get the last. God runs that one every time. But I didn't. I didn't say any more about priests. Jennifer was dead and Mam had stopped believing in God.

That was the best race. The race to save Father O'Keefe. They didn't get any better than that. I'd have told Sam Appleby about it, too. 'Saved a man's life, once,' I'd have said. 'Ran so fast, I even beat God.'

But what kind of story is that to put in a local rag?

15

Friday, 21 May, 2.45pm

Washed out after talking to Sam, Harry goes to the front room, sits down and reads the paper. This room is much lighter than the study or the kitchen and Harry enjoys relaxing under the bay window, feeling the warmth of the spring sun on his face and hands. He has not yet had a shower after his jog. This is probably what he would wish to do next; however, after scanning the headlines his fatigue gets the better of him and he falls asleep in his chair.

In that restless sleep Harry stands once more by his mother's side, the snow deep beneath his feet, watching Father O'Keefe being stretchered into the back of the ambulance. They remain there, motionless, respectful, until the ambulance reaches the bottom of the street and turns the corner. Despite the cold, Harry would be content to stay a while longer. With the departure of the priest, he has become aware again of the absence of a man in the house. Father O'Keefe was only half a man, it's true, and a dismal little half man at that, but half a man filled half an absence, and that was better than nothing.

'Should we say a prayer, Mam? To help him get better?'

But his Mam says, 'Come on in, Harry. You'll catch your death out here.'

Harry returns to the kitchen, picks up his *Wizard* and reads about William Wilson, the fastest runner in the world, because even a man in a comic can fill some sort of gap. But Wilson isn't running, not today. There's a war on and he has to go and fight the Germans, just like all the other men. It's the dead of night over there, of course, not the middle of the afternoon. It's a very special night, too. This is the first time Wilson has been out in a Lancaster Bomber. Until now he's flown only Spitfires and Hurricanes, and acquitted himself well enough, shooting down more enemy planes than anyone else, even Douglas Bader in *Reach for the Skies*. But this is a new challenge and the sleeping Harry thrills as the episode plays out again behind closed eyelids. His lips tighten. His feet twitch.

This is what Harry sees. The Lancaster Bomber flies through ink-black skies. Suddenly an engine explodes, spits nuts, bolts, shredded propeller. The flight engineer shouts 'Fire! Fire!' Flames dance in his goggles. The navigator throws up his arms, yells through his handlebar moustache, 'We've been hit!!' The pilot, brow tightly knit, jaw set, wrestles with the control column. Grimaces. The Lancaster Bomber nosedives.

But who is this?

It's Wilson.

Wilson grabs the fire extinguisher. Climbs out of the cockpit. Crawls along the wing of the aircraft. And in the nick of time, dodging flack from fifty Messerschmidts …

Then, in his dream, Harry turns the page and reads the following words:

> *'If you wish to run, not only today, but tomorrow and the day after and every day after that, you must slow down your heart … Slow down your heart and you will run for ever.'*

Harry thinks, Well, that's an odd thing to read in a comic and no mistake. What can that possibly have to do with Lancaster Bombers and killing Germans? There must be some secret here. He repeats the words. 'Slow down the heart and you will run for ever.' He repeats them until he has them off pat. Although little Jennifer has died of Pulmonary Atresia and Father O'Keefe has gone to talk like a fish, William Wilson is 145 years old and still in his prime. The war has ended. Harry's hero has returned, unscathed. And he's running faster than ever.

It's just possible, of course, that the sleeping Harry has got confused, that in the unpredictable ebb and flow of his dream he has turned to a different number of *The Wizard*, a different month, perhaps even a different year. For otherwise how can one possibly explain Wilson's sudden return to Blighty? How can even he step so effortlessly from the wing of a Lancaster Bomber to the Olympic track at Wembley and run as though he were still airborne? But to Harry, there is no mystery. In his dream, everything is possible.

'Slow down the heart, Sam. That's the secret. Slow down the heart.'

Beached in his front room, dreaming of his boyhood hero, Harry's mouth opens and closes, opens and closes, like a fish.

16

Friday, 21 May, 3.50pm

An hour later, his chin now resting on his chest, his newspaper crumpled in his lap, Harry hears a knock at the front door. As he eases himself out of the chair, he hears the voices of his daughter and granddaughter. He knows it must be almost four o'clock. That's when they call by every Friday afternoon, after Cati's finished school. But he's still taken aback. He thinks, My God, where did all that time go?

'Meh, meh.'

Cati, his five-year-old granddaughter, carries a small toy sheep in her hand. Harry affects surprise.

'Well, hello, Mrs Sheep, and a fine sheep you are and no mistake. Do you want to come in for a cuppa?'

'Meh, meh.'

'Well, and a very polite sheep, too ... Come on in, but remember to keep an eye out for Mr Wolf!'

Emma, Harry's daughter, uses her Friday visit to make sure her mother is coping. Sometimes, when Beti is under the weather, or is having trouble breathing, she will do the hoovering and prepare a meal. The shopping, however, she leaves to Harry: this is a task that can be safely entrusted to a man. It is a convenient enough arrangement: Cati's school is close by and only a small detour is required on their way home.

'Your mother's gone to see Auntie Amy.'

As he utters these words, Harry realises that it's high time Beti was back, because this too is part of the Friday routine: Beti's home to chat with Emma, to tell her what needs doing, to draw pictures with Cati, and he doesn't recall anyone saying that today is any different. Sensing that a fuller explanation is required, he adds: 'They've gone to town ... Shopping ... She won't be long.' Fearing then that even this molification is not wholly satisfactory, he says: 'I rang her, I rang Amy, to ask her, to see when ...' And he feels a little better: at least he has made an effort and it isn't his fault that his wife his decided to abandon the customary arrangements.

'Where does Mr Wolf live, Grandpa?'

'Just by here, Cati ... By here ...' Harry rat-tat-tats his knuckle against the door of the understairs cupboard, cocks his ear. 'But I think he's having forty winks at the moment, so Mrs Sheep will have to keep very very quiet so she doesn't wake him up.'

Emma and Cati go into the kitchen and sit down. Harry puts on the kettle. The Welsh cakes are still on the counter, following Sam Appleby's visit. He takes these over to the table, then fetches the milk from the fridge. He expects to find Cati's apple juice there, too, and is dismayed on realising that there isn't any juice, nor indeed any other drink suitable for a child. This is also part of the Friday routine: he buys a carton in the morning, ready for the afternoon visit. And he must buy it fresh, because once opened, its contents have to be drunk within three days. Beti is always insistent on this point. But there it is: between the business with the trousers, and having to go through all those photographs with Sam Appleby, today has not been a normal Friday. He goes to the cupboard, disregards a jar of Ovaltine, finds the unopened bottle of Lime Cordial that Beti had from her sister at Christmas.

'Lime Cordial …? With a drop of water …?'

Cati looks at the bottle, the bright green, and shakes her head.

'What do you say to your Grandpa?'

'No thank you, Grandpa.'

'Have tea, the same as us.'

'I don't like tea, Mam.'

'Water, then. Have water.'

Harry has already started to fill a beaker from the tap when he sees his daughter moving the David Lewis shopping bag to the other end of the table, where it will be out of Cati's reach. He approves of this precaution. At the same time he feels a slight queasiness at the thought that he still hasn't brought this matter to heel. He is cross, too, that Beti isn't here to help him look after Emma and Cati and to advise him about the trousers. Then, as he carries the drinks over to the table, he thinks, Well, Beti may not be here, but Emma is, and surely her nose is every bit as good as her mother's. Better, perhaps. A young nose. A nose that hasn't got worn out. With this in mind, Harry gives Cati a grandfatherly wink and points a thumb towards the door.

'I think there might be something upstairs for Mrs Sheep … What do you think, Mrs Sheep?'

'Meh, meh.'

This is part of the routine, too. Although Harry has forgotten the apple juice, he has arranged this particular treat well in advance, a week ago to be exact, just as his granddaughter left after her last visit. He has done this every week for amost two years. Cati, although she is only five, is now familiar with the ritual and has been waiting for the wink and the pointing thumb since she sat down. Her grandfather's teasing dialogue with the sheep is just a playful variation on the established order of events.

Harry escorts Cati safely past the cupboard under the stairs. He is always unsure whether she is genuinely afraid of the wolf he has conjured up, or is merely pretending in order to extend the game. Either way, he is happy to demonstrate to her that the cupboard is locked, that the bolt is on the outside and much, much too steely strong for even the most ferocious wolf in the world to break through. Nevertheless, Cati still holds Harry's hand and pleads with him to go upstairs with her. But Harry has things he needs to discuss with his daughter so he promises to stand there, in the passage, and keep an eye on the door, a hand on the bolt, until his granddaughter returns.

'Promise?'

'Promise.'

* * *

'Can you smell anything?'

Emma holds the bottom of one of the trouser legs under her nose and sniffs. 'Where was the smell?'

'I don't know ... She didn't say.'

Emma takes the other trouser leg and sniffs again. She moves to the waist band, runs it through her fingers, sniffing every two or three inches, but more hesitantly this time, drawing her nose back every once in a while and frowning.

'Nobody's worn it, Emma, I only tried it on ... I only ...'

Emma says 'Hsssh!' and Harry obeys without demur, knowing that words drown out smells.

'Well?'

'There's something.'

'What?'

'Not sure. Let me have another go. It was just here ...'

Emma takes hold of the waistband near one of the pockets, sniffs and shakes her head. She turns the pocket inside out and tries again.

'There. That's where it is. In the pocket.'

'In the pocket? What's in the pocket?

'Not sure ... Garlic, maybe.'

'Garlic?'

'Here, right at the bottom.'

Emma passes the trousers to her father. He holds the pocket in both hands, examines the folds and seams.

'Here?'

'Right inside.'

Harry lifts the pocket to his nose and sniffs, waits a moment, pulls the material tight and sniffs again.

'Can't smell a thing.'

'You haven't given it enough time. Have another go.'

Harry tries again. Shakes his head. 'You sure you haven't

got anything on your fingers, girl? You been cooking today? Smell your fingers, Emma. Go on. Smell them.'

'Meh, meh.'

Cati puts the sheep on top of the dressing table in her grandparents' bedroom and takes hold of the curtain cord. Her Grandpa has shown her how to use this but until today she hasn't had a chance to do so by herself. As she pulls the cord she feels a sense of power, of accomplishment, that a little girl like herself can move curtains of such size and weight, of such folding opulence. So she does it again, opens and closes the curtains, feels the power coursing through her arms.

'Meh, meh.'

The sheep is walking along the glass surface of the dressing table. She takes a sudden turn to the left and pokes her head over the edge.

'Don't fall, Mrs Sheep.'

The sheep tries her level best to open the drawer but her feet are too small to get a proper grip on the handle, so Cati must help her. She opens the drawer half an inch or so, just enough to let in a shaft of light. The sheep jumps up and down in excitement, bounds and capers from one end of the drawer to the other, pokes her nose through the crack.

'Meh, meh.'

Cati pulls the drawer out further. She knows that her Grandpa will have hidden the Rolos under his handkerchiefs over on the right: it's what he always does. The sheep, however, is not privy to this information: this is her first visit to Grandpa's bedroom and Cati hasn't shared the secret with her. Setting out on her own account, the sheep quickly gets lost amongst the socks so that Cati must ask her, with a mix of anxiety and reproach, 'Where have you got to, Mrs Sheep, where *have* you *got* to?' The sheep answers, 'Meh, meh. Meh, meh.' At last, she finds the Rolos. She wrestles clumsily with the wrapping. 'No, no, no, Mrs Sheep,' Cati says, 'you can't have any Rolos until you ask Grandpa. They're Grandpa's Rolos.' She puts the Rolos in her skirt pocket.

On turning to leave, Cati sees her Grandma's head on the pillow. This gives her a start – finding Grandma in bed isn't part of the Friday afternoon visit – and she stands for a moment, pondering what to do next. At first she is anxious that she might have woken her with all her chatter and her rummaging through the drawers, and Grandma must be very tired indeed to go to bed at this time of the afternoon. But no, on moving closer, she can see that her eyes are closed and her hand, the one hand that is visible by the pillow's edge, is quite still. Cati stands for another few seconds, then places the sheep gently on the side of the bed and says, 'Meh, meh,' by way of introducing the new creature to her Grandma. She fully expects that the eyes will open presently because the lips have already parted, she can see that clearly now. And that's fine. It's what Grandma always does when they're playing pretend sleeps. A hand will shoot out and grab her arm. The voice will say, 'Boo!' That's what Cati expects.

'Meh, meh.'

But the hand and the mouth remain still. Cati, realising now that Grandma isn't playing pretend sleep but is in fact sleeping properly, says, 'Ssssh, Mrs Sheep.' Then she goes back and closes the curtains. Cati's quite happy to do this, too, because that's what's expected when someone's in bed, asleep. It also gives her another chance to pull the cord. But she does so more slowly this time, just an inch at a time, with hardly any noise at all, and she doesn't allow Mrs Sheep a single bleat.

Harry and Emma are standing by the front door when Cati comes downstairs and tells them that Mrs Sheep has found the Rolos, and with only a little help from her, and that she kept nice and quiet, too, so as not to disturb Grandma. And Grandpa says, 'There's a good sheep she is.' But his mind is on other things. He has a plastic bag in his hand, the bus leaves in ten minutes, and he'll have to hurry or the shop will be shut. By now Emma has reached the gate. She says, 'Come on, then, Cati,' because she, too, has jobs to do. The three of them walk through the gate. Harry says, 'Bye-bye, Mrs Sheep. Bye-bye, Cati.' The sheep replies, 'Meh, meh.' And when Cati asks her mother why Grandma's asleep in bed this time of day Harry has already disappeared around the corner and Emma is listening to a telephone message from her husband.

17

'Wilson ran with his long, swift, rhythmic stride, and I kept up with him.' The Wizard, 25 May 1946

1947 was the best year, you might say, if you've set your mind on weeding out the best of everything, not just the best races but the best years as well. And there are different kinds of best, I'll grant you that. Different kinds of first, and different kinds of best, too. And a year will tell you more than a race. The best year up to that point, mind you, because I was only fourteen. But best years are bigger then, when you're young, when you haven't got too many under your belt, weighing you down. 1947. The year Wilson of *The Wizard* won the Philadelphia decathlon with the highest score ever. Higher than your Daley Thompsons, your Jürgen Hingsens.

And me setting off to follow, joining the Harriers, building up to my second wind.

That's when I started on the list. Which meant not just the races but the high jumps and the long jumps as well, and the javelin and the boxing and the swimming and the weightlifting, because Wilson did the lot.

VENUE & DATE	EVENT	NOTES
6 March '38 Stamford Bridge	Mile 3:48	Beat world record by 17 seconds!
19 May '38 Athens Olympics	Javelin 262 ft.	After going to Lathos to study sculpture of Hermes
3 Sept. '38 New York	440 yds 0.44	Despite breaking 3 ribs
22 April '39 Berlin	Half Mile	In front of Dr. Goebbels

Etc.

Why keep a list? Well, to start with, Wilson had got lost in the war. Shot down in flames and everybody shrugging their shoulders, saying, That's him gone, poor dab. Won't see the like again. End of an era. So we needed a record, for posterity. And if Harry Selwyn didn't do it, who would? That's why I kept a list. To get it all down on paper, so it wouldn't be forgotten, or misremembered.

Right enough, you say, very meticulous. But didn't you still have all the back numbers? Couldn't you just look at the comics if you wanted to check your facts? Of course I could. They were all there, under the bed, in boxes, in chronological order, too. *The Wizard*, *The Hotspur*, *The Hornet* and the rest. And Mam under orders not to mess them about when she was doing the hoovering or changing the sheets. But who wants to wade through a box full of comics just to check a single fact? Imagine somebody at school claiming Wilson wasn't the first four minute miler. I couldn't say, 'Oh, I'm sorry, please come back tomorrow, we'll have a chat then, after I've looked under the bed.' Who'd have believed me?

So, a record. An *aide memoire*. Short, sweet, portable. That's what I needed. Something I could point to and say, 'Look. Stamford Bridge, 6th of March, 1938. The first to break four minutes. There's the facts for you, right there.' It was more than one sheet of paper afterwards, mind you, because Wilson just went on winning. The Philadelphia decathlon was the best, like I said. It took ten lines to write it all down, even using one of the new biros, with their thin letters. But then there was the Black Olympics, when he went over to Africa and beat Chaka and all the Zulus. And some might say that was the best, because there were over a million Zulus and just one Wilson. The whole shabang went on for months and I needed two sheets to get it all down. There's more than one kind of best. That's all I'm saying.

In the end I gathered the sheets of paper together and sat back and thought, God, look at him, on his feet since 1814 and still at it. And that was the best of all. Not the score. Not the winning. Just that Wilson had waited until he was one 152 years old before reaching his peak. Which meant that even though he was fast, faster than anyone else in the world, he still lived in the slow lane. That's where his true home was. He bided his time, waited his chance. Fast in his legs, you could say. But slow in the heart. And there's nothing like running if you want to slow down the heart. It's a paradox, but there you are.

That's why I want you to keep your own record, a little inventory of the things I tell you. In case someone asks about me and I'm indisposed. 'Harry Selwyn, did you say? Who's he, then?' Or perhaps they'll have a stab and get it wrong. 'Isn't he the feller there was that fuss about...?' After reading the *Gazette*, maybe. Or talking to Raymond. 'Wasn't he out there himself, way back ...?' And you'll be there to put them right, to tell them that all Harry Selwyn ever did was keep to the slow lane, ease his heart and prepare for the long haul.

18

Friday, 21 May, 5.45pm

'I'd like to speak to the Manager, please.'

Having waited his turn in the queue, and then waited a further two minutes while the sales assistant consulted her computer, Harry has decided to speak plainly. A paying customer has his rights, a company has its responsibilities. Plain speaking is called for.

'You mean Mr Beynon?'

'Could be. Young chap ... Dark hair ... He was working here earlier ... Over by there ... You went to speak to him about my trousers.'

'Ah, yes. Mr Beynon. He's gone home.'

'Home?'

'He finished at five. Is there some way I can help you, Mr ... Mr ...'

'Selwyn.'

'Yes. I remember. Mr Selwyn. The trousers. You brought the trousers back.'

'Because of the legs.'

'The legs ...'

'The legs were too short. My wife said ... But that doesn't matter now, I've come to tell Mr ... Mr ...'

'Mr Beynon ...'

'Yes, to tell Mr Beynon how it happened, to tell him ...'

'How it happened?'

'Yes, how it happened.'

'I don't understand, Mr Selwyn. How what happened?'

'How the ... How the ...'

Although Harry has decided to speak plainly, he had hoped to do so in the company of someone in authority, someone who would afford him the courtesy of a private hearing, in an office with a door that could be closed. He is in a quandary: Mr Beynon isn't here but Harry has already wasted half a day on this tiresome errand and his message – the explanation he has been composing and refining since he spoke to Emma – demands a voice and an ear. This is why he leans over the counter, makes a come-here gesture with his finger, and starts whispering slowly and with great deliberation. What he has to say he will say once, and once only.

'To tell him ... how ... that smell ... got on the trousers.' Harry pauses a moment to make sure the girl is following, to assess whether her silence is a sign of attention or, as he fears, mere indifference, the boredom of late afternoon. 'To tell him … that it wasn't me… *It was someone else …*' He pauses again, clears his throat, draws breath. 'Someone else bought these trousers and then returned them, changed them for another style, another size, perhaps. And I'm not saying it was you who served him, it might well have been a colleague of yours, but be that as it may, he brought the trousers back, and the smell was already on them. *It was already on them.* But he got to change them anyway. Yes, and they went back out into the shop, onto the rail, to be sold again. Do you follow me? The trousers were put out to be sold again, and that's how I bought them, with the smell already there. *Already there. On the trousers.* And it's odd, I'm not saying otherwise, because you said you couldn't put them out again, not with that smell on them. But listen to this, listen to this, what if the girl who was working here at the time couldn't smell the smell? Mm? Couldn't *smell* the smell. She had a cold, perhaps. A bunged-up nose. And she said to the chap, Well, there you are, then, your wife says they're too small – or too big, of course, on that occasion, with the other chap, or maybe a bit tight in the waist – yes, and she says, there you are, then, you'd best go and choose another pair and we'll do a swap. Go and get another pair and you'll be right then, we'll change them for you, we'll …'

To show how this scene might have unfolded, Harry turns and points over to where the trousers are displayed on their hangers. In doing so, he is shocked to see that a long queue has formed behind him. He is shocked, also, to realise that his discreet whisper has swollen into a declamatory boom. He turns back to the girl, leans over the counter again and resumes his *sotto voce*. 'You see what I mean?' He waits. Looks into her eyes.

'Do you know this other gentleman, Mr Selwyn?'

'I beg your pardon?'

Harry's 'I-beg-your-pardon' is meant to convey surprise only, but the girl takes it literally, decides that this troublesome customer is hard of hearing, and raises her voice accordingly, speaks more distinctly and, by now, with perhaps a little rasp of impatience.

'Do you *know* the gentleman who brought the trousers back the first time?'

'*Know* him?' Harry reins in his voice again in an effort to get the girl to do likewise. 'Of course I don't know him. I'm only saying ...'

'But if you don't know the gentleman ...'

'And I'm not saying he's got to be a man. It could be a woman, came in to get a pair of trousers for her husband and got the wrong size, a touch too small, a touch too big, he tried them on at home, and they didn't fit, so back she comes ...'

'But Mr Selwyn, if you don't know who the lady is, or the gentleman, how do you know that's what happened? How can you prove it? How ...?'

'Prove? How do you mean, *prove*?'

'Prove that someone other than yourself has worn these trousers.'

'But how else *could* it have happened? If it wasn't me, it must have been somebody else. And it wasn't me.'

'Alright, Mr Selwyn, I'll have a word with the Manager on Monday.'

'Monday?'

'When he comes back. He isn't working this weekend.'

'But they're too small ... The legs ... My wife says ...'

'I'm sorry, Mr Selwyn, that's all I can do for you today.'

'Is there another manager I can talk to? Is there someone who can ...'

'Mr Selwyn, there are people waiting. The store closes in a quarter of an hour.'

Harry descends the escalator and turns for the exit. It is a quarter to seven and an amplified voice from above instructs all customers to take their goods to the nearest checkout. It thanks them for shopping in this branch of David Lewis, wishes them a good evening, a pleasant weekend, and expresses the hope that they will return soon. 'Good evening to you, too,' says Harry, under his breath. And perhaps that is the tipping point. Instead of proceeding to the exit, which is now only a few yards away, he turns abruptly and retraces his steps.

Harry alone ascends the escalator. This makes him nervous: he can feel the gaze of the descending shoppers upon him, their unspoken judgement. Good Lord, they're thinking, who's the old codger in the tracksuit? Has he lost the plot? In fact, Harry half expects someone to call over to him, to tell him, in a friendly if slightly condescending voice, that he's going the wrong way, he needs to go down, not up. But no one says anything. They have their shopping to think of, their buses to catch, their teas to make.

On returning to the first floor, Harry is glad to see a cluster of people at the checkout and others, too — women in the main, although this is the men's section – still wandering amongst the jackets and shirts and trousers. This is encouraging. It feels perfectly natural, then, to go and join them, for who is to say that he, Harry, isn't related to one of those women, still seeking that elusive present for husband or son? Who is to say he isn't the husband himself? And having made his way over to join these other last-minute shoppers, it is natural, too, that he should simulate their now rather rushed and fumbling scrutinies, taking a pair of trousers off its rail, looking at the label, the price, the waist size, the leg length, replacing it, moving quickly to another.

So this is what Harry does. For a minute or so, he fails to locate the Taupe 'Charleston' Herringbone Flat Front Trousers. They have no doubt been moved, he thinks, to make room for the more seasonal styles, the chinos, the shorts and the Farhi Linen Trousers which, Harry notices, are now for sale at a 20% reduction. He knows that this is the way of things: a stratagem to keep the customers on their toes. In fact, for that one minute, part of him is convinced that the Taupe 'Charleston' Herringbone Flat Front Trousers have ceased to exist, that the line has been discontinued, the company gone to the wall. What is more, he feels, deep down in the pit of his stomach, that this has all been done quite deliberately just to prevent him from returning his trousers and restoring justice and good order to the world. A foolish notion, of course, but that is how terror afflicts a man unaccustomed to illegality and ill-prepared for the act he must shortly commit.

Despite his discomfort, Harry continues moving from row to row, from unit to unit, considering this item and that, wondering whether he dare ask a member of staff. Would that make him appear more authentic? Or would it merely draw unwelcome attention? He lifts up a leg of the Charcoal Birdseye Premium Suit Trousers and rubs the material between finger and thumb. He inspects the quality of the stitching on the inside seams. This is what he has seen women do, it is what is to be expected in a clothes shop: close examination of the product, a little humming and hahing over the price. It mustn't be overdone, of course: what is natural for a woman is not of necessity natural for a man. No, not by a long chalk. And Harry, despite his years, is an amateur in the world of clothes shopping.

He finds the Taupe 'Charleston' Herringbone Flat Front Trousers in the furthest corner, between the window and the jeans. He remembers standing here before, on his first visit. They have not moved. The memory affords him a little balm of comfort, encourages him to believe that the world is not so capricious as he feared. He is buoyed up, too, by the realisation that this location is well suited to the little manoeuvre he has in mind. He stands with his back to the window. Over his spectacles he can see the queue at the till, now reduced to the last handful. A security guard is positioned strategically at the top of the escalator, where he keeps an eye on a group of teenage boys, idling amongst the trainers. They, in turn, keep a watchful and slightly provocative eye on the security guard.

Harry examines the label. Waist 32 Leg 30. An inch longer than the other pair. An inch longer than he is used to, as well, which is odd, he thinks, given that age will surely tend to reduce a man, not augment him. But Beti knows best. There has been a mistake somewhere, no doubt. Harry lifts the trousers off the hanger and puts them into his David Lewis shopping bag. Then he takes out the old Taupe 'Charleston' Herringbone Flat Front Trousers – the deficient ones, too short in the leg and also, allegedly, infected by an inappropriate smell – and drapes them over the top of the unit. He would prefer to hang them neatly, so they could exactly mimic the pair he has just removed. But this, he decides, is too risky. Even if he had the time, he would never be able to fold them in the officially prescribed way and then feed them through the narrow apertures. The David Lewis hanger is a much more exacting contraption than those in the wardrobe at home. So he leaves them where they are, on top of the unit. He looks at his watch. He looks through the window at the busy street below. He sizes up his escape route.

The security guard remains at his post by the top of the escalator. He's sharing a joke with one of the sales girls. His smile says that his shift is about to draw to a close. The suspicious looking boys have disappeared, so he can relax and look forward to going home. The air of vigilant surveillance that he generated has also receded. Despite this, and even though the offence has already been committed, Harry feels an instinctive compulsion to distance himself from the deed, to draw some kind of curtain between himself and its maleficence. On the wall to his left there is a small display of bright orange jackets. He removes one of these, reads the label – Craft Performance Running Jacket – and carries it over to the till. There is only one person in the queue but the few seconds' wait allows Harry to hold the garment up in front of him, to examine the sweat panels under the armpits, to read the washing instructions, so that all may witness the seriousness of his intent. On reaching the counter he asks the sales assistant whether perhaps they might have something between the Medium and the Large, because the one is rather tight across his shoulders and the other a little too long. And he doesn't mind when she says, 'No, I'm sorry, sir, that's all there is.' By now, everyone knows that he is a customer, no more, no less – somewhat hard to please, perhaps, and a trifle odd, too, in his tracksuit and daps, but the genuine article, nonetheless.

Harry is relieved then that he doesn't have to take the jacket back to its hanger. That would mean returning to the furthest recesses of the men's clothes section and the temptation to unwind time, to undo his transgression, might be more than he could resist. Onward, he thinks. Onward, and don't look back.

As he passes the security guard Harry ventures a modest smile and receives a 'Good-day now' in return. He is, after all, an old man, and who would suspect an old man with a David Lewis shopping bag in his hand?

19

Heart time v World time

'You'll be the oldest in the race tomorrow, then, Harry, will you?'

Thinking, well, if there's somebody older than you, tell me now so I can be off for a quick word before they pop their clogs. No point wasting my time talking to the *second* oldest.

I told him, 'You're older than me, Sam. In heartbeats. There's a lot will be older than me tomorrow, in heartbeats. Put that in your paper, Sam. Teach people a thing or two.'

He threw me a quizzical look.

So I told him. Wrote it all down.

$$3,000,000,000$$

Just like the kids, back at school.

Three billion, I said. The biggest number they'd ever seen. A blackboard-full. So I'd have to walk right across, one end to the other, just to show them how many kinds of nothing there were. The nothing that's really nothing, then all the nothings that aren't nothing at all, but different kinds of something. But only one number at the end of the day. And one question. If everybody's got three billion heartbeats, then why do some live longer than others? Wrote that up on the blackboard, too.

If everybody has three billion heartbeats, why do some live longer than others?

Nobody knew.

So I made everybody put a hand on his neighbour's chest and start counting. Waited till a minute was up, then shouted 'Stop' and told them to get their number and write it down, and no cheating. Then went round the class.

'Simpson?'

'68, sir.'

'Preece?'

'74, sir.'

'Ellis-Jones?'

'73, sir.'

'Lovell?'

'65, sir.'

Up they went on the blackboard then, name and number, name and number. And there'd always be a little Jenkins in the back row would shout out '79, sir!' As though he'd already won, thinking his heartbeat was a score, like a cricket match. I'd tell him, 'Well, well, Jenkins, 79 not out! That's a lot of heartbeats to squeeze in to one minute. Well done, boy!'

Then turned to his neighbour. '63, sir,' he'd mumble.

'What's that, Evans? What's that you say? Only 63? That's not many, is it?' And move on.

'71, sir.'

'76, sir.'

'68, sir.'

Until the blackboard was full of heartbeats. And I asked them again. Why do some people live longer than others? And they'd shuffle their bums and they'd pick their noses, because they'd had a bellyful by then. Like little Sam Applebys, didn't want to learn anything, just wanted to hear another story.

But then it dawned. A face lit up. And another. Just one or two to begin with, but they made little pools of light, and the light spread. Evans told Williams, and Williams told Roberts, and Roberts told Dodgson, and even Jenkins and Beynon knew by the end.

I asked them again. 'Do you understand? Do you see why some people live longer than others?'

And the one who'd said '63' looked a lot happier than the one who'd said '79'.

I had them write it down in their exercise books then, to practise their long division, to see how many 63s there were in three billion, how many 76s and 68s, and so on. And when they'd done that, 'So, what's the answer, Lovell? What will they put on your gravestone, when you've done with sums and heartbeats?'

And the wind's in his sails now. It's last shall be first time, and winning from behind is twice as good.

'90, sir! I'll be 90 years old!'

Which is older than his Grandpa, older even than his Great Uncle Billy who lost a leg at Passchendale. But as for Jenkins.

'What will be on your gravestone, Jenkins?'

'72, sir.'

'Speak up, boy!'

'72, sir.'

Live fast, live short. That's the rule. And it was a good way to learn your long division.

I wrote it all out so Sam could follow, so he'd know what I meant when I said the heart had its own time. 'I'm younger than you,' I told him. 'A lot younger. In heartbeats.' It might be true, as well, I can't say for certain – I didn't have the gumption to put my hand on his chest and count. But how long would you give a tubby journalist who's just turned fifty-five and has no idea how to slow his heart?

'You're talking to a youngster here, Sam,' I said. 'Come back in a couple of years when I've had a bit more practice.'

20

Friday, 21 May, 6.20pm

On his way out of the store Harry passes two young women handing out leaflets to promote the David Lewis Loyalty Card. He is glad of this parting opportunity to reassert his status as an insignificant and benign consumer.

'Leaflet, sir?'

The woman on the left smiles at him. Harry takes a leaflet and smiles back.

'Thank you.'

In fact he smiles more fulsomely than is necessary for such a rudimentary exchange. He looks into her eyes, too, as though trying to borrow from them some of her own authenticity. But she has already turned to another customer.

Everyone is in a hurry to get home, to show their new frocks to husbands and partners, to prepare tea. Perhaps, Harry thinks, she is planning to go out tonight, if only to the pub, or to a friend's house, and that's where her mind is now, far from leaflets and shoppers. She has no interest in the contents of bags. She doesn't even notice the slight fret of perspiration which he can feel now, dampening his brow.

When the alarm sounds, Harry does not at first understand its significance. The high-pitched bleep is less bell-like, more subdued and remote than might be expected of a device designed to repel thieves; it is also less insistent, less intrusive than the ambulance siren that Harry and the other shoppers can now hear, spilling into the store through the wide-open doors. So for a couple of steps the *beep, beep, beep* is drowned out by that other, more urgent alarm. And even then, when the ambulance has passed and Harry's ears have identified the shop alarm for what it is, he is not too perturbed. Several others pass through the doors at more or less the same time and all, on hearing the *beep, beep, beep*, look at their bags, shrug their shoulders, shake their heads, to declare their innocence, to show that there's been some mistake, that someone else must be to blame.

Harry does likewise: he looks at the trousers in his bag, shakes his head and continues on his way. A minute later he is walking though the town centre, neither hurrying nor dawdling, but adopting the measured, slightly distracted aura of a man preoccupied by other things. Harry has a further reason not to be overly exercised by the alarm. Although only an occasional visitor to large clothes stores, he is certain he knows what a security tag looks like and he is equally certain he saw nothing of the kind when he took the trousers down from their hanger. Such tags are, in his experience, invariably big fat chunky things, telling you to beware, to watch your step. He would have noticed.

Despite persuading himself that all is well, Harry decides not to walk up to Castle Street and catch the bus home, as he would normally do. Instead he takes a sudden turn to the left, into Paget Street, and begins to run. Why does he do this? There are several possible explanations. Perhaps he doesn't wish to stand at the bus stop and be the object of others' scrutiny, their huddled, behind-the-hand comments. 'Isn't that what-d'you-call? You know, that teacher fellow. Gracious, he's not looking too hot, is he? And what's that he's got in his bag, I wonder?' Or maybe, after all, he's simply obeying his instincts. Harry is still wearing his tracksuit and his New Balance RX Terrain running shoes and the meaning of this, after so many years, is that he is about to run. Perhaps Harry himself would find it difficult to explain why he starts running. But that is what he does.

Harry jogs gently at first but soon increases his speed. By now the adrenalin and the cortisol are telling him that he is no longer a mere shopper, casually wending his way home. Nor is this merely another jog. It is a race. Although Harry cannot see the other runners he knows they are there somewhere, out of sight, waiting to make their move, and he must hold on to his lead. Running at speed, however, the shopping bag becomes an encumbrance, swaying and flapping with each step, disrupting his rhythm. So, without slowing, he rolls it up and holds it in his right fist, just as though it were a baton, and thinks, There, that's better. He's relieved, too, that the name David Lewis is no longer visible to the world, primed to betray him. He takes another turn, into Garth Road, and then, after a hundred yards, he reaches the south gate of the park.

Harry can begin to relax now. Here, in the park, no one will look askance at a man wearing a tracksuit and trainers. He slows to a brisk walk. He knows he has done quite enough running today, that he mustn't push himself too hard only a few hours before a race. On reaching the tall chestnut trees by the river he pauses a while and lets his gaze wander: to a scatter of children throwing a frisbee; to a middle-aged couple out for a walk, hand-in-hand − they too contemplating the frisbee-throwers; and then to three men in orange overalls, raking the flower borders. He savours their indifference, the knowledge that he is quite invisible and insignificant to them.

His composure restored, Harry unrolls the plastic bag, intending to carry it once more by the handle, in the conventional manner, and resume his progress. In doing so, however, he yields to the temptation to have a quick peek at the trousers within, to make sure they haven't creased. It would be a pity if he had to iron them before going out tomorrow night; and even rigorous ironing cannot wholly restore newness once it has been lost. A pity, and a sign of negligence, too, which Beti would no doubt chastise him for. But in order to do the job properly, and to ensure he won't accidentally drop the trousers on the dusty path, Harry must sit down. So he walks on until he reaches a wooden bench. He draws a hand along the wooden slats, then examines the palm: it is dry and clean. Clean enough.

Harry sits down and lays the trousers out flat on his lap. He thinks, Well, that's not too bad, not too bad at all. He lifts the trousers up with both hands and allows the legs to hang down in front of him. He considers the shallow folds at each knee and judges that these will surely come out quickly enough with the heat of his body, that this is the difference between a fold and a crease: a fold will right itself without recourse to an iron. Then, instinctively, and merely to enjoy the newness further, he moves his finger along the waistband. He feels the seam inside, its taut, discreet stitching. It is a great deal more complex than he had anticipated, comprising several rows and layers which it is difficult to disaggregate. He puts on his glasses so he can make sense of it all. So much stitching, he thinks. For such a simple garment.

Harry turns the trousers over, examines the legs, first the left, then the right, and thinks, Fine. Smooth as glass. He returns to the waistband, undoes the button and opens the zip. That is as it should be, too, although the zip is rather stubborn. He would have preferred buttons, but the Taupe 'Charleston' Herringbone Flat Front Trousers were not available in a buttoned model, so that was that. Harry opens and closes the zip three or four more times and is pleased when it begins to move more smoothly. Good, he thinks. That's all very good. That's just as it should be.

It is at this point that Harry notices the small black disc, no bigger than a button, attached to the seam above the left pocket. It is, to all intents and purposes, and especially to the casual observer, indistinguishable from the real button on the waistband. Then, turning the trousers over, he sees a second small disc, attached both to the same seam and also – as is now clear – to the first disc. He looks at each in turn. He squeezes them between finger and thumb. He realises that they are, in fact, a single unit, or at least so tightly bolted together as to make no difference. He grips them between the fingers and thumbs of both hands and tries, first, to turn them, and then to pull them apart. But to no avail.

The trousers lie flat in Harry's lap. He looks over at the men in orange overalls. He looks at the seagulls that have begun to gather on the grass. He looks at the litter bin on the other side of the path, at the grey squirrel perched on its rim, scavenging for titbits amongst the refuse. The *beep, beep, beep* has begun to sound again in his inner ear and he knows well enough, despite his years, that the world has shrunk, that the little things have become the big things, and the smallest are the biggest of all. He gives the little discs another tug, says 'Blast' under his breath. But he isn't surprised. What, after all, is the point of a security tag that comes loose as simply, as willingly, as a common-or-garden button? He looks at the litter bin. Who, he thinks, would be any the wiser? One casual turn of the wrist, and his bag will become just another item of rubbish, evidence of nothing but the general, impersonal superfluity of things.

The squirrel runs off to a nearby tree. Harry has the bin to himself. He rehearses the act in his mind. The turn of the wrist. The fingers opening. The drop. He does this over and over, each time devising a slightly different way of releasing the bag, of deflecting attention. On balance, he feels that it would be best to drop the bag whilst walking, so that the one disguises the other, a little ballet of seamless nonchalance. He will walk, neither too fast nor too slow, and perhaps whistle as well, and let the bag fall into the bin without pause. Without undue attention either: he will exercise only the minimal care that any bag of rubbish would warrant. Like the remnants of a picnic. Banana skins. Crumbs. Crisp packets. The bag would, of course, remain exposed on top of the bin. That couldn't be helped. Indeed, Harry decides, it would be a great mistake even to try to conceal the bag, to be seen scavenging amongst the refuse, like some vagrant. A gently paced walk, therefore, accompanied by an equally gentle whistle. Drop the bag without stopping, without even slowing down. Then carry on.

That is what Harry decides to do.

But despite his careful planning, Harry remains seated on the bench. He realises that his decision, firm though it is, relates to the method of disposal only. Indeed, it is the very finality of that decision that allows it to drift to the back of his mind now and be replaced by other, more abstract considerations. He hates wasting money, and throwing a new pair of trousers into a litter bin would be like throwing two twenty pound notes into the fire. He makes a mental picture of himself doing just that, and flinches at the idiocy, the wickedness, of it. Harry knows, too, that he has justice on his side. He, and only he, has a moral right to these trousers. No matter what the girl in the shop says, or her cheeky young whelp of a manager, or even the security tag itself, that right is indivisible and indisputable. And why should a man be punished for standing up for his rights? Why should he be compelled to burn forty pounds because his trousers are too short?

More important, however, is the fact that Harry, rightly or wrongly, now suspects that one of the men in orange overalls is looking at him. Is he laughing, too? It's difficult to be certain, and Harry doesn't want to stare, but he can see the white of the man's teeth. He can see him turn, say something to the orange man at his side. Does he look over, too?

It's time to go home.

Back at David Lewis's, Brian, the security officer on the ground floor – a tall, gangly young man who looks uncomfortable in his starched uniform and peaked hat – whispers to the girl who has been distributing the leaflets: 'No worries. I know the guy. He used to teach me in school. Real head case. Lives up by the park. I'll sort him out later.'

The girl, whose name is Connie, has no interest in Brian or what he has to tell her. Like everyone else, at this time on a Friday afternoon, her mind is on other things. And anyway she knows that Brian is only trying to sound cool, to make her think he knows stuff.

'Later?'

And she says that much only because it's high time someone cut the preening know-all down to size.

Brian shrugs, says nothing.

'And what d'you mean, sort him out? You're not the police. You can't sort people out.'

Brian still says nothing. He taps the side of his nose with his finger. He gives Connie a wink.

21

Whistling v. The World

'So then, Harry,' said Sam. 'How's it done? How do you slow down your heart?'

As though there was a secret, and if I whispered the secret in his ear he'd be able to do it himself.

'Do you do iso ... Do you do iso ...'

And looked out through the window, as though the word was hiding amongst the dahlias.

'Isometrics?'

'No.'

'Isotonics?'

'That's it. Isotonics. Are you one of those isotonic types?' And perked up a bit then, thinking he'd got there, that the secret was out.

'No, I'm not,' I said.

I'd half a mind to go and fetch the cutting as well, the one with the apology in it, to jostle his memory, in case he thought isotonics was just a new fangled sort of strychnine. But I didn't. Instead, I said, 'Do you know what the Kalenjin eat, Sam?' Because the Kalenjin are about as far as you can get from strychnine and isotonics.

'The Kalen ...?'

'In Kenya,' I said. 'In Africa.'

And had to explain who they were, that the Kalenjin could run three marathons, one after the other, without a break. Three marathons, I said, and at night, too. Run right through the night and up about their business in the morning, same as usual. I asked him again, did he have any idea what the Kalenjin had for their supper, before they went out for their three marathons, what they ate to keep up their strength?

Of course he didn't.

'Maize,' I told him. 'A bowl full of maize and a pint of beer.'

He laughed at that. Not a belly laugh, just a wheezy snigger through his nose. 'It's no laughing matter,' I said. So he laughed again, thinking my sudden earnestness a mere pretence, a part of the joke. That's why I said no more about the Kalenjin. (I should never have mentioned them in the first place.) I changed tack and said, 'Whistling.' I thought, Well, if it's a secret he wants, and he's not impressed by the maize, whistling's as good as anything, he can have a good snigger at that. It's a pretty safe bet, too. It doesn't have any strychnine in it and nobody's going to send me a letter saying I've broken the rules because I've been overheard having a sly whistle.

'Whistling, Sam,' I said. 'That's how it's done. That's how you slow the heart.'

You had to choose the right tune, of course. Strike the right balance between inhalation and exhalation. Keep a smooth legato. Then I whistled 'In the Still of the Night', to show him how. Let each line float in its own time, turned the notes on my tongue for a while before setting them free. Made him wait for his story.

'Conserving the breath I call that, Sam,' I said, when I finished. 'Keeping a penny's worth in the fist, so you last out until the end of the line. Maybe tuppence, or threepence, just in case, because it's a long line, the air in your lungs gets less and less, every note tries to swallow up more than its share. Just a few pennies. Keep them tight in your fist. To last you out.'

I whistled it again, 'In the Still of the Night'. Made him wait a bit more. Whistled it like Dad used to, not the beginning so much, but later on. 'At the moon in its flight, My thoughts all ...' Can't remember how it went then. Dad never sang it, couldn't sing to save his life. Whistled it on our way down to fetch the fish, and both of us knowing it was a joke, because it was morning we went for the fish, not the still of the night. But you could see the moon sometimes. In the winter. Still, too. Quiet. 'My thoughts all stray to you.' That's how it went. And Dad's lips in a tight O so you'd swear he really wanted to sing the long 'Yoooo' but could only do the whistle.

'Give it a go,' I told Sam. 'Try it for yourself.' He'd need a good lungful before he got started, I said, to keep it going, to keep that note up in the air, flying right to the end.

Why don't we whistle like we used to? Now there's a question. The milkman, first thing in the morning. Bottle on the doorstep and a little warble to go with it, so in time you couldn't think of the milk without hearing the whistle too.

The window-cleaner, then. Up with the ladder. Time for a whistle. Dip the rag in the bucket. Another whistle. Everybody whistled.

No, not everybody. Women didn't whistle that much. Too common. And priests. Priests weren't great whistlers either. Too common for them as well, probably. But everyone else. So where's it gone? Are they still whistling but we can't hear them because of the din? Or don't they know the songs? Can't whistle their punk and their rap?

'That's the secret,' I told Sam. 'That's how you get your heart to bide its time. You whistle 'In the Still of the Night', legato, breathe slow and soft so you'd scarcely shift a feather. Everything else follows then. Get your breath right, I said, and the heart takes up the baton. I could hold my breath for two minutes, I told him. Back in the early days. Two whole minutes.

'So, Harry,' he asked me, 'do you whistle when you're running? Does it help your rhythm?' And started sniggering. Thinking, What's this halfwit prattling about again?

'You think I'm a halfwit, Sam?'

22

1945 Dad v. Uncle Jack

Dad came back. I walked into the house and smelled his cigarette smoke. Heard him then, upstairs. A man's feet sound different to a woman's. They're heavier, they know where they're going . Different to a woman. A woman's feet go this way and that, over by here then over by there. Stop every now and then because she's doing the dusting, giving the flowers some water, making the bed. These were a man's feet, no doubt about it, straight across the bedroom, into the bathroom, no stopping, no dillydallying. And heavy. Floorboards creaking under the weight.

'Dad back?'

Mam was in the kitchen.

'Harry? What ...?'

Because I was home early from school. We were all sent home early. The snow was deep, getting worse.

'The snow,' I said. 'It's starting to drift.'

Which was bad news if you lived out in the sticks, got stuck in the lanes. And anyway, it had all happened before, when the snow was heavy, so I couldn't understand why she was bothered.

'Dad home?'

She didn't answer. She went to the bottom of the stairs and shouted: 'Jack! Come on down, Jack. Harry's here. Come and say hello to Harry.'

It wasn't Dad at all. 'Your Uncle Jack,' she said. 'Called by to have a cuppa and a chat.' Heard him upstairs again, out of the bathroom, into the bedroom. 'And to see to the cistern,' she said. That's where he was now, upstairs, fixing the cistern, getting it to work properly.

'What's wrong with the cistern?' I said.

'The pressure,' she said. 'The ballcock.' Which surprised me, that a butcher would know about cisterns and ballcocks and suchlike.

He came down then and shook my hand and said I'd grown into a big boy and took a shilling out of his pocket. 'Buy yourself some sweets, Harry.' And smiled.

'What do you say, Harry? What do you say?' said Mam.

I said 'Thank you', but I said it more to the clothes horse than to Uncle Jack because I didn't want to look at him and have to be smiled at again. Then he took a packet of cigarettes out of his blazer pocket and said, 'Is the boy big enough to smoke yet?' And when Mam shook her head, he said, 'I'm sure he has the odd drag with his mates.' And turned to me. 'Do you, Harry? Do you have a sly smoke after school? With your mates, eh? Behind the bike sheds? In the toilets?' Then lit up. Stood in front of the fire, flicked his ash back into the grate and asked me if I liked football, did I think City would get promotion. Took a drag on his cigarette, blew smoke into the kitchen, talked about the snow, the black ice, the need for more grit. Flicked his ash into the grate.

That's when I saw it, just as he put the cigarette back in his mouth. The top of his middle finger had gone. The middle finger on his left hand, nail and all, and the skin grown back over just as though that's how it had always been.

'Wounded in action,' he said. He'd caught me staring. And he held his hand out in front of him then, so I could have a better look.

Mam said, 'Don't talk nonsense, Jack.' Because Uncle Jack hadn't been in the army or the RAF or anything. He'd been cutting chops, she told him, as though he didn't know already. The knife had hit a bone and slipped, and nobody to blame but himself. She looked at me. 'Nobody to blame but himself.' And cutting off the top of your own finger in your own butcher's shop was nothing when men were losing legs and arms and heads on the other side of the world.

He had white eyelashes, Uncle Jack, the same as his hair. White eyelashes and a pink face, just like a pig's, and I thought, Yes, that's how butchers are meant to look. That's how they all go after spending so much time in the company of pigs. Pity he wasn't a bit fatter, though. You've got to be fat to be a real pig. Fat like Sam Appleby.

'Brought your Mam a bit of bacon,' he said, all nice-nice, sorry he'd made her cross. 'Bit of butter, too.' And no mention of cisterns or ballcocks.

23

Friday, 21 May, 6.40pm

Harry opens the front door and shouts, 'Beti!' He has prepared himself to say 'Sorry', too, for being late, and he has already fashioned a plausible enough version of events at David Lewis's to present to his wife. He goes to the bottom of the stairs, puts a hand on the newel post and shouts again. 'Beti?' And listens to the silence.

Harry hangs his David Lewis bag on one of the hooks in the passage and takes off his anorak. He hangs this on another hook and makes for the kitchen. He switches on the kettle, drops a teabag into a mug and fetches the milk from the fridge. While waiting for the water to boil he sits at the table and opens today's post. The smaller of the two envelopes contains a bank statement. Harry puts this to one side. In the other, he finds a leisurewear catalogue. *Summer Edition 2012. Exclusive Welcome Discount of 15%.* He flicks through the pictures of young men and women, their beaming smiles, their gleaming kit. As his glance falls on the Ron Hill Men's Advance Contour Close-fitting Tights, he remembers the trousers, tut-tuts to himself and returns to the passage. He takes the bag off the hook, then throws the catalogue into the rubbish bin.

Harry makes his tea and sits down at the kitchen table. He lays the trousers out in front of him. Fearing that Beti might not approve, he picks them up again and hangs them over the back of a chair. He lets his right hand linger there a while, to remind himself that the fiasco at the shop is behind him, finished, settled, that everything is back to normal. He takes a sip of tea and glances at the bank statement. Then he goes over to the phone.

A woman's voice says that he has two messages. The first is from Sam Appleby, reminding Harry that a photographer will be calling at seven, or thereabouts. 'He'd like to get a shot of the two of you, Harry, you and Beti, in the house together.' Harry plays the message again. He remembers nothing of this arrangement and he thinks that seven o'clock is an odd time for photographers to be calling by. 'A shot of the two of you, Harry, you and Beti, in the house together. Just a reminder, in case it wasn't clear …' And although Harry remembers nothing, he is cross at Sam for thinking he needs reminding, for leaving a message that merely repeats what, it appears, has already been said and agreed.

Harry looks at his watch. It's a quarter to seven. He wonders whether Sam might mean seven in the morning. He considers for a moment whether that would be more plausible than seven in the evening. It's unlikely, but it's possible. And how can he find out? By phoning Sam, of course. But Harry has spent enough time today talking to Sam Appleby.

In the second message Raymond, Harry's brother, says 'Beti, just to let you know …' And explains that he'll be a little late for his Friday supper. He needs to take the bandsaw back to Dennis, and Dennis won't be home until six, and he might get held up in traffic. Harry's never heard of Dennis, so he listens to the message again. 'Dennis won't be home …' But it's a message for Beti, not Harry, so perhaps that's only to be expected. Beti will tell him who Dennis is.

Hearing the sound of feet walking across the floor above his head, Harry shouts out again.

'Beti!'

He opens the kitchen door.

'Beti!'

Only when the footsteps retreat does Harry realise that he has been duped. The sound is above his head, but the feet are next door. Neighbours share floorboards in these tight terraces. And Harry is aggrieved that even his house should conspire against him. He shakes his head. 'Where the hell?' He goes back to the phone. He must share his agitation with someone, if only to fill the dispiriting silence that has taken the place of the footsteps. He picks up the handset and dials his sister-in-law's number.

'Hello?'

The instant reply takes Harry by surprise. He realises he hasn't prepared himself, his mouth is devoid of words. He has been here once already today, dialling the same number, and he'd half expected the same result. He wants to chide Amy for being so inconsiderate, so thoughtless, as to take Beti into town without letting anyone know. But how can such a thing be said without full knowledge of the facts? Instead, he must be content with a single, stabbed question: 'Beti ... Is Beti there?' When Amy says that she's seen nothing of her sister all day, that she's been over at McArthur Glen with Alun, her husband, Harry is reluctant to believe her. 'Are you sure? Didn't she call by after she had her hair done?'

Amy has learned to tolerate her brother-in-law's truculence. Rather than risk storing up trouble for Beti later on, she suggests, gently, as though speaking to a fractious child, that he phone his daughter, Emma. She invites him to consider, too, whether Beti might have arranged to meet a friend. Can he think of anyone ...? Did she mention ...? And then, has he perhaps thought of ringing the hairdressers? Some of them are open late on Fridays, she knows this because she's been herself. 'She might even still be there, Harry.' Even if she isn't there, Amy explains, they'll surely have a record of her appointment. Her name will be in a book. The time, too.

Harry thinks for a moment, then says: 'The hairdressers. Yes, of course. Thanks, Amy, I'll give them a ring now.' Although Amy has offered a number of possible reasons for Beti's absence, all of them quite tentatively, he seizes upon this, the last of them, as the most authoritative. Hairdressers are women's matters: they know about such things. In any case, his thirst for explanation must be slaked from whatever source is to hand.

Not wishing to admit that he has no idea where his wife has gone to have her hair done, Harry draws the conversation to a close with a curt 'Good-bye then'. He leans both hands against the edge of the counter, bows his head, closes his eyes, and tries to think of hairdressers. He's sure Beti once mentioned some girl or other who cut her hair too short and that it was time to try somewhere else. But who that girl was, where she worked, and where Beti has gone since, are things he probably never knew, or was not conscious of knowing, and he realises it is futile to speculate.

Harry picks up Beti's little red telephone book. He looks under 'H' for 'Hairdressers' but finds nothing. He checks 'D' to make sure that Beti's system is as he supposes it to be. He finds the doctors coralled together, and the dentists, too. He returns to 'H', thinking he must have missed something, runs his finger down the two pages of Hendersons, Healeys, Howells and hospitals, but still finds no hairdressers. He ponders what other word she might have used. Coiff ... Coiff something or other. Coiffure? Coiffurist? He looks under 'C'. Nothing. Then he looks for Ladies Hair Stylist. He's seen this himself outside one of the shops in town and thought, Well, that's careless, leaving the apostrophe out of Ladies'. Drawing another blank, he tries to recall whether Beti said anything last night when he phoned her from the pub: something he missed because of the noise; or something he has since forgotten. 'I'm going to have my hair done tomorrow, Harry. At … At …' Something along those lines. But why would she? Why would she bother? Harry's memory short-cuts to his own voice, saying 'Don't wait up for me, *bach*. You get off to bed. I'll see you in the morning.'

Now flicking at random through the little red book, Harry's eye catches the letter 'K'. This letter stands out for two reasons. It is at the exact centre of the book, so the stitched binding allows it to remain open more easily at this page. There are also only three entries under this letter. He can ignore Kitchenware and Kevin Scott. He doesn't know who Kevin Scott is, but instinct tells him that he is unlikely to be a ladies' hairdresser. Which leaves Karen. Karen has no surname and, in the frustrating absence of other clues, Harry decides this is significant. It means she is on terms of some familiarity with Beti: she belongs to her daily round, her circle of acquaintance. He says the name out loud. 'Karen.' In his mind's eye he sees this Karen at work, scissors in hand, hair cuttings on the floor, Beti herself in the chair, making conversation. 'Thank you, Karen,' she says. 'Perhaps a little more off at the back …?' Karen. Just Karen. In Harry's reconstruction, Karens of this kind have no surname. He takes hold of the phone and dials.

'Karen?'

'Who's that?'

'Is that Karen? Karen the hairdresser?'

'Sorry?'

'The hairdresser … Are you the …'

'Who's speaking, please?'

'It's Harry Selwyn here, Karen. Sorry to bother you. It's about my wife. I'm not sure where she's got to. I was wondering, did she have, did you … Karen …? Hello …? Are you there, Karen?'

24

Harry v. The Quickening

Uncle Jack brought Mam some bacon. We ate it for breakfast and Mam said, 'Nice of your Uncle Jack, wasn't it?' I said yes, it tasted good, especially with the potatoes she'd fried up from the night before. I asked if Uncle Jack was going to bring any more. She said maybe, but I wasn't to tell anyone, with it being wartime and not much bacon to be had and some people might get cross that they didn't have a butcher in the family as well. I asked her where the bacon had all gone, and she said the Germans. Which made me think, was Uncle Jack a German too? Was that how he got his hands on it? And I thought, if that's right, no wonder Mam didn't want me to say anything.

I ate my bacon and it was crispy and salty and nice. Mam ate her bacon and a little piggy grew inside her. I didn't know at the time. You need a big sister to tell you things like that. Then I heard her being sick in the toilet. When she'd been sick three days running she started to cry as well. I asked her if she was going to see the doctor. She said, 'We'll see.' And carried on being sick. And even when she wasn't being sick her face looked like rice pudding, so she didn't want anybody to see her. That's why I couldn't let Robert Bramwell Number

Four come round and play with my new Meccano. I had to say, No, Mam was sick, and nobody was allowed in the house. When I told him the same thing a week later he said, She having a baby, then? Because his Mam was sick for months before she had Bernard, almost puked him out before he had a chance to get born. I told him to shut up. But it got me thinking.

The week after that we went to Grandma's. Mam put lots of make-up on, to cover up the rice pudding. The two of them went out into the back garden and I had to stay indoors and listen out for the plumber. But nobody called, so I think that was just a fib, to keep me in the house. I could see them through the window then, dead-heading the dahlias, nattering about things, standing still for a bit and looking glum. I took her *Home Doctor* out of the bureau and had a skim through. Looked up 'Sick' and 'Vomit' and 'Puke'. No wiser, though, couldn't pin it down. There was vomiting everywhere. Vomiting from food-poisoning, vomiting from heat, vomiting from this and that. Vomiting from pregnancy, too, mind you. But how could you tell? How could you know it was one and not the other? And not a word about tears.

I looked through Grandma's other books: her *Mrs Beeton's*, her *Lives of the Saints*, her *Gentlemen Prefer Blondes*, which promised me the intimate diary of a professional lady and had a doctor in it, right from the start. But two hundred pages were too much, and Mam wasn't blonde, and there were only so many flowers she could dead-head. Then I noticed the book next to it. It was turned back to front, so you couldn't see the title, just the pages, all brown and dusty. And you'd hardly know it was there because it was pushed right to the back of the shelf. So that made me think, Well, at last, this might be the business. If Grandma's turned it back to front, tucked it out of the way, it can't be just any old book. Not like the Bible. The Bible was staring you right in the face. *Mrs Beeton's*, too, and the rest. No, this was the only shy fellow. *Advice to a Wife on the Management of Her Own Health* it was called, can't remember who by. Dr Pie. Professor Pasty. Something like that. Something with a crust. It didn't have anything about tears in it, and I had to wade through a lot of stuff about the evils of tight lacing and pendulous bellies before I got to the morning sickness. But there it was. If you've got a baby inside you, it said, the vomiting stops after a while and the quickening starts. I'd no idea what a quickening was, but it sounded fast, and I thought, that's what I'll do, I'll look out for the quickening. Better bet than the tears, got to be. And I'd know then, one way or the other.

And how would I recognise the quickening? The pie man said it was just like the fluttering of a bird inside you. That's what he'd been told, anyway, by the ladies. So I wrote that down inside my comic. *Vomiting stops. Quickening starts. Like a fluttering.* When Mam and Grandma finished dead-heading and nattering, and I told them I'd listened out for the plumber but he hadn't come, we went back home and I waited. And I waited some more. And it stopped, right enough. The vomiting dried up.

'You better, Mam?'

'A little,' she said.

And she stopped looking like a rice pudding, too.

Then I listened for the fluttering. I sat with Mam in the kitchen, right up close, listened out for the little flip-flap. But heard nothing. I thought the fire was crackling too loud. Or maybe the tea and toast had filled her so much, the little wings couldn't work up a proper flutter. I looked in her eyes then, wondering if it might show itself there, just a blink, a quick flicker of the eyelashes. Or maybe a sudden gasp. Because that's where the wings were, down in the middle of her. So a quick gulp of air. Or a hiccup. Even a belch.

'What are you looking like that for, Harry?' she said.

Yes, a belch. That's what would have proved it. The bacon inside, telling you it's in there, turning back into a pig.

25

Friday, 21 May, 7.00 pm

Harry is about to ring his daughter to tell her about Karen, the hairdresser, and her inexplicable rudeness, when he hears a knock on the door. For a second he plays with the idea that Beti might have lost her key, perhaps left her purse in a shop, and here she is, returned home at last after hours of futile searching. The question is already beginning to form on his lips, 'Where, where have you been all this time?' But no, as he leaves the kitchen he sees through the bevelled glass in the front door the outline of a tall, thin man. He opens the door. The man has a large grey bag slung over his shoulder.

'I see you're all ready.'

'I'm sorry?'

The man looks down at Harry's running shoes. 'Your kit. You're ready for off?'

Harry looks down, too. 'Off?'

'Didn't Sam say?'

'Sam?'

'Sam Appleby. *The Gazette*.'

Harry struggles to associate the gaunt figure before him with the overweight journalist. Then he remembers the telephone message, realises the significance of the grey bag.

'Yes, yes. Of course. Sam. The pictures. Come on in, come on in.'

To compensate for his lapse of memory, Harry ushers the visitor into the house with exaggerated zeal. 'The wife's not back yet, mind ... She went out ... Went to town and hasn't ... Do go through to the kitchen ... That's it, through there.'

For the next twenty minutes the photographer takes pictures of Harry in various locations, both in the house and outside. He directs him to lean on the cast iron gate that opens onto the pavement. 'Look at the camera now, Harry ... That's it ... Now over to the left ...' He makes him pose by the Victorian fireplace in the lounge. Here, on the mantelpiece, stands a black and white photograph of Harry as a young man, attired just as he is today, in tracksuit and running shoes. 'Look at the picture, Harry ... At the eyes.' They move to the kitchen, where the photographer takes a number of close-ups of Harry at the long wooden table, his eight medals and two cups arrayed before him. In one, he spreads his arms wide, as though embracing his trophies. In another, he leans forward and rests his chin between cupped hands so that you would swear his head was itself a trophy. In another, he leans back in his chair, arms folded, the cups and medals left to speak on his behalf.

'Do you have any more, Harry? Are there any more cups?'

Having taken a dozen or so shots, the photographer finds himself still seeking ways of arranging his subjects. He senses an asymmetry. Here is Harry Selwyn, the oldest runner in Wales, by common consent. The pictures will confirm as much. They will capture, in particular, the sharp contrast between the smooth, flawless blue of the tracksuit and the wrinkled, weathered face of the man wearing it. But then the cups and medals will tell their own story, will pose their own questions. 'Is this all he has achieved?' they will ask. 'Is this the reward for sixty years of assiduous training, of dogged competition?' And this is not the story they are supposed to tell.

'Have you kept everything, Harry? You know, were they all yours for keeps? Or did you have to give some back, at the end of the year, that sort of thing ...?'

There must be something in the way the photographer asks this question that conveys his disappointment. Harry would normally say, 'Good gracious, no, I've hardly won a thing. Nothing worth mentioning, anyway. I've stuck at it, that's all. Stuck it out longer than the rest.' Then give a self-deprecatory chuckle, to show how little concerned he is with matters of winning and losing. He has done this before, and his audience has generally chuckled with him. They've found the unexpected combination of advanced age and humility quite endearing. But Harry doesn't like the patronising tone he detects in this man's voice. He bristles at the implication that he must do more to justify himself, as though it were he who had sought these irksome attentions. That is why he shakes his head, rises from his chair and asks the photographer to excuse him, but his brother is about to arrive and he must prepare supper.

The photographer closes the gate behind him.

'I'll see you in the morning, then.'

'Mm?'

'In the morning ... To take a few more pictures ... You and your wife ... Your wife will be there, won't she?'

'Yes, yes, she'll be there ... There we are, then. Goodbye, now.'

The photographer drives away and his voice is replaced by another, the nagging whine in Harry's head that says, 'Come on, Beti *fach*. Where have you got to? Where *on earth* have you got to?' He closes the front door, picks up a flyer from the mat.

PIZZA PARADISE

Two-for-one Special Offer
Free delivery on orders over £10

The pizza puts Harry in mind of supper, and the fish he has left in the fridge. Thinking of the fish, in turn, prompts him to consider the other items that must be got ready: the potatoes, the broccoli, the sauce, the parsley that will have to be chopped and mixed into the sauce. Is there any parsley left? He can't remember.

And where is Beti, to take charge of these things? Where has she gone? And why doesn't she come back?

Harry looks at the flyer, tries to remember whether he's ever seen Raymond eat a pizza.

26

1945 Harry Selwyn v. The Piglet

Raymond had started crawling before I noticed the pig in his face.

I was sitting in the garden. Summer, must have been. He was on the grass, playing with a bowl of water and nothing on but his nappy and a vest. Bowl full of water and two toy boats. And me keeping an eye on him so Mam could get on with her jobs in the kitchen. Every now and again he'd go on all fours and have a scout about, crawl through the leaves, look at the worms and the ants, and I'd have to carry him back before he got into the flower beds. That's when I heard them in the garden next door, Mr Bennett and another chap I hadn't seen before. Round as a plum, the other chap. Had little round glasses, too, just like the Sheriff with the Two-gun Tonsils in *The Wizard*.

Mr Bennett said, 'He's nothing like his brother, is he?'

The round little man said, 'What do you expect? Is a soldier like a butcher?'

Mr Bennett said, 'Right enough, right enough,' and laughed.

And nobody thought a twelve-year-old lad dragging his little brother out of the roses had ears, had already started collecting evidence.

I didn't understand, not on the day. It sounded like the plum man with the glasses was telling a joke about soldiers and butchers, but I thought maybe I'd missed the beginning, so didn't catch the drift. I didn't understand the next day either. But then it rained and Raymond was crawling on the kitchen floor because it was too wet to go out, and I had to watch him while Mam did the ironing. Crawling on the floor and stopping every now and again to look round. Rocked back and forth on his little pink hands, so you'd swear he was weighing things up, planning his next move.

Then I saw it. The pig in his eyes. And maybe a pig's eyelashes aren't white, not like milk is white, or snow, but they're whiter than mine or Mam's or Dad's, that's for certain. Rocked back and forth on his hands and knees, looked up at me with his piggy eyes, and giggled. That's when I saw it. In his eyes, in his cheeks, in the little white curls on his head. And I half expected to see the top of his middle finger gone as well, nail and all. Saw it and understood.

'Contented baby you've got there, Barbara,' they said. 'Right little charmer.' Like he was king of the bloody sty.

Then Mam. 'Give your brother a little bite of dinner, will you, Harry, there's a good boy ... Take him for a walk round the block ... Wipe his nose ...'

And I tell you straight, it was a struggle to hold my nerve with those little piggy eyes looking up at me, those little piggy smiles.

I asked Mam if we could to church that Sunday. 'We haven't been for ages,' I said. Which was true. We hadn't been since Father O'Keefe turned into a fish.

It was Whitsun, too, and Father Hurley at school said that was more important than all the other Sundays put together. God got close to you at Whitsun, so close you could feel his breath on your neck. And he showed us a picture of a lot of old men with their heads on fire, to prove it. 'It's Whitsun, Mam,' I said. But Mam said it was too much bother, that she had Raymond to look after, and the washing to do. 'Too much bother,' she said.

'So can I go by myself, Mam?'

'By yourself? Why do you want to go to church by yourself?'

I told her I went to school by myself every morning. I told her I went shopping, too, and buying bread and milk and potatoes and making sure I got the right change was a bigger thing than standing in church doing nothing. And anyway, Father Hurley at school said that children who missed Sunday mass went to hell if they fell under a bus Monday morning, it said so in the Bible. And that was just an ordinary Sunday. So Whitsun would be worse, bound to be. 'I don't want to go to hell, Mam,' I told her. Made a bit of a song and dance, too.

'Hell lasts forever, Mam, doesn't it?' That sort of thing. Turned away then, stayed quiet for a bit.

So I got to go. And Mam came with me, because she didn't want people to think she'd sent her little boy to church by himself. Which was a shame. I was looking forward to sitting in the front row, to have a better view of things. But we had to stay at the back, Mam said, to get out quickly at the end. It didn't feel right having Raymond there, either, cwtched up in Mam's lap, looking like the baby Jesus. But he started whining in the middle of the sermon so Mam had to take him out. I felt better then.

By the time the priest lifted up the bread I had all the words ready. Everything came together, just as I'd planned. The altar boy rang his bell. The congregation bowed their heads, mumbled their *Domine non sum dignus*. Then it was my turn. 'Heavenly Father,' I said, in my head, 'I want to talk to You about Raymond. He's outside with his Mam at the moment but he'll be back presently. Raymond Vincent Selwyn. That's what people call him. But it's not right. The Selwyn shouldn't be there. Selwyn's Dad's name. Mine, too. Raymond's different. You've only got to look at his eyes and you can see for Yourself. He belongs to the butcher. The butcher came in to our house without permission and he had no right. Piglet I call him. Raymond the piglet.'

Then I had to stop for a second. Some of the words had left my head and slithered out onto my tongue, bold as brass, without me noticing. The woman in the row in front looked round to see what the noise was and I could feel my face burning. And it was a good job Mam had gone out, or that would have been it. But it's hard to keep the words in your head, especially if you're only twelve, and haven't had the practice. Like keeping your feet still. Not picking your nose.

I started over again. This time I didn't mention the piglet. I was worried that maybe God didn't want to hear about piglets first thing in the morning, what with Him being so busy up there on the altar. 'Heavenly Father,' I said, and buried the words right down in my belly so they wouldn't slip out again. 'Raymond Vincent has come into our family through the sin of the butcher, and it's not fair on Dad because he's away in the war and he can't do anything about it and I'm too young to do anything myself and that's why I want You to give Raymond Vincent a really bad dose of Pulmonary Atresia, so he can die quick, before Dad comes back.'

I was happy with that. I'd managed to get sin in, and war as well, on top of the Pulmonary Atresia. Which made it nice and heavy, so it stayed down inside, didn't leak out. And I said it again. 'Pulmonary Atresia'. It wasn't as good as the *Domine non sum dignus*, but I was pretty sure it was Latin and I said it three times then, so it would stick.

'Pulmonary Atresia

Pulmonary Atresia

Pulmonary Atresia.'

Because that's how they did things back in those days, when they had something important to say, they needed God to pay attention. They said it three times, to make it stronger. And when I went up to receive communion I said it again. Swallowed God's body and said it three more times, just to make sure.

'Pulmonary Atresia.

Pulmonary Atresia.

Pulmonary Atresia.'

And I thought, Yes, that's where the words settle best, down in the belly. That's where God goes, after you've swallowed Him. He'll hear every syllable.

I waited six months then, getting my hopes up. Bit of a cough, a wheeze on the chest, red cheeks, a touch of fever on the brow, and I thought, that's it, it's happening, God's answered my prayer. Even afterwards, when the cough had gone, when the cheeks were just piggy pink again, I thought, not to worry, He's probably just softening him up, wearing him down bit by bit, so the Pulmonary Atresia gets a better grip when the time comes. And you can't go rushing God. He's always been one for the slow lane, has the Almighty Father.

Six months. Then Mam said that Dad wouldn't be coming back.

'Never?'

'Never.'

So now I knew why she didn't want to go to church. And why she wanted to sit at the back. Because everybody else could see the pig in Raymond's eyes, too.

27

Harry Selwyn v. Mr Pig

I can hear you. You're asking yourself, how can this Harry Selwyn be so sure that Raymond was *that* piggy's piglet? Where's the evidence? Mr Bennett next door didn't mention *that* butcher's name, did he? He didn't give his address. He didn't say, 'the one with the chopped-off finger'. Aren't there pigs oinking their way around every town and village, every church and chapel in the country? And who has such finely tuned ears that he can tell the difference between one oink and another? Apart from the sow, of course. Yes, I dare say the sow can tell the difference. Can *smell* it, too, more than likely, every time the little piglet pulls on her teat. It's possible, I say no more. I'm a townie when all's said and done. I'm not versed in the ways of pigs.

Then you ask, how does this Harry Selwyn know there wasn't a pig oinking away somewhere in his *own* family? Some Great Grandpa who was just biding his time before he stuck out his stub nose again, his big pink belly, his curly-wurly tail. Kept them in reserve for a generation or two, knowing we'd pay him more attention then. 'Well, he doesn't take after his father, does he?' we'd say. 'No, nor his mother, either, poor dab.' Until Auntie Brenda, ninety-six years old and never heard of DNA or genes, starts chortling into her Ovaltine. 'Well, hello, Grandpa,' she says. 'Welcome back. Come to have another stab at it, have you?'

Yes, you say, that's the answer. The Selwyns have been little piggies all along. So no need to go poking about in other people's middens.

How could I be so sure that Raymond was *that* piggy's piglet?

This is how.

Mam used to take Raymond and me to town every Friday morning to buy fish. Fish, then school, in that order, because it was wartime and there were long queues, even at eight in the morning, and Friday worst of all. Fish on Friday, war or no war, queues half way up the High Street.

And always the same way into town, come what may. Down to the bottom of the street, up the hill, and turn into Darren Terrace. Walk past the Star Garage then, where Mr Mitchell next door would shout out, 'Hello, Harry. Come to help me fix this gearbox?' Only his teeth in sight, his face all oil, and his hands as well, just like the Black and White Minstrels. Past **DAVIES BROS CARDBOARD BOX MAKER & PRINTERS** then and I'd say 'Bros for Brothers'. I'd say 'ampersand', too, later, after I'd learned about it in school. It had 'and' in it, so it was easy to remember. And 'hamper' was a kind of box. I said 'hampersand' then, for a laugh.

That's when we passed the butcher's, just after I'd said 'hampersand', at the corner between Darren Terrace and Blenheim Street. We never bought anything there, not on a Friday. Friday was fish. No meat, only fish. We just walked past, and came out in the middle of the High Street. And we'd see the queue from way off, even at eight in the morning, with it being the war, and Friday, and no fridges, just a slate bench in the back pantry. But that's not the point. The point is this. To get to the fish shop we walked past the butchers. Always did. No reason not to.

But that morning – that particular Friday morning – was different. We went to the bottom of the road and climbed up the hill. Mam carried a shopping bag, I had a satchel on my back, and I was pushing Raymond in his pram. That's how we did it. I pushed him on the way out, Mam pushed him on the way back, after I'd gone to school. How old was he? I don't know. But he was crawling, and the piggy had started to show, belly and all. I had to hold my arms straight out in from of me to get the little fat piggy up the hill.

We came to the corner of Darren Terrace, but instead of turning we carried straight on.

I said, 'Aren't we buying fish, Mam?'

She said we were going a different way today. 'Just for a change,' she said.

'It's further this way,' I said.

'A little change,' she said again.

Which was fine. A change is nice.

Maybe it was still alright the week afterwards when Mam pretended she'd locked us out, said she had to collect the spare key from Grandma's. But when it happened all over again the week after that, and no explanation, only 'Come on, Harry, we haven't got all day,' and the rain dripping over my collar, I knew it was the butcher's fault. Mam had his little piggy in the pram. His secret little piggy.

I hear you. 'Circumstantial evidence!' you say. 'Jumping to conclusions! Falling out with the butcher doesn't mean you've had his baby!'

Right enough. Even in short trousers, I knew that *suspicion* wasn't *proof*. That's why I went up to Mam the day after and told her I was going to take Raymond over to Robert Bramwell's, Number Four. She said 'That's nice.' Robert Bramwell had a sandpit in his garden and anyway she was starting to get a migraine, so she was glad to have the house to herself and lie down for a bit. We did go to Robert Bramwell's, too, because I didn't want Mam to call me a liar. But we didn't play in his garden, we went down the town instead, me, Raymond in his pram and Robert Bramwell. We took turns pushing the pram. And when it was my turn I shouted, 'Race!' and blow me, I picked up speed and Robert Bramwell couldn't keep up, even though I was pushing the pram and the piglet in it, bouncing about, wriggling and kicking. And on the downhill I thought, Jesus, the bloody pram's going faster than me. And how can that be? But that's wheels for you. Not a muscle. Not a sinew. But they'll leave you standing. Which proves something else. And I'll come to that in a while.

When we got to the butcher's shop I undid the straps on the pram and lifted Raymond up to the window. You'd scarcely know it was a butcher's shop, mind. The window was almost empty, with the war, and it being late in the morning. Only a couple of sausages and a piece of rump, maybe the odd liver. Nothing hanging either, like there normally was, so you could see the look on a pig after he'd been scrubbed inside and out. There was only one pig in the butcher's shop that day and he was wearing a stripy apron.

So I held him up, the piglet, stuck his snout against the glass, and stuck my own right next to it, so there'd be no confusion, so he'd know it was *that* piglet. Had to hold him for a good stretch, too, wriggling and squirming all the while, until the butcher's mate gave the butcher a prod and pointed at the window.

The little piggy saw the big piggy and started to cry. The big piggy saw the little piggy and went red. That's when I noticed his big ears. They went red, too. I thought, Well, that's what must happen to butchers' ears. That's how they go when they stand amongst the carcasses all day, all that blood in the air, that chopping. The ears soak it up. Swell.

So, his ears went red, too, and his nose and his cheeks, until his head was just like a big slab of meat itself and we'd have been happy enough to see it hanging on one of the hooks, because there were plenty to spare.

That's how I know Raymond was *that* piggy's little piggy. And you need to write this down on your piece of paper, in case somebody asks and they need the proof.

28

Friday, 21 May, 7pm

Harry looks at the flyer.

> *10" and 12" Pizzas*
> *Select Four Toppings*

He's surprised that they still use inches. Inches were done away with long before he retired. Feet and yards, too. He spent years teaching nothing but metres and centimetres. So why are pizzas different? Who knows what ten inches are these days?

Harry puts his hand on the counter, spreads his fingers and tries to picture a pizza of the same width. The span of his hand is only nine and a half inches, but it's close enough. He studies the photograph on the flyer, the melting cheese, the tomatoes, the mushrooms, the olives.

Free delivery on orders over £10

Harry folds the flyer in two, then folds it again, intending to throw it into the rubbish bin under the counter; but he pauses, reconsiders, then walks over to the dresser and places it behind the wooden elephant, with the other papers. He opens the fridge door, looks at the fish in its paper wrapping and thinks, I've bought it now. When will it get eaten, if not tonight? And Beti won't eat pizza, not for love nor money.

29

Harry Selwyn v. God (2)

Six months I waited, through the coughs and the snivels. Through the measles, too. Six months, and church every Sunday to show God I was serious, it wasn't just a childish whim. But Raymond got better every time. His piggy eyes looked up at me, as if to say, Ha! I've caught you out again. You don't think God listens to the likes of you, do you? After your Mam turned Father O'Keefe into a fish!

I did a Novena then. I thought, right You are, then, the price has gone up. And you don't get to haggle with God. Pay the asking price or out on your arse, that's how it is with God. So a Novena it had to be. And that was tricky, going to nine masses on the trot, one day after another. Sunday was alright. Through the week, too. You could go to mass every morning in the school chapel, if you wanted to. And that was eight of the nine out of the way. It was a bother, mind you, getting up at seven to catch the early bus, and I didn't dare be late or else it might have cancelled out the whole novena. You couldn't pull the wool over God's eyes, not in those days, the days of the Latin and the priests in their black socks.

So weekdays were fine, and Sunday, too. Saturday was the problem. Saturday didn't belong to anybody, neither church nor school.

'Mam, I want to go to church today.'

'It's Saturday, *bach*, not Sunday.'

'I want to go Sunday *and* Saturday, Mam.'

How could I say such a thing? I felt sick just thinking about it. And you've got to run them together, one after another, like a running flush, or else it won't work. You can't just add an extra one at the end, on the Wednesday, say, and pretend it's a Saturday. God wouldn't stand for that.

So when the Saturday came, the novena Saturday, I said, 'I'm off for a run, Mam.' It wasn't a lie, either. And that was just as well, because you're on a sticky wicket asking God a favour and then telling your Mam porkies.

'Keep warm,' Mam said. That's all. 'Keep warm.'

'I will,' I said.

I had to wear the tracksuit she'd given me for Christmas then, a black woolly one. It was too warm, really. Mam didn't know the difference between tracksuits for running and tracksuits for just standing about the place, waiting to throw something. So she just got the warmest. That's what mothers do. Whatever else, make sure you're warm. So I did as I was told.

'Off for a run,' I said. And not a word of a lie. Ran down to church for the ten o'clock mass and stood at the back, behind a pillar. Over-egged it a bit as well, the hiding behind the pillar. Caught the priest squinting at me once, when he was down at the communion rail. Just a peek. Bit of a frown. Hiding behind a pillar's all well and good if it's fat enough. But a Catholic pillar's more of a pipe than a pillar, these days. Henry the Eighth took all the fat ones. And half-hiding's worse than not hiding at all.

I finished the novena. Nine masses on the trot. And offered it up to Our Lady. Not to God, but to His Mam. Father Hurley at school told us that prayers got a better passage that way. God was more likely to listen to His Mam than some maculate youths. That's what he said. 'Maculate.' I looked it up in the dictionary and found out it only meant spotty and he just said it to show off. But I was glad then, for a while. I didn't have any spots, not one, so I could say I was immaculate, just like Our Lady.

A year went by and another telegram came from Uncle Tom. 'Little Janet taken,' it said. Nothing about who'd taken her, not in so many words. Just had the letters PA at the end. But I knew it was the Pulmonary Atresia again. Had to be.

'Runs in the family,' said Mam. 'Poor little thing. Poor Dot.'

I must have gone pale then. Mam told me to sit down and she'd fetch a glass of water. I started to shake a little, too, had to stuff my hands under my armpits so she wouldn't see the tremble in my fingers. Brought the water then and put her hand on my forehead, asked if I felt ill. I shook my head. I didn't dare say anything because I knew it would all come out a jumble, and if I started there'd be no end to it, I'd have to say, No, Mam, it's got nothing to do with running in the family. It's Our Lady's fault. I'd prayed to her and she'd misunderstood, got hold of the wrong end of the stick, garbled the message when she passed it on upstairs. Like Chinese whispers. She'd heard the Pulmonary Atresia and thought, Right you are then, we'll sort out the other little girl. And I was half tempted to ask Mam to send a telegram back to Uncle Tom right away, telling him he mustn't feel down, explaining it wasn't his fault, or Auntie Dot's either, or anybody else's in the family. It was just Our Lady, getting her wires crossed.

Or perhaps, after all, Our Lady had heard it right, had understood about Raymond and his piggy eyes and his piggy father, and the whole caboodle, and thought, Jesus wept, this Harry Selwyn's got a cheek, hasn't he, asking me to do away with his own brother! Never heard such a thing. On my life I haven't. High time I taught that lad a lesson.

30

Friday 21 May 7.10 pm

Harry opens the fridge door, sees the fish in its paper wrapping, and a bottle of milk, nearly empty. Sam Appleby and Emma and the photographer have all drunk tea today, and Harry with them, and no one has thought to fetch another bottle. Then he sees half a lemon, lying on its side in the fridge door. He picks this up, studies the condition of its flesh, gives it a gentle squeeze to bring the juice to the surface, looks anxiously at the pock marks his fingers and thumbs have left on the skin. And shakes his head.

He closes the fridge door, walks over to the counter and

reaches a hand into the shelf below. He names the items he can feel there. 'Potatoes ... Carrots ... Broc ...' Remembering the parsley, he returns to the fridge and looks in the plastic bag in the base compartment; sees a lettuce, the stump of a cucumber and two tomatoes. There is no parsley. He picks up the lemon, squeezes it gently, holds it to his nose.

31

Harry Selwyn v. God (3)

I went and made my confession to the priest. Not Father O'Keefe, he couldn't talk any more, but the other one, the curate that looked like a mouse. I told him I'd been nasty to my little brother and that I was really really sorry. I said nothing about the novena or Pulmonary Atresia or Janet or Auntie Dot. I was pretty sure God knew about them already, without me having to humiliate myself in front of the mouse.

He said, 'I see,' and told me to meditate on the Holy Family. I didn't get his drift at first. Had no idea Jesus had a little brother. But the priest said, yes, he had more than one, but you don't get to hear about them because it was only Jesus got crucified. 'For our sins,' he said. I wasn't sure who the butcher would be, either. Joseph was a carpenter and Gabriel an angel and the Holy Ghost didn't even have a body. And I couldn't remember anything in the Bible about aunties and uncles.

Then he said something that made more sense. 'A little brother is a gift from God,' he said. He talked about other presents we had from God as well, so you'd think it was Christmas all year round. But that was the one that stuck in my mind. 'A little brother is a gift from God.' And I thought, well, if he's gift, why can't I give him to somebody else? Like pass the parcel. That's what a present was, to my mind. It didn't belong to anybody really, not like your shirt or your shoes or your glasses. And that meant you could swap it, if you wanted to. If you already had one, say. Like the Triang clockwork steam tip lorry I got from Uncle Tom. Swapped that because Dad had given me one for my birthday. Swapped it for a holster, to carry my gun. And nobody got told off. Didn't say anything to Uncle Tom, of course. That would have been bad manners. And I wouldn't have told the butcher, either, that I'd given his little piggy to somebody else.

The more I thought about it, the more certain I became. It was time for another swap. God had ordained it. He'd decided this was how to get the job done. It was odd that He'd chosen the little mouse of a curate to pass the message on. But that's what God was like in those days. Always one for the mysterious ways.

And what exactly did He want me to do? Well, once I sat down and put my mind to it, it was easy enough to work out. On the one hand you had Auntie Dot and Uncle Tom. They had no children left and couldn't have any more because the Pulmonary Atresia would get them, too. And on the other hand you had the Selwyns – me, Mam and Raymond – and the trouble with the Selwyns was that there was one too many. *Surplus to requirements* they would have called that in the army. Send the surplus back to stores then, and cross it off the inventory to make sure the same thing didn't happen again. That's what God wanted me to do. He wanted me to help Him get his inventory straight.

I waited until Mam went over to see Grandma and I wrote a letter.

Dear Auntie Dot,

Happy birthday. I hope you have a nice day and get lots of presents. I have a very special gift for you to make up for losing Jennifer and Janet. His name is Raymond. I'm sorry he's a boy. He smiles lots and can count to a hundred and you can have his clothes as well and his Thunderbolt tricycle but Uncle Tom will have to raise the seat. Raymond hasn't wet the bed for over a year. He likes listening to Listen With Mother on the wireless and he can sing Three Blind Mice.

etc.

I bought a birthday card with my own money, too, a big one with a thatched cottage on it, and put it in with the letter.

The reply came a couple of days later. An 'extremely touching gesture', it said. Mam said nice things as well. She'd spoken to Auntie Dot. Don't know whether she saw the letter but she'd got the gist alright. I was a very considerate boy, she said. Very generous, offering my only brother to make Auntie Dot happy. She gave me half a crown, too.

'Is Raymond going to live with Uncle Tom and Auntie Dot now, then?' I asked.

It was a fair enough question, I thought, judging by all the nice things people were saying about me. But she shook her head. Told me I wasn't to send letters like that again. Wasn't to send any letters at all without talking to her first. And that was that.

Which put everything on hold for another ten years.

32

Friday 21 May, 7.15 pm

As he picks up the phone, Harry rehearses his lines. 'I'm sorry, Raymond, Beti's gone over to her sister's ...'

Although he knows this is untrue, he's sure it is the most serviceable explanation available. Beti and Amy have been out all day and haven't come back yet so they won't be able to enjoy supper together this evening. 'I'm really sorry, Raymond ...' A credible story. And he won't need to trouble himself with pizzas or fish or the absence of parsley or any of that nonsense. 'I think they're having a bite to eat in town.' That's it. And what would be the point of having supper with Raymond unless Beti were there, too?

Harry has already begun dialling Raymond's number when he spots the flaw in his story. He makes a mental picture of Raymond and Amy meeting during the week – while out shopping, perhaps, or fetching a prescription from the chemist. Raymond says, 'But Harry told me you went to town with Beti, had a meal out …' Amy shakes her head, looks puzzled. 'No, you've got it wrong there, Raymond.' How would he get out of that? No, he decides, it would be a mistake to drag Amy into this business.

Harry replaces the phone and thinks, Well, if I don't tell Raymond that Beti's gone out with Amy, what do I tell him? He returns to the fridge and looks again at the fish and the lemon. He takes out the milk and tries to calculate whether there is enough left for three cups. Shakes his head. And what of tomorrow morning? Then, his eye falling on the gap in the fridge door where a carton of juice should have been, Cati comes to mind. He says her name out loud. 'Cati.' Hesitantly at first, then triumphantly. 'Cati, of course.'

As he dials Raymond's number again, Harry rehearses this story, too. 'Emma … Emma's asked Beti to go and keep an eye on Cati … Short notice… The usual babysitter's gone down with some bug … Sorry about that, Raymond, can't be helped. Have you got food in the house?' It doesn't matter then if Raymond meets Emma because Emma will be happy to keep his little secret. And that will be the next step, after speaking to Raymond: he'll phone his daughter and share with her the little white lie he's had to tell Uncle Raymond. Then he'll say that Beti's feeling a bit under the weather after being out all day and the last thing she wants is Raymond going on about his flowers and his jazz and all the rest of it. She'll understand. They'll have a little chuckle. 'Between us and the four walls, Emma, OK?' 'OK, Dad.'

That's how it'll be. Another white lie, but no harm done.

The phone rings five times before Raymond's recorded voice asks him to leave a message. 'Harry here, Raymond. Just to say that Beti's had to go and look after Cati … Short notice …' He fumbles for the remainder of his story, forgets his lines. 'Sorry about that, Raymond … Er …' Suddenly impatient with the piece of mute plastic in his hand, he says, 'Not to worry, Raymond, I'll ring back in ten minutes.' Then, as an afterthought: 'Ring me first if you get the chance.'

Harry isn't too disheartened. This is how telephones work these days, he knows that well enough from his own experience. The phone rings, he's at the front door, looking for his key, and although he makes what haste he can, he reaches the kitchen just after the fifth and final ring. 'Please leave a message …' Or in the bath. And you can't be expected to jump out of the bath, just because somebody wants you on the phone. So he'll ring back in ten minutes. Enough for Raymond to finish whatever it is he's doing.

To fill those ten minutes, Harry takes a tomato and a piece of cheese from the fridge and cuts two slices of bread. He will have these for supper in a while, as soon as Beti returns. He fetches a jar of Branston's from the cupboard and sits at the table. He begins to relax in the knowledge that he won't have to cook anything this evening after all. He decides, on reflection, not to cut any bread for Beti, just in case she has, indeed, gone somewhere for a meal, to a destination he has forgotten, with a companion he doesn't know.

The ten minutes pass. And then another five. By now, Harry has spotted the flaw in this plan, too. If he asks Emma to back up his white lie, just to keep Raymond satisfied, what then will be the truth? Or, rather, what will be the other, over-riding lie that he will have to tell Emma when she says, 'Poor

Mam. Can I have a quick word with her?' What can he say then? 'Oh, she hasn't come back yet, Emma ... Hasn't come back from the hairdressers ... ' How can he possibly say such a thing at a quarter past seven in the evening?

Harry decides that Beti must indeed have gone for a bite to eat. What other explanation is possible? Perhaps she said something last night. I'm going to town ... I'm meeting ... Perhaps she even asked him to let Raymond know.

It's possible.

Harry cuts a small cube of Red Leicester. He spoons a portion of pickle onto the side of his plate.

33

12 September 1953 Penwyllt Round 10 miles

```
H.Selwyn Taff Harriers S 14 1.43
```

'And Raymond?' Sam said. 'Raymond was never a runner, was he?'

Expecting an emphatic 'No'. Thinking, he's not much of an athlete, not by the look of him. Nothing like his brother. Wondering how two brothers could be so different.

'Raymond was faster than me,' I told him. 'A lot faster, too, when he was young. Didn't get the opportunities, that's all. Same as Dad.'

What else could I tell him? That the little piggy oughtn't to be here at all? That God had cocked things up? That a piggy didn't stop being a piggy just because he played the saxophone, or because he'd set up a new sty somewhere else?

And that I knew he was still just biding his time, calling by to keep an eye on sow number one, wondering how long he'd have to wait.

What kind of story is that to put in a paper?

34

Friday, 21 May, 7.40 pm

Harry opens the front door. Raymond enters, bag in hand, bottles clunking.

Harry says, 'Didn't you get the message?'

Raymond says, 'Didn't you get mine? I was over at Dennis's. Had to take his bandsaw back.'

'Dennis?'

Harry remembers. Raymond hasn't been at home. He's going to be late. That late has already arrived.

'Yes, of course. The bandsaw.'

So Harry must repeat his explanation. 'Beti's gone to look after Cati ... Emma's out ... Somewhere ...' He says this rather brusquely. He has lost all faith in the story, and recites it only because he has no other story to hand. And in any case, he knows it's too late to delete its central lie. Raymond will go home later and listen to his messages. Harry's voice is there, an indelible affidavit.

They make their way through to the kitchen.

'You eaten already, Harry?'

They both look at the pickle-stained plate on the table, the knife, the packet of cheese.

'Eaten? No, no ... Haven't cleared away, that's all ... Running a bit behind.'

Harry takes the plate over to the sink. Then, seeing

Raymond in his smart, if slightly garish, check jacket and white shirt, he becomes conscious that he hasn't shaved or showered or changed out of his tracksuit. He draws his hand across his chin.

'Been out myself, see ... Not had a chance to ...'

And he's put out that he should feel at such a disadvantage in his own home.

Harry rarely cooks supper, and Beti alone assumes responsibility for fish. Fish can so easily be overcooked and spoiled. She normally poaches it in the oven, in an appropriate sauce: parsley, cheese or Béchamel, depending on the kind of fish Harry has bought. Harry would never attempt to make a sauce. He prefers not to use the oven, either, because he is nervous about getting the times and temperatures wrong. Nor is he always sure when to cover a dish or how much cheese to use or how much flour. Harry prefers to cook his meals on the hob or under the grill: bacon, eggs, rarebit, porridge in the morning. Vegetables, too. He can give a hand with potatoes, carrots, peas, and the like. Foods that a man can test with a knife or a spoon. Foods he can feel in his fingers whether they're ready or not. This is Harry's preference.

Harry puts on Beti's apron to show his brother that everything is under control, that he is master in his own kitchen. It is a dark blue apron, without flowers or frills. He would feel better if he were wearing it over something more appropriate than a tracksuit. He would be happier, too, without the cords, hanging loosely on either side, but he has always found it difficult to tie knots behind his back. Beti normally does this for him, when the need arises. Harry doesn't consider asking Raymond. Tying the cords of his apron is not the kind of task he would easily entrust to his brother. He shows him the fish.

'Lemon sole tonight.'

'Looks nice.'

'Just fried, mind you.'

'Fried's fine. Looks good.'

Harry's relieved that he can then stand at the sink, wash and prepare the vegetables, take the fish out of their wrapping, put the butter in the frying pan. In this way he gains another few minutes to gather his thoughts and consider the implications of his latest story.

'Put some music on if you like.'

While Harry busies himself with the food, Raymond goes over to the dresser and browses through the small collection of CDs. He passes over *James Galway: Man With the Golden Flute* and *Christmas With Nana Mouskouri* and chooses *Kenny G's Greatest Hits*, a collection which he himself bought as a Christmas present for Harry and Beti, some years ago. He slots this into the small black radio-CD, presses PLAY and waits until the first notes of 'Songbird' fill the kitchen. He turns down the volume a little, returns to his seat at the table and opens the *Mail*.

Despite the music, the two brothers are uncomfortably aware of the silence it is intended to fill. Generally, on a Friday, it is Beti who keeps the conversation going, asking Raymond about his garden, his musical activities, his children – all grown up now, pursuing their careers in other worlds. Harry has no interest in any of these matters. Neither does Raymond have any desire to talk about them with his brother. As a result there is nothing between them but the gap left by Beti and the voiceless songs of Kenny G.

So, ten minutes to gather his thoughts. And at the end of those ten minutes, as Harry places the fish in the frying pan, he suddenly realises that the damage has already been done. Beti will arrive home presently and say, 'Sorry I've been so long ... Terrible traffic ... So-and-so kept me talking ...' Raymond will say, 'Hold on, Harry told me that Emma ... that Cati ...' And what will happen then?

Harry lights the gas under the frying pan. As he does so, his brother lifts the plastic bag off the back of the chair and looks inside.

'New trousers, Harry?'

Raymond is taken aback then when Harry suddenly turns off the gas, strides across the kitchen floor and takes the bag out of his hands.

'Before I start cooking,' Harry barks. 'Got to take them out ... Before the smell ... Before the fish ...'

Raymond is startled at the vehemence in his brother's voice, at the urgency with which he closes the bag and makes for the kitchen door.

'Special trousers are they, Harry?'

35

Harry v. No one

'Tom Courtenay,' Sam Appleby said, still looking for an angle, juggling the clichés. 'Do you see yourself a bit like Tom Courtenay? Do you feel sometimes that it's just you against the rest of the world?'

Sam thinks he knows about running because he's seen *The Loneliness of the Long Distance Runner*. Maybe *Chariots of Fire* as well, I can't say. He didn't mention it and I wasn't going to bring it up myself and make the day any longer than it had to be. Loneliness, he said. Tom Courtenay against the rest of the world. That's the kind of story he wants from me, too, to put in his paper. So I told him I'd never robbed a baker, or been to Borstal either, thank you very much. And anyway, what's loneliness got to do with it? Nobody ran to be by themselves. We ran for the company, I told him, the cameraderie. Which was obvious enough. If people wanted to run by themselves then there wouldn't be harriers and athletics clubs all over the place, would there?

'I haven't been to Borstal,' I told Sam. 'But I've run with the Kalenjin and they've got a name for it.' Wrote it down on a piece of paper then to make sure he'd get it right.

RIIRII

'Riirii,' I said. 'That's what the Kalenjin call it. Running together. None of your loneliness there. None of your Tom Courtenays. That's it. "R" double "I", "R" double "I". Riirii.'

'The Kalenjin, you say?'

I made a bit of a meal of it then, gave my tongue too much rope. The teacher in me, no doubt. Seeing the ignorance in front of me, a gaping black hole. Wanting to fill it with light. And sometimes you need to get the facts out into the open, and all the facts, too, otherwise you've only yourself to blame.

'When I was in the army,' I said.

Because it was in the army I took it up seriously, the running. Although you might say it took me up. The army way. Everybody out together, single file, eyes on the man in front, ears on the stamp of his feet. Yes, that would be nearer the mark. It took me up. Showed me how you could run and run, left, right, left, right, run all day if you wanted to, and still enough breath to see you through the night. That's what happens when you run with your platoon. Eyes on the man in front and you don't feel a thing. No pain. No anything. Even though you're in your boots and you've got a heavy sack on your back, you just kept your eyes on the man in front and the feet look after themselves. Everybody breathes together. From one big lung. Left, right, left, right. The army way. So I was only telling him the truth.

'The army,' Sam said. 'What part of the army would that have been then, Harry?'

'National Service,' I said. 'Like everybody else. Just National Service.'

36

Friday, 21 May, 7.50 pm

Raymond scans the *Mail*'s TV pages. On the CD player, Peabo Bryson is singing 'By the time this night is over ...' with Kenny G accompanying on sax. The song is a little too sweet for Raymond's taste – he chose the disk with Harry and Beti in mind, not to please himself – but he relishes the faultless technique, the velvet intonation.

In the passage, Harry takes the trousers out of the plastic bag and lays them over his left arm. He draws his right hand across the material, enjoys its smoothness, congratulates himself at getting this far without mishap. He picks up a speck of fluff between finger and thumb and thinks, There we are, then. Start again.

As he passes the study door, Harry pauses. Should he leave the trousers here for the time being and take them upstairs later, when he goes to bed? The smell of the fish will surely not travel this far, not from the kitchen, not if he shuts the door. He looks again at the trousers. By the bright shafts of evening sunlight that are now piercing the glass in the front door he can see that there are, after all, creases in the material, tiny wrinkles that he hadn't noticed before. He presses a finger against the cloth. A wrinkle shifts. He takes a step towards the door, repeats the experiment, wonders whether it is merely a trick of the light. He decides that prudence is best. Maybe, after a night on a hanger, the wrinkles will disappear of their own accord.

At the bottom of the stairs Harry fingers the security tag. He would be glad to get rid of it. Even through his shirt and vest he is sure he will feel the hard little disks chafing his skin, becoming more and more uncomfortable as the evening progresses. He tries to estimate how far it is protruding from the waistband, at what angle it will rub against his stomach, whether it will be worse sitting down or standing up. But without wearing the trousers, how can he possibly answer such questions? And wearing them, too, not merely trying them on. He resolves to do this as soon as Raymond leaves. In the meantime, he consoles himself with the thought that he alone will be aware of the secret button. A belt will be sufficient to conceal it. No one will be any the wiser.

On entering his bedroom the first thing that Harry notices is the window, and more particularly the curtains. These hang untidily, not quite closed, the bottom of one bunched on the sill. A ray of sunlight enters through the gap between them, casting heavy shadows across the room. As he places his trousers on the back of the chair, Harry notices that the drawer of the dressing table, too, has been left half-open. Then he remembers. 'Cati ... Of course. The Rolos.' He opens both curtains and sees a brief commotion in the ash tree outside, where a thrush is returning to her nest. He notices, too, in the horizontal light, that the window is covered in greasy streaks. He tutts. 'Shame on you,' he says, and makes a picture in his mind of the negligent window cleaners, leaving the job half done, thinking, Oh, it's only pensioners. He'll have words.

Harry picks up his trousers, turns towards the wardrobe and sees his wife's hand resting on the coverlet. A moment later, his eyes now accustomed to the shadows, he sees her head, too, a dark, ill-defined presence on the pillow.

'Beti?'

He moves closer.

'Beti?'

There is no doubt that Harry is startled, even perturbed. And yet it is not so much the thing itself – seeing his wife in bed at half past seven in the evening – that prompts this reaction. Beti has had a nasty turn – a migraine, no doubt – and gone to bed for a little nap. She's drawn the curtains, closed her eyes, tried to sleep it off, and slept a little longer than she meant to. It's happened before, it will happen again. So, not the thing itself, but the fact that this has happened without warning, without a message: that is what perturbs Harry.

'Beti?'

Harry says his wife's name a little more loudly this time, hoping that she will wake. He wants to explain that supper is almost ready, and she needs to eat something if she's been poorly all afternoon. A little fish, to build up her strength. Even if it is only fish from the frying pan and there's no sauce. And anyway, Raymond's waiting for her.

As his thoughts turn to his brother, Harry realises that he now has another problem to contend with. In a few seconds he will have to go back to the kitchen and say, 'I'm sorry, Raymond, I made a mistake. Beti's been upstairs all the while. Had a bit of a turn earlier on. She'll be down in a minute.' And Raymond will answer: 'But Harry, you said earlier …' And how will he respond then? He's already told him that Beti's over at Emma's, minding her granddaughter, that she's been out all day, getting her hair cut, shopping in town. How can he possibly take it all back?

This is why Harry decides to let his wife sleep on. Instead of going to the wardrobe and risking a squeak of the hinge as he opens the door, he hangs the trousers on the back of the chair. He would like to close the curtains: he regrets having opened them. But then, newly sensitised to every little noise he makes just walking around the room, he thinks, best not, best leave things as they are. He goes out, turning the doorknob behind him as slowly and as quietly as he can. He walks to the bathroom on tip-toe.

37

The Kalenjin v. The World

It was a mistake, talking about the army. The army's got nothing to do with running. I just happened to be there. And running with your platoon's no better than running with the Harriers. No worse either, I dare say, but no better.

And then, 'Tell me about Kenya, Harry.'

'How'd you know about Kenya?' I said.

'You said, Harry.'

'Me?' Because I hadn't said a word.

'In Kenya you were fighting?'

Not a word. I'm sure of it. Not to Sam Appleby. Not about Kenya. Which proves my point. Somebody had been stirring things. Who? Well, there's a question.

'National Service, Sam,' I said. 'Everybody had to go somewhere. And I didn't do any fighting.'

So I told him about Kenya. And maybe that was a mistake, too. You want to get the facts out, but then each fact has got another fact tucked away inside it, and you can only say so much.

He said, 'That's who you were fighting against, was it, Harry? These Kalenjin characters.'

'The Kalenjin were on *our* side,' I said. 'The *Crown's* side.'

He nodded. Wrote it down in his book. Said, 'Did you have a gun?'

'What?' I said.

'A gun,' he said. 'Did you have a gun, when you were in Kenya? You know, a rifle of some kind.' As though I didn't know what a gun was.

'Everybody had a gun,' I said. 'Mark Four Lee Enfield.'

Wrote that down, too.

'And a photo?' he said. 'Have you got a photo of you carrying the gun? In your uniform?'

'No, Sam, I haven't,' I said. 'I guarded the compound. Patrolled the perimeter. Kept an eye on things. Checked people in and out.'

'But surely you …'

'I'll show you what I've got.'

So I looked in the box, got out the list. 'There you are,' I said. 'There's the Kalenjin for you.' Thinking, not a bad story to put in a local rag like the *Gazette*. Three million people and they've won more medals than anybody. As though Wales had beaten the world. As though The Incredible Wilson had come back to life.

Here's the list, so you can see what Sam saw, so you can show it to anyone who doubts what I've told you.

OLYMPIC GAMES 1964 — 2004 RUNNING (Men)		
	All Medals	Gold Medals
KALENJIN	30	10
Ethiopia	10	5
USA	10	3
UK	8	1
Kenya (except Kalenjin)	7	4
Morocco	7	3
Germany	6	1
Finland	4	3
New Zealand	4	2
Tunisia	4	1

Had to say 'I'll give you the Beijing figures tomorrow,' and I was cross about that. A list's no use if you don't keep it up to date. I left the piece of paper out on the sideboard, so I'd remember to get back to it later, to make amends. 'Pop it in the post,' I said. 'If you like.' And said it quickly, waving my hand in the air, so he'd understand that I'd already spotted the gap, that I had the information to hand, but it had been a busy day and he shouldn't expect all his facts and figures on a plate, just because he worked for the *Gazette*.

* * *

It's a pity we don't have a word for *riirii*.

I remembered then. A summer's evening. Left the camp in Cwm Gwdi, just me and four other squaddies. Ran up Cefn Cwm Llwch to the top of Pen-y-fan. Steep pull at the end, but took it steady. Eyes on the man in front, even if it was just his heels. Stood a while, then. Looked over the mountains, the valleys, the sea as well, way down to the south. Didn't care we were out of breath, legs aching, and getting up at six for more square bashing. The morning would take care of itself. Just me and the four others and the mountain, and the whole world at our feet. That was *riirii,* even though I hadn't heard the word, hadn't been anywhere near Africa.

Pity I don't have a photo, too. I'd have shown it to Sam, so he'd understand. To set the record straight.

38

Friday, 21 Mai, 8pm

Harry's brother, Raymond, is a stocky man with bright eyes and a short neck. Despite his sixty-seven years he still boasts a tight crop of grey curls on the crown of his head. He has also kept the sideburns he first grew in the sixties. 'A tribute to Sonny Rollins,' he says, whenever someone draws attention to them. He must then explain who Sonny Rollins was, and that he also sported a beard in his later career. 'He only had the sideburns when I saw him, mind you.' Which gives him the opportunity to say when and where that was, to reminisce about his greatest hero on the sax.

Looking at the two brothers sitting opposite each other at the kitchen table it is difficult, at first, to detect any resemblance. Only through studying them at close quarters –

much closer than politeness would allow — and then comparing them with the black-and-white photographs on the dresser, would you begin to suspect, perhaps, that both had inherited the full, fleshy lips of the mother. If you'd known the mother you might also remark on the way each brother tilts his head slightly to the left as he speaks; the way he tucks his napkin into his collar and rests his knife and fork on the plate as he eats. This is how she brought them up. No one would remember the father. Even if they looked at the dresser they'd be none the wiser. The picture on the dresser shows a man in army uniform, and all men in uniform look alike.

'Fish is good.'

Harry shakes his head. 'A bit dry ... Bet ...'

He wants to say, 'Beti would have made a sauce,' partly by way of apology, but also to study Raymond's reaction. This is merely his custom. He has always measured the temperature of his brother's regard for Beti, even in her absence, and even in connection with such mundane matters as the kind of sauce she might have made for the fish. It is difficult not to resist the dictates of entrenched habit. But this evening is unusual. Beti is asleep just a few feet above their heads and Harry feels uncomfortable speaking of her as though she weren't there. Instead, he says, 'Better with a bit of parsley, mind. Would have got some, but there was none left.' Raymond makes a quick 'no matter' gesture with his hand, then looks out through the window.

'Dahlias coming along well.'

39

New Year Race Mountain Ash 1958 4 miles

1958 was the best year for Wales, I told Sam. It's supposed to be a Welsh paper, the *Gazette*, and I'd had enough of Kenya. So I showed him a picture of Herb Elliott winning the mile at the Empire Games. 'The Arms Park,' I said, in case he didn't recognise it. The place looked different, with the track and the flags and the marshals and everything.

A pity I couldn't find a photo of John Merriman, too. He was the first Welshman to win a medal, or the first I heard about. But I couldn't, so I had to make do with Herb Elliott, and the old programme with the scribbles on it where I'd copied down the results.

And the envelope. That was in the box, too, for the stamp. I gave it to Sam. 'There's the stamp,' I said. 'Sixth British Empire and Commonwealth Games. See where it says?' And pointed to the big ribbon in the dragon's mouth.

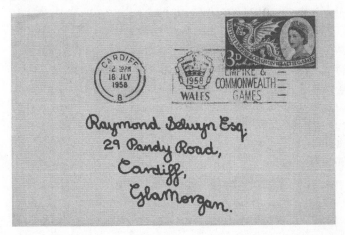

I was impressed by that, the way they'd squeezed all the words into such a tight space. Very clever. Although I wasn't happy with the VIth. Didn't look right to me, mixing the Latin and the English. On the wrong side of the ribbon, too, for it to read properly, if it were a real ribbon. And it was a bit of a shock seeing Beti's handwriting again. Just like a little girl's, even though she must have been coming up to her eighteenth by then and left school long since. A little girl trying to make an impression.

Sam looked at the envelope. 'Letter to your brother, Harry?' he said, as though he had rights, could hold you to ransom, just because he wrote for a newspaper.

'Only the envelope, Sam,' I said. 'And the stamp. No idea where the letter went. Or who sent it, for that matter.' I took the envelope from him, held it upside down, gave it a shake. 'Nothing, see?'

1958 was the best year for Wales. Best for me as well. Saw Herb Elliott win in Cardiff. Then the New Year race started up in Mountain Ash. Finished in the top thirty in that, which was good going, given the numbers, bearing in mind the calibre. Might have done better, too, but I took a tumble, just as we turned for Pont Siôn Norton, and had to hold a hanky to my head for the last mile, to stop the blood. No photo of that, thank God. But that was the best year, no two ways. The first best year, I mean. Twenty-six and all that running still to do.

Then the letter came. I had my own place by then, but I went over to Mam's to put the television in, so she could follow the Games on the BBC. Opened the door and there it was, the envelope, on the mat. I picked it up, saw the Raymond Selwyn Esq, the flowery loops, and I knew

146

straightaway. The piggy had a sow. Only seventeen and he had his snout in the trough. So I opened it, read the letter, there and then in the passage. The sow thought a lot of her piggy. Not that she said as much, not in so many words, but that's what she meant. She thought he had 'kind eyes'. She liked his 'sweet smile'. I took the letter home and read it again. And I thought, Yes, she's fond enough, you can't deny it, but there's something missing. There's nothing here except lips and eyes. Face love. It was only 1958, I know, they were both only kids, but I wondered whether the lips and the eyes stood for something else, just that the piggy's little sow couldn't bring herself to say it. Or maybe she was afraid his Mam would pick it up from the mat and ask him, Who sent this, then, Raymond? Someone I don't know about? A secret admirer?

I put the letter in another envelope and wrote Raymond's name and address on it. Copied her handwriting, too, best I could, so he wouldn't suspect. Felt a bit queasy doing that. A bit like wearing somebody else's clothes without permission. But I made a fair fist of it. I was a teacher, after all. I saw those little loops every day of the week, all nervous and wobbly. And anyway, it wasn't difficult. You could say it already looked as though it had been copied, that's how much care she'd taken. My copy just made it look more what it already was.

Beti's writing told me something else. It told me that, even if she was going out with a little piggy, even though she might well think the world of her little piggy, it wasn't her fault. She was young and innocent. She'd been duped. She deserved better. Don't ask me how I could tell. I felt it in my hand as I copied the big round 'C' in 'CARDIFF'. I felt it again as I worked the 'M' in 'GLAMORGAN', which was just a touch too big. There are four strokes in the letter 'M' and Beti had spent a long time getting each one right. Too long. And that's what happens when you think too hard about something, it grows big in your head, then bigger still on the paper. And that 'GAN', drooping at the end. She was doing her best but no one had shown her how to use a ruler to keep her words straight.

I posted the letter again, but I kept the envelope, for the stamp, to remember the Games. And that's why it's still there, in the box, with the cuttings and the picture of Herb Elliott.

'Nineteen fifty eight,' I said. 'Big year for Wales.'

For me, too. Just twenty-six, and all that running still to do.

40

Friday, 21 May, 8.10 pm

Harry looks through the French windows. 'Slugs are bad this year. With the rain.'

Raymond nods. 'Dry now, though. Good to have it dry.'

Harry takes a slice of bread and spreads some butter on it. 'Bread's too thin as well.'

'Mm?'

'The bread ... Can't spread the butter ... Goes into holes.'

'You need to warm it.'

Harry bites off a crust and shakes his head. 'Doesn't last then.'

'Doesn't last?'

'The butter. It doesn't last. Not if you warm it up.'

Raymond cuts a potato, puts half in his mouth, rests his knife and fork on his plate, shakes his head. 'Not all of it.'

'What?'

'You don't have to warm it all. Just a little bit. As much as you need.'

Harry considers this. He makes a mental picture of his mother, long ago, cutting a knob of butter, putting it on a plate, placing the plate in front of the range in the kitchen. He remembers how the butter would sweat, and when you saw the beads collect on one side it was time to turn it around.

'Can't stand marg.'

Raymond nods. 'Easier, though.'

'Lot easier.'

Then Harry remembers how sometimes she'd put the butter on the mantelpiece. There was less heat there but it penetrated the whole knob of butter, not just the one side. Fine if you've got all day. No good at all if you're catching the early bus to school and need to make your sandwiches.

'Healthier, too,' Raymond says. 'For the heart.' He pats his chest.

'Mm,' says Harry. 'But the taste. The taste. '

'It's better than it used to be.'

'Better?'

'Lot better.'

Harry chews a piece of fish, decides it isn't too bad after all, for fried. 'When?'

'Eh?'

'You say it's better than it used to be. Better than it used to be when?'

Raymond thinks for a while. 'Stork,' he says, triumphantly, as though remembering the name of a long-forgotten friend. 'That was the first. Stork margarine.'

Harry frowns. He is reluctant to acknowledge his brother's

right to opine on the origins of things. 'You can still get Stork,' he says. 'Tesco's. You can buy Stork in Tesco's.'

'Not the same, though. Not the same as it used to be. Name's the same, but it's different inside. They've changed the ingredients.'

Harry frowns again. Nevertheless, he is, for the moment, quite happy to talk about butter and margarine, if only because it's better than talking about Beti, than thinking about Beti, than trying to work out when the devil she went to bed, and what she did when she got back home after having her hair cut, and why on earth she didn't leave a message on the dresser.

'It's you that's changed, Raymond, not the Stork. That's what happens when you get to your age. Things start to taste different.'

41

Harry Selwyn v. Raymond Selwyn

'Brian James,' I said, and pointed to the photo. 'From Penrhiwceiber.'

'Ah, yes, Brian James,' Sam said, pretending he knew things.

Maindy again. I wasn't running, only watching, and I wanted a shot of the boys together, before Brian left for Canada. Brian and me in the front row, with Clive Phillips and Dave Pugh. Ron Jones at the back with somebody else, don't remember his name. And Chris Suddaby on the end, smile like a five bar gate because somebody said he'd get a kiss from the photographer if he smiled nicely.

'Beti took this one,' I said. And tried to remember whether

she was laughing too, behind the camera. Probably not. Not in front of all those men. And her just starting out to work on her own account.

'Were you together by then, Harry?' said Sam. 'You and Beti … Were you an item?'

I turned the picture over.

H. R. LISTER PHOTOGRAPHER
17 CHURCH ROAD, RHIWBINA, CARDIFF
Weddings, Portraits, Schools, Commercial

'It was her job, Sam,' I said. 'Same as her father. H. R. Lister. He was a Harry as well … Harry Lister … Plenty of Harrys to be had in those days.'

It was a mistake, turning the picture over. I thought it would clarify matters. Show the connections. School, the photographer, the photographer's daughter, the teacher. So he'd understand how these things can happen, of their own accord. That events just took their natural course. But he said, Well, did I have pictures of us all together, Beti and me, the mammies and the daddies, the whole tribe?

So, let me tell you again, in case Sam gets hold of half the story and turns everything on its head. *I didn't do anything with that letter.* I posted it on and nobody was any the wiser. I didn't do anything with the envelope either. I put it by, for safe keeping. For the stamp. To remember '58.

Beti started coming round to Mam's house then. Of course she did. That's where her little piggy lived. I went there, too, to see Mam. And that's how we'd run into each other, Beti and me, just for a minute of two, a quick hello-goodbye before they went out. Raymond sometimes took her to hear his band.

She wasn't too keen on that. Too shrill for Beti's taste, although she didn't complain. She wasn't one to complain, not in so many words. But more often than not it was a film. *Ben-Hur*, *North West Frontier*, *Some Like It Hot*. That sort of thing. I remember them all. Not that I went much to the pictures myself, but Raymond would always tell Mam what they were going to see. He'd have plenty to say when they came home, too, about the plot and the actors and so forth, as though he had to prove they'd really been there. I expected him to produce the ticket stubs, even an empty popcorn bag. In the end I wondered whether they'd been anywhere near a cinema. On second thoughts, maybe not popcorn. I'm not sure they had much popcorn in those days.

So, just a quick hello-goodbye. I'd be on my way in, to see Mam, Beti'd be on her way out, to the pictures. Or else she'd be on her way in, to say good night to Mam, and I'd be setting off for home, after hearing what Elizabeth Taylor or Montgomery Clift had been up to. Did I say I had my own place by then? Anyway, that's another one. *From Here to Eternity*. Beti was a big fan of Montgomery Clift. Raymond did all the talking, mind you. And that set me thinking, too – the way she'd stand there in her grey raincoat, studying the pattern on the carpet, playing with her fingers, Raymond doing all the talking. Too bashful by half.

A year went by, all films and playing with fingers. Then Raymond went off to do his National Service. I was anxious that they'd get rid of it before he'd done his stint, but the bother in Aden broke out, then Iraq and Libya and Cyprus and a couple of other places, so they must have thought, Well, best keep a couple of squaddies in reserve, just in case. Let's pull in that Raymond Selwyn chap. He'll teach them a thing or two.

He sent Mam a photo of himself in uniform, him and his platoon over in Pirbright. Pirbright Raymond went for his training, not Brecon. Don't know why. There was no telling where you'd get sent for your training. Mam wasn't pleased. She wanted to write to the MOD, to complain, to say, How did they expect him to get back home to his Mam from there? Beti persuaded her not to, even though she was in tears herself. No, her eyes were red. Beti was too bashful to cry in front of others.

Now then, if Sam Appleby were telling this story he'd boil it all down to a couple of hundred words. A little paragraph in bold at the beginning describing the Soldier and his Betrothed, saying how shocked everybody was to see them torn apart. Then a comment from the Soldier himself: 'I don't know how he could ... My own brother ...' A few crumbs of gossip then about the brother's love life. 'Not a stranger to scandal ...' And finish off with the date of the wedding, because everybody likes a wedding.

But that would have been a lie. I didn't break up Raymond and Beti. I didn't go to Church Road, Rhiwbina and tell Mr and Mrs Lister that their daughter was going out with a piglet. And I said nothing to Beti, either, when Raymond went off to do his training. I said nothing. I did nothing. And I did it over and over again.

Did it over and over again? What does that mean? you ask. How can you do nothing over and over again? You can't have more of nothing. Harry Selwyn's lost the plot.

I've said it before and I'll say it again. There's more than one kind of nothing. There's the nothing that's only nothing. And then there are all those nothings that aren't nothing at all, but different kinds of something. This is one of them.

Beti came over to Mam's a week after Raymond left for Pirbright, to have a chat, to compare letters.

'He said they had to get up at six ...'

'Do drill all morning ...'

'Had to get his hair cut...'

'His curls! His beautiful curls!'

And laughed at the photograph. So handsome, Mam said. So cute, Beti said. Beti didn't bring her letter with her. It wouldn't have been fit for a mother's eyes. Just the SWALK on the envelope would have made Beti blush. But she recited excerpts from memory. Had the whole thing off by heart.

Mam read out her own letter and stopped every time she didn't understand something. 'What's jankers, Harry? What's this? What's that?' Because I'd been through it myself. I'd explained it all before, too, but she'd forgotten, after so many years. Or maybe she hadn't forgotten, just wanted to spin it out a bit longer, think of Raymond playing at soldiers.

'I hope he'll be alright,' said Beti.

I picked up the photograph and smiled. 'Of course he'll be alright, Beti ... You can tell by his face ... He's settled in just fine.'

That's all. And went to fill the kettle.

Here's another example. A month later. A hot summer's day, Beti came over to the school with her father to take photographs: each class in turn, Standard I to Standard IV, then the portraits. The headmaster contracted the Listers for the job. All I did was mention to Mam, in passing, how much the last outfit had charged. Daylight robbery, she agreed. Did Mam say something to Beti? Did Beti pass that something on to her father? It was none of my business. Quotes were procured. Mr Lister got the job.

I spent a lot of time with Beti that day, the day they took the pictures. We didn't talk a great deal – indeed, I specifically eschewed too much idle chit-chat — but we got to see each other go about our business. We gathered impressions, we reflected upon them. She saw me telling off a boy in the back row for chatting to his friend instead of looking at the camera. Firmly, but fairly, not making a fuss. I helped a little girl tie her hair back, to be at her best for the photograph. I fetched water for another, who was complaining of the heat. Put my hand on her brow, asked whether she felt unwell. I did what it was appropriate for me to do, what I was expected to do, no more, no less.

Or perhaps, in the end, you might consider that I did somewhat less than expected, under the circumstances. And rather more, too. After the Listers finished taking their pictures I helped them carry their gear back to the car. This was a new green and white Triumph Herald. Quite striking for its time. 'Duotone,' said Mr Lister, who'd noticed me eyeing his purchase. 'Because of the two colours,' he said. 'Duotone.' I nodded. Kept a straight face. Afforded him due respect. Then stole a glance at Beti, who was grinning. 'Duotone, ' I said. 'Very smart.' Looked at Beti again.

So, a little less, and a little more. But not too much either way.

The next time Beti came to Mam's house she said she hadn't heard from Raymond for over a week. I told her not to fret, Mam hadn't heard anything either. But she wasn't pleased. Beti has a way of looking at you when she isn't pleased, when she wants to show she's hurt. She turns her face down, just a touch, so that her eyes are angled upwards. She isn't angry, but she wants you to know she's disappointed in you, she'd expected more. I don't know where she got that from. The films, perhaps. Marilyn Monroe did it in *Some Like It Hot*. So that was it, more than likely. The films. But since it was Beti pulling the face, she looked more like Bernadette than Marilyn Monroe. Mam took me to see that one. *The Song of Bernadette*. Can't remember who played Bernadette. Jennifer something or other. No matter. Bernadette was peeking up at God, of course, not at Jack Lemmon. But then, you could say there was something quite pious about Beti, too, back in those days.

It was the eyes that lured Raymond. Beti's eyes looking up at him. I'm certain of it. Another Bernadette, baiting her own little god. A man's an easy fish to catch, even for a shy little thing like Beti. And I was glad to see that look for myself, the tilt of the eyes, the come-closer-but-not-too-close look, because I knew what had hooked him. More to the point, I knew Raymond would miss it, that thing, if it were taken away. Would grieve its loss. Which was just as well, because if it wasn't there, that thing, why was I wasting my time?

It didn't bother me, then, when people said, 'Isn't that Beti girl a bit on the quiet side for Raymond? Tell me, what does he see in her?' Maybe they were remembering the films, too, and thinking, 'Yes, that's who she is. Another Bernadette. White as the driven snow.' I didn't mind when Mam said, 'Yes, a nice enough girl, I suppose ...' And went back to her ironing or her baking, not wanting to trip over the 'but' that would follow. I didn't mind because none of them had seen that look in the eyes, the look that proves there isn't much difference, sometimes, between your Marilyn Monroes and your Bernadettes. And I'll tell you this for nothing, if I'd wanted to fall in love that evening, if I'd had some inclination in that direction, that look would have clinched the matter.

'How long's he been gone?' I said. 'A month, is it?'

'Six weeks,' said Beti.

'Ah … Right you are, then … And when's he due to go to Germany?'

'The end of the month,' she said. Then the look. The face looking down, ever so slightly, the eyes looking up. Wanting her lover. Wanting to tell him off, too.

'Well, then,' I said, 'he'll have a lot on his mind … He'll get round to it, you see if he doesn't. Tomorrow, perhaps. By the weekend, I'm sure.' Waited a second. Offered a reassuring smile. 'He isn't … He's never been … There's no harm in Raymond, none at all, but …'

One more example.

Raymond came home for a week's leave before he went to Germany. We all had a slap-up meal at the Royal: Mam, Beti, Raymond, me and Yvonne, the girl I was going out with at the time.

'Steak for me,' said Raymond, and gave his belly a squeeze. He'd lost weight in Pirbright. Looked quite the dapper gent for once, in his uniform and crew-cut. The Basic Training had done him good, and he knew it.

'Well, Raymond,' I said. 'Tell us what you've been up to.'

And he told us about night training.

'Close your eyes,' he said.

We closed our eyes.

'What's this, then …?'

He started making noises.

'And this …?'

Closed our eyes and had to guess. Sometimes you'd guess it was his fingers, flicking the table cloth. Or maybe his knife and fork, rattling on the plate. Sometimes you'd be right, sometimes wrong. And that would be a puzzle. But the ear's less of an ear without an eye. That's what the night training taught you.

Then he said, 'What's this, then?'

Nobody had a clue. Opened our eyes and there he was, tapping the buttons of his jacket with a spoon. Which should have been easy, because a spoon's just a spoon, and a button's just a button. But a button *and* a spoon. Now, there's the difference.

'So?' he said.

'A spoon and a button,' we said, because there was nothing wrong with our eyes.

Raymond shook his head. 'Enemy reloading, sir!' he barked. 'SVT 40, three feet to the left, sir!' And then, in a Sergeant Major voice, 'How can you tell, Private Selwyn? How can you be sure that it's an SVT 40?' 'Because the SVT 40 sounds just like a man hitting his jacket buttons with a spoon, sir!'

We laughed.

'Night training,' Raymond said. 'Knowing your spoons from your SVT40s.'

And then, when he'd tired of the night training, he told us about the jazz band he was in, and the inventories he had to keep, and the way he had to rub Number 3 Green Blanco into his kit, and it was jankers if he got smudges or streaks. Then he described how the squaddies asked him to write their letters for them. Letters to their Mams sometimes, but their sweethearts mainly. And the things he had to write! They would make a crow blush!

Beti bit her lip. I touched her sleeve. Asked, could I get her a drink?

But no, on second thoughts, that's too noisy a story to finish with. Consider this. A fortnight went by. Raymond had returned to Germany. Beti called by one Sunday afternoon while Mam was over at Antie Dot's, helping her look after Uncle Tom. I opened the door and saw her standing there, hands in her coat pockets, eyes downcast.

'Your Mam in?'

'No, Beti, she isn't.'

Came in, sat down and told me that Raymond had asked her to marry him.

'And what did you say, Beti?'

A pause. Then, 'Probably.'

'Probably?'

'Probably, I said. I'll probably marry you.' Another pause. 'He'd get seven shillings a week more if he was married. That's what he said ... If we got married now.'

'He thinks the world ...'

'Seven shillings ... Like it was a joke.'

And again. Whitsun. Three months later. Mam over at Auntie Dot's after Uncle Tom died. Beti brought a sprig of parsley to plant in the garden. 'Just a little something ...' I was standing in the kitchen, waiting for the kettle to boil, looking out through the window. Beti was at the table, pretending to read the paper. I took the cups down from the shelf, fetched the milk from the pantry. Beti got up, came over and put her hand on the back of my shoulder, leaned her head on my arm. I turned.

'Hold me, Harry. I'm so ...'

The words quiet but clear, almost stilted, as though she'd been practising them. Even the drifting off at the end, it sounded as though she'd practised that, too. Or as though she'd heard it in a film. Borrowed words. Elizabeth Taylor turning to Montgomery Clift, asking him to comfort her. Something like that. As you'd expect from a shy girl like Beti, who didn't know her own words yet. But she'd broken her heart, so what did it matter that she'd borrowed someone else's? Words have got to come from somewhere.

I put my arms around her. I said nothing.

My pupils kept tadpoles in a tank in the corner of the classroom. Two gave them their food, two changed the water, two others kept the records, wrote down how much they'd altered from one day to the next. Not the same two, of course – there was a rota, so everyone got a turn.

I'd ask them, 'So, is it a frog yet? Has it stopped being a tadpole?' They'd stand for a while, look at the little stumps and shake their heads. Disappointed. Irritated, too. Children are impatient creatures.

Came back the next day. 'The tail's got smaller, sir! Is it a frog yet?' But a frog doesn't have a tail, does he, not even the remnant of one?

The following day the front legs were starting to poke through, just little black nodules under the skin. The day after, the children shouted, 'The head's changed shape, sir! And the eyes! Look at the eyes, sir!'

Another week and I asked them again: 'So, what have we here?'

There was the frog, standing on his little stone. The whole frog and nothing but the frog. The tadpole was less than a memory.

'When?' I said. 'When did this happen?'

Nobody knew. All they knew was that they'd lost the moment. It had happened when they were at home, in bed, asleep. Or perhaps when they were here at school, practising their writing, but they were too busy trying to join the w and the p, keeping their words straight.

Anyway, who has such sharp eyes that he can see a leg growing? And a frog's leg at that. Who has such keen hearing that he can detect that first intake of breath? Ear to the mouth, everybody quiet, shut your eyes now, boys and girls, and listen ...

You'd need the patience of Job to catch that first bubble of air.

Some tadpoles take eight months to turn into frogs. I thought I'd done well, turning Beti around in a year and a half. And all I did was stand in that little gap between the tadpole and the frog and wait for the moment, the first breath. And she came to me. Two years earlier I would have thought, Well, God has answered my prayers. Better late than never. But I knew now that God was just a character in the old black-and-white films and I had nothing more to say to Him.

Jennifer Jones. That's who played Bernadette.

As I say, if Sam Appleby wrote this story he'd want to boil it down to a couple of hundred words – a bit of scandal here, a few tears there, a ringing condemnation of the gutless paramour, for stealing his young brother's happiness while he was away serving queen and country. That's what he'd want to do. But how could he? There was no story. No evidence. And what newspaper man is going to sit for a year and a half, twiddling his thumbs, waiting for that first breath to break?

42

Friday, 21 May 8.40pm

'What do you mean, things taste different?'

'You lose it,' Harry says.

'Lose it?'

'You lose your sense of taste. You know … You've got to use more salt, more ketchup, more everything, because it all tastes the same. You can't tell the difference between one thing and another.'

'Like what?'

'Eh?'

'You say you can't tell the difference between one thing and another … Like what? Can't taste the difference between what and what?'

'Like … Like…'

Harry and Raymond are sharing a bottle of Badger Golden Glory. Harry turns the bottle around and reads the label.

'Like this. *An award-winning premium ale, well balanced with distinctive bitterness and a delicate floral peach and melon aroma* … Can you taste that?' Harry says. 'Can you taste the *floral peach and melon*?'

Raymond picks up his glass, takes a sip, lets the beer settle on his tongue and swallows. He takes another sip and shakes his head. 'There's something …'

'But peach …?' Then, more quietly, 'And melon?'

Harry knows he must keep his voice down. What would happen if Beti came into the kitchen this second and said, 'Why didn't you wake me, Harry? Goodness, you surely haven't eaten already, have you?' It doesn't bear thinking about. But nor must he speak too quietly. That would sound unnatural, it would prompt questions he couldn't possibly answer. Anyway, the alcohol is beginning to loosen his tongue.

'There's something …' Raymond says. 'There's something different about it … Peach, did you say?'

'And melon. You mean you can taste the melon? You can taste melon in the beer?'

43

Harry v. The Saxophone May 18, 1968

Raymond's been talking to Sam. Putting ideas in his head. There's no other explanation.

It's odd he's decided to do it now, mind you. That he's let it drift so long. But there's no telling, is there? A man will bide his time, wait his chance.

Raymond didn't come back from Germany. He found out that Beti and I were together and he didn't come back. Or, rather, he came back from Germany but he didn't come home. He went to work in England, in Halifax. Halifax was the place for concrete in those days, and that's what Raymond was doing by then, testing concrete. Kept his distance, so he didn't have to face the truth, that he'd lost Beti, that she'd chosen someone more considerate, less immature. Good luck to him, too, I thought. At last, the piggy has found a sty of his own, he won't come snorting around our midden any more.

So it was odd that Raymond decided to come to the wedding. The oddest thing, you might say, was that we invited him. But what else could we do? What would Mam have said? And anyway, part of me liked the idea of Raymond, over in Halifax, opening the envelope and seeing it in black and white, that it was all finished between them, that Beti would be more of a Selwyn than he'd ever been. Imagined his fingers, leaving smudges of concrete dust on the paper. Childish, I know. But I've promised to tell you the truth. Isn't everybody childish at some time or another?

As I say, two years he stayed away. Came back for the wedding in his big new Jaguar, all of a swagger. I'd no idea there'd been such a run on concrete. Turned round then, of course, and there it was everywhere, the whole world was made of the stuff. Raymond had seen it coming. Must have. New Jaguar and new girlfriend, too. Margaret. 'Call me Mags,' she said. And her Labradors, a whole Jaguar full of them. He shook my hand, gave Beti a peck on the cheek, half a crown each to the bridesmaids, strutted about the place so you'd think it was him getting wed, not me. As though it was his due.

Mam said, 'There's nice he doesn't bear a grudge. Isn't it, Harry?'

Raymond said, 'I can play at the reception, if you like ... Bring the band as well.'

So I started to think, Jesus, he's won again. I've taken my eye off the ball, and he's won again. He's put his resentment on the back burner, out of sight. He's holding his fire until the time is ripe. And when will that be? When *will* the time be ripe? How will I know? And who would have believed that a piglet could keep it up for so long?

So they all came. Raymond, the bass player, the piano player, the drummer, the whole troop. And Raymond standing out in the front, with his sax, filling the hall with his sweet exhalations. That's what the sax does with your breath, it dresses it up, gives it fancy twirls and twists, and people think it's really you they're hearing, not just air going through metal. Had to go out on to the floor then, just Beti and me, make a spectacle of ourselves in front of everybody, dance to the piggy's tune.

At the end they all went up to him and said, Wonderful, Raymond. Just like the old days. Thank you so much. And left the hotel humming 'In the Still of the Night'.

And then, outside. A grand night, they said. A splendid send-off. But muttering behind their hands, too. Beyond earshot, but I could tell. What's wrong with Harry tonight? they were saying. A bit dour, don't you think? A bit on the glum side? Doesn't take after his brother, does he?

No, he doesn't.

How could I?

And I was the cuckoo in the nest.

Two years later, Raymond came back for good.

'More space for the dogs,' Mags said.

'Roller Compacted Concrete,' Raymond said. 'And Plasticizers. That's the future.'

Mam said, 'There's nice, the family back together. Isn't it, Harry? Isn't it nice we're all back together again?'

Of course he came back. A man bides his time, waits his chance. But he can't hold his breath in for ever, can he? Two minutes I managed once. And what's two minutes? That's why I say Raymond's been talking to Sam. He couldn't keep it up any longer. And you've got to breathe out before you can breathe in. So he breathed it out, all that black air, emptied his lungs, out with the old, in with the new. And Sam was there, that's all. Ready to take the black air, put it in his little book.

44

Friday, 21 May, 8.55 pm

'Sam Appleby came over earlier.'

'Who?'

'Sam Appleby … Called by this afternoon … Doing a piece on the race.'

'Sam Appleby?'

'From the *Gazette*.'

Harry opens another bottle of Badger Golden Glory and pours some into his brother's glass.

'He thinks I'm too old. Thinks I'm going to do myself an injury.'

Harry waits for the froth to settle, then fills Raymond's glass and pours the remainder of the beer into his own.

'Aren't you worried you'll get hurt? he said. Hurt? I said. I've been pissing blood since I was twenty years of age, I said. Pissing blood since before you were born, Sam, and I'm still here to tell the tale.'

'Sam Appleby you say?'

'Eh?'

'This chap you're talking about. From the *Gazette*. Appleby, you say?'

'Sam Appleby. Why? You know him?'

'The Appleby that used to go out with Jim Bentley's girl? What was her name? Fee … Fee something.'

'Stephanie, you mean?'

'No, no. Not Stephanie. The redhead. Fee. Fee something or other.'

'Stephanie had red hair.'

'No, not Stephanie. It was Fee … Definitely Fee.'

Harry uses a knife to scrape the pieces of fish skin from Raymond's plate onto his own. Then, stacking one plate on top of the other and rising to his feet, he asks, in a matter-of-fact voice, 'You spoken to him recently?'

'Spoken to him?'

'Sam Appleby. Have you spoken to Sam Appleby?' Harry

reins in his voice, which has suddenly become loud and terse. 'Have you seen him around? Has he phoned?'

Raymond shakes his head. Smiles bemusement. 'Why would I want to speak to Sam Appleby?'

45

21 September 1962 Amman Valley 10m

```
1 Bob Crabb Glos AC SM 53.02
2 F. Aspen AH SM 53.13
3 H.Selwyn Taff Harriers SM 53.26
4 Tom Jenkins Swansea AC M40 53.28
```

I've pissed blood, Sam, I said. But never coughed it. Not a drop.

He was asking about accidents, injuries, mishaps. The worst, the longest, how many, that sort of thing. Did I ever stop for treatment in the middle of a race? Was running more dangerous now I was getting on a bit? I lifted my foot up. A bit of bother with the Achilles every now and again, I said. But it was under control, I did the exercises. Would you like a picture of my heel? I asked. But he wasn't interested. And the nose, I said. Sinusitis. That was a nuisance, too. He wasn't interested in my nose, either. So I thought, Well, then, I'll give you a drop of blood. Your readers might like a drop of blood.

'I've pissed blood,' I told him. 'Run so hard I dried out, like a dishcloth in the sun. Like an old leaf. Like a frog that can't find his way back to the pond. Bladder empty, so just dry skin against dry skin. Rubbing. Only blood left.'

He raised his eyebrows.

'Haematuria,' I said. Then said it again. 'Haematuria.' He liked that. A bit of Latin. He started believing me once he got the bit of Latin. Spelt it out for him then so he could write it down in his book.

'Did you get over it?' he asked.

'No, Sam,' I said. 'I'm still lying there, in a ditch up by Gwaun Cae Gurwen. You'd best put a step on it or the crows'll have my tongue out.'

But that's what happens. It's hot, you sweat, you've got a thirst the size of a desert but you daren't stop or you'll lose position. And that would be a pity. The man in front is starting to tire, you can hear his breath. *Oof, oof,* he's going. You think, This is it, this is my chance, I can pull ahead now. So your thirst goes to buggery. An hour later you have a pint in the Mount Pleasant. You've come third and that's better than you've ever done before. You have another pint, and another. You go for a piss and the urinal's all red and the others just stand there, staring at the blood flowing past their feet, staring at you, thinking, Christ, he's a goner.

I've pissed blood, I told him. But never coughed it. Beti's coughed blood, mind you. Coughing scrapes the inside of her throat, so there's little streaks of red in her sputum then. Red on her hanky.

She was like that from the beginning, even on the first night, after the saxophone had stopped and everybody had gone home, and the two of us were lying in the big bed they kept for the newly weds. Beti on her side, her back to me, trying to bury the noise in the blankets, hold it in her fist. *Psh, psh* of the inhaler then. Ten minutes' peace. Then started all over again. And me, pretending to sleep, lying on my side, my back to her, thinking, Jesus, I've caught her, what the hell am I going to do with her now?

46

Friday, 21 May, 9.10 pm

Harry clears the plates, puts them down carefully on the counter.

'Sorry, Raymond, no pudding tonight ... Haven't had the time.'

Raymond shakes his head. 'No need ...'

'Bananas ... We've got plenty of bananas.'

'No need, Harry, I'm full.'

'Sure?'

'Full as an egg.'

Harry goes to the dresser, takes a pack of cards from the middle drawer and brings them over to the table. Conversation stops and for the next ten minutes the brothers concentrate on winning tricks. Indeed, so deep is their concentration that, after a minute or two, as a card is played, one or the other will pause to allow Beti to take her turn. It is some time before they adjust to the gap she has left and the disruption this has caused to their routine.

'Will she want food when she gets back?'

'Food?'

'Beti. When she gets home. Are you keeping some supper for her?'

Harry takes a card form the pack, places three kings on the table, straightens his remaining cards and shakes his head. 'No. She'll have had food. Emma will have made her something.'

Another five minutes pass. Harry, prompted by Raymond's questions, is now trying to work out exactly when Beti went to bed and how long she's been there. Raymond's right: she'll need something to eat. When did she eat last? Has she eaten since breakfast? Did she even *have* breakfast? Or was she already ill, even then? He can answer none of these questions.

'How many?'

'Eh?'

'Five cards this time, is it?'

'Five.'

He went to town at ten o'clock. Was Beti in bed then? Yes, she was. Fact. And when he returned? Where had she got to by then?

'You to choose, Harry.'

'Mm?'

'Trumps. Your choice.'

When he returned, Beti had already gone out to have her hair done. Yes. Of course. She must have done. Another fact. And then he went out for a jog. So that's the answer. Beti came back when he was still out running. An unfortunate coincidence, but undoubtedly the case. Beti returned from town, worn out, felt a migraine coming on, saw those lights behind her eyes, took a Panadol and went straight to bed. What time was that? Twelve? Half past twelve? Before one, certainly, because that's when Sam Appleby arrived, give or take. What happened then? He had a banana. He showed Sam Appleby the pictures, the cuttings. That's all he remembers. Banana. Sam. These are the facts.

'Diamonds.'

47

5 October 1967 Ras y Frenni 8m

1 Phil Marks Pemb AC SM 46.08
2 C. Philpott Milford Harr. M40 46.13

3 H.Selwyn Taff Harriers SM 46.26
4 P. J. Roberts Bridgend AC SM 46.27

Beti said, 'You don't love me any more, Harry, do you?'
Looked up at me. Looked away.

As though I were watching a film.

Winning's usually enough. You go up and receive your cup, your medal, someone takes your picture, a couple of lines in the paper if you're lucky, and that's that. Put your cup on the mantelpiece and get yourself ready for the next race. That's the deal. But not this time. Not with Beti. I'd won her fare and square. All the paperwork said so. The pictures, too. I'd won her, but I hadn't the faintest idea what to do with her. As if the cup said, No, thank you, I don't want to stay put on the mantelpiece, I want more than this. And there wasn't another race to turn to.

We were over in Pembrokeshire. Crymych. Ras y Frenni. Awful weather. Course like the Somme. Which was in my favour, mind you, being on the slight side, low centre of gravity, good at keeping my feet when everybody else is slithering about like ducks on ice. I wrapped duct tape around my shoes, just in case. That's the worst with mud, your shoes can take off without you. And running barefoot never appealed, even though I'd run with the Kalenjin, and the Kalenjin didn't have a shoelace between them. Duct tape around my toes as well, to stop the blisters. I came third, and that got me a medal.

Beti said, 'You don't love me any more, Harry, do you?'

And I thought, Jesus, how does she know that? What's changed?

'Why do you say that, Beti?'

She shook her head. 'You don't love me, not like ...'

Then looked up at me with *that* look. The look that would touch something deep inside you if you had the inclination. And you wouldn't mind then if she couldn't find the right words. That look was enough. It had been enough for the last five years, you could say, because even if I didn't have an inclination to fall in love with her I had plenty of other reasons to go through the motions. You can't call that love, I know, but it had got me by.

'Not like what, Beti? Not like *what*?'

They say that the desire to love is similar to the real thing. That people can't tell the difference. They want to be in love so much that the want becomes the love. They fool everybody. They even fool themselves. I'd hoped that Beti and I could be like that. Not that I wanted to *love* her, not as such. I was *obliged* to love her. But the obligation made its own want. An inferior want, but real nonetheless. So I hoped that might do the trick. If I went through the motions often enough, day after day, I might even forget the difference myself.

Like joined-up writing. I worked hard at that, when I started out teaching. It's a big jump from pen and paper to chalk and blackboard, and if the teacher can't do it properly what hope is there for his pupils? Talking of hope, here's one I used.

hopefully

Only nine letters, but six of them looped, so plenty of ups and downs. Spent a lot of time showing them how to move from the *p* to the *e*, so you couldn't see the join, no white space, no crossings out, no corrections, no wobbles. And the others, too, but the *p* and th *e* are the hardest to get right, to make them look natural so there's no break in the flow. And getting it right without lifting your pen from the page. That's hardest, because there's a lot of ink goes into just that one word. Open it out and you'll see. Only nine letters, but a whole foot of ink. Twelve inches. Like this.

——————————————————————————————

——————————————————————————————

——————————————————————————————

——

But best if you do it yourself, on a big sheet of paper, so you can get one long line. There isn't enough space to do it justice here.

It became second nature after a while, so that I didn't have to practise any more, I could write just as well on the blackboard as on paper. That's what love's like, I thought. Wanting to love. Having to love. Pretending to love. You apply yourself and in a month or two, a year or two, it will happen. Go through the motions, join the *p*'s and the *e*'s and there'll come a time when you can't see the join.

But five years went by and she said, 'You're a long way away from me, Harry.'

I looked puzzled. She said, 'You've become cold, Harry. So cold.'

'Cold?'

'You don't love me any more, do you?'

Over in Pembrokeshire, after Ras y Frenni, in the mud and the rain, pulling off the duct tape, getting myself ready to collect the medal, and Beti caught me off guard. She saw that

I didn't care, I'd stopped even going through the motions. She looked away. She looked up at me again. With *that* look.

'Not like …'

'Not like what, Beti? Not like what?' Perhaps I said it a little abruptly, but I had to go to the marquee, to collect my medal. The photographer was waiting, there were protocols to observe.

'Like Raymond used to,' she said. 'You don't love me like *that.*'

'Like *that?*'

I dare say I blushed. A man doesn't expect to hear such things in the rain and mud, amongst the runners and the marshals. This was bedroom talk. Or perhaps, there again, it might have been kitchen table talk. When you run out of things to say, and you look out through the window, hunt for something to fill the gap. The birds. The flowers. Whatever's there. But you've got bugger all to say about them either. That's when you might come out with things of that sort. When all the other words have run out and the silence takes over. And it knocked me back. As though the frog had decided to become a tadpole again and hadn't let anybody know. Had lost its legs and lungs, had grown a new tail, and me like one of the little boys, too busy to notice.

I probably went to fetch my medal then. I can't remember. I don't remember anything except thinking, Well, that's a voice I haven't heard before. Where did that come from? I tried to work out what 'like *that*' meant. Whatever it was, I needed to get hold of it and do the job properly. I confess I was a little irritated, too, that she used such a slippery phrase. Like *that*? Like *what*, exactly? Be more specific, child, I wanted to say. I held my teacher's instincts in check, but only just. I would have to work it out for myself. And I had no idea what that would mean.

It must have been when I came back from the marquee,

when I'd had time to think. I said, 'Of course I love you, Beti.
I love you more than anything. Than anyone.' And it's odd, I
know, but I wanted to believe it myself. If I didn't believe it,
if I didn't really love Beti, then how could I say I'd beaten
Raymond? It dawned on me then. This was a race without a
tape at the end of it, because it couldn't have an end. No tape,
no photograph, no medal, no headline to say, it's all over,
you've won or you've lost, but you've run the last lap and
you don't have to run it again. It wasn't enough to put a ring
on her finger. To beat Raymond, I had to win Beti over and
over again. That was the real long haul.

'Do you, Harry?'

'I ... I just ... I have trouble expressing my feelings ...
Always have, perhaps, but Kenya ... You know, seeing all
that ... It made it worse, I'm sure it did ... You couldn't give
in, you see, you couldn't let yourself feel ...' Quietly, too.
Hesitantly. I bowed my head and left it at that. No more words.

She looked at me. But not *that* look. Nodded.

So no more words. And that became part of the joined-up
writing, too. The silence. Accepting that there were things
words couldn't touch. Or touched them only to make them
worse. No words, no lies. And if that was the case, then
perhaps the cold wasn't cold after all. It just masked
something else, something deep down, beyond words, that
only Beti could get at, and then draw to the surface, to feel
its warmth. That's how it had to be understood. That's how
Beti had to understand it.

And I kept the nib on the paper all the while, so she wouldn't
see the gap between one letter and the next, so it would all be
a single long line. Beti wanted to believe me, too. Of course she
did. And wanting to believe is a bit like actually believing, I
should think. Just like love. She put her arms around me. She

did it without conviction, I could tell, but it was the start – the start of her embracing the weakness in me. I think she came to love that weakness more than anything else. You know where you stand with weakness, it doesn't raise your hopes. It tells you you're needed, you're important. She tried to love enough for the two of us after that. Told herself I couldn't cope without her. Like one of her dahlias. Put a cane down in the earth so the flower would grow straight. Tied it then so the head wouldn't drop too much when it came into bloom.

And what did I do? You could say I did nothing. I accepted the cane and the watering and the weeding and everything else in its season. I accepted the piece of string, knotted just tightly enough to hold me up straight against the buffeting winds. But sometimes I did a little more than nothing. Once in a while I'd offer a flower or two in return, to say thank you, to show Beti her efforts weren't in vain. That it was a long haul for both of us, but we were getting there. And that was all part of the joined-up writing, too.

Was that a kind of love? Not love 'like *that*', of course. How could it be? But was it as good? I mean, in its own terms, was it as good as what had been between Beti and Raymond? Would it become as good, given time, with steady application, in the long run?

Because if it didn't, it was worth bugger all.

48

Friday, 21 May, 9.15 pm

'I'd best go and …' Harry points a thumb at the dishes. 'Best get rid of the scraps.'

Although it is Harry who speaks, Beti is the true custodian of these words. This is her custom every Friday night: as soon as the meal is finished, she will say, 'Best clear the dishes.' Then she or Harry will throw the leftovers into the recycling bag and tie it fast. 'Get fish everywhere otherwise,' she will say, or some variation on these words. Raymond might respond: 'That's the worst with fish.' Or perhaps: 'Got a cold. Can't smell a thing.' And then, as one washes the dishes, the other will take the fruit salad from the fridge, or the apple tart from the oven, and put it on the table. Raymond will say, 'Looks good, Beti.'

Tonight, none of this happens. There isn't any pudding, there isn't any Beti. As a result, for a while, Harry forgets about the dishes, the scraps, the fishy smells. But then, as soon he remembers, he moves with unprecedented haste. He knows that Beti may come downstairs at any moment and discover the mess her husband has made, the obligations he has failed to meet. 'And fish, Harry. Fish!'

Harry lifts the lid of the recycling container. With the side of a knife he scrapes the remains of the food into the bag inside. Then he removes the bag and ties it tight. It isn't half full yet, but that can't be helped: he dare not leave the bag open and risk the smells escaping, infecting the rest of the house. He ties it tight, then puts it into another bag, just in case. To Harry's mind, the recycling bags supplied by the Council are too flimsy, barely fit for purpose, especially where fish is concerned.

The CD draws to a plaintive close. Silence resumes.

'Ten years old,' Raymond says.

'Mm?'

'Kenny G … Started playing the sax when he was ten … When he was still in junior school.'

'Well, you've got to …'

'Could hold a note for forty-five minutes.'

'Hold it?'

'Non-stop. Not a break.'

'Circular breathing, Raymond. It's a trick.'

'But still ...'

'Hold a note for as long as you like with circular breathing.'

Harry fills the sink from the hot water tap, adds washing up liquid, puts on his yellow rubber gloves.

49

Warm Breath v. Cold Breath

You ask, how can that be done? How can you make the cold seem warm? You say you've heard enough about joined-up writing. It's all so much flummery. Smoke and mirrors. It's just Harry Selwyn at his old game, making pretty patterns out of words. He think he's still standing in front of his class, showing the little brats how clever he is, bamboozling them with his big numbers, his far-fetched tales. Cold is cold, you say, and warm is warm. It's as simple as that. If the warmth isn't there – *really* there, deep down inside you, beyond the words – where will you get it from? Saying something doesn't make it true. Doesn't make people believe you, either. So who's kidding who?

That's what you think. I can hear you.

Well, listen to me. Down inside's got nothing to do with it.

Try this. Hold a hand up in front of your mouth, not too far, just a couple of inches. Open your mouth wide and breathe out. Wide, remember. A big 'O'. It's warm, isn't it? The air is warm. Your very own air, from deep down. Warm enough to melt an ice-cube.

Do it again, but this time tighten your lips. Just a little 'o'. Barely enough to let the air through. Then breathe out. It's cold. Same air, same mouth, same lungs, all the same deep down, but the warmth has gone.

You close your lips. You open them again. Like a fish. Nothing but lips. That's the difference between warm and cold. You learn how to use your lips. Face love.

50

10 May 1973 Wenallt Round 12m

```
9 H.Selwyn Taff Harriers V40 1.39.38
10 A.Cronin NAC S 1.39.45
11 W. Williams Rhondda AC S 1.39.47
12 S. Pierce Swansea AC V40 1.40.05
```

I told him he'd got the wrong end of the stick. 'I'm not seventy-nine, Sam,' I said. 'I'm fifteen and a half.'

He wanted the truth. I gave him the truth. Whether he believed it or not wasn't my problem.

He said, 'So then, Harry, when are you thinking of hanging up your daps?' Biro in hand, ready to write another number in his notebook, thinking that would be the answer. A number. A year. An age. 'After the Bryn Coch?' he said. 'It'll be fifty tomorrow, won't it?' I didn't answer. 'Or are you going to celebrate your eightieth first? Eh? Is that what you have in mind, Harry? Reach eighty and have a big bash?'

As though numbers meant anything.

'Why eighty?' I asked.

He thought. 'You've got to stop somewhere.'

'You retiring at sixty-five, Sam?'

'Thereabouts.'

179

'Why's that?' I said.

'Because ...'

'Why not sixty-seven? Or forty-nine? Or ninety-two?'

'Because ...'

'You don't make children stop, do you?'

'Children?'

'A number's just a muscle, Sam,' I said. And watched him wince.

That's when I told him my age. 'I'm not seventy-nine, Sam,' I said. 'I'm fifteen and a half. Put that in your paper. Harry Selwyn will be running with the juniors tomorrow because he's fifteen and a half again.'

He looked flummoxed. It was only to be expected. So I showed him how to measure age properly.

'When were you at your best, Sam?' I said.

'At my best?'

It wasn't a fair question. I suspect Sam has never had a best. Or, to put it another way, there was probably little difference between his best and his worst. He lived on a plateau. No mountain terrors, no fertile valleys either. And anyway, what does 'at your best' mean for a journalist? That he writes more words than ever before? That he writes them faster? Or is it just that one scoop, a comet crossing the night sky, the curtains closing over again? Sam didn't know. I didn't know.

'OK, Sam,' I said. 'Here's another question for you.'

I was more careful this time. I asked him a question I could answer. And I had the figures to hand, to prove it. 'What about a runner?' I said. 'When is a *runner* at his best? Let's say he runs the Wenallt Round every year ...' Because those were the photos I was showing him at the time: the Wenallt Round, above Caerphilly. 'Let's say he runs it every year. How old will he be when he gets up one morning and says to his wife, Well, here we are then, the day has arrived. A year ago I was scrambling up the last rocky outcrops. Next year I'll be picking my way down through the scree. But today, this morning, I'm at the peak. I'll never be as good again. If I don't win today, I'll never win. When does that happen, Sam? When's a runner at his best?'

He crossed his arms and looked up at the ceiling, as though the answer were there, scribbled on the side of the lampshade. Then, 'Twenty-five!' Said it with conviction, too, so that I began to wonder what he'd been up to at that age to make him so certain.

'Close enough, Sam!' I said. 'Well done.'

I told him the right answer was twenty-seven. He seemed pleased. Smiled. Straightened his back. Like a little schoolboy, all bright and bushy tailed, eager for the next question. So I said. 'Here's another one for you.'

I knew the answer to this question, too, even though it was a lot more difficult and flew in the face of common sense. 'A man is at his best at twenty-seven,' I said. 'It's downhill from then on. But ... *But* ...' And I raised a finger to show that the big one was coming. 'But how much downhill will he have to do before he runs again as he did when he was eighteen? How old will he be when he completes the Wenallt Round in an hour and a half, like he did nine years ago, the year he left school, went to college, played at being a man?'

Sam creased his brow. I swear I could hear the acid in his stomach, digesting the digits. I knew what he would say. He thought he was only doing sums, simple addition and subtraction. Like the boys and girls at school. If a man's at his best at twenty seven, when will he be eighteen again? Well, then, it takes nine years to go from eighteen to twenty seven. It must take another nine years to go back again. And there you have it, your answer. 27 + 9 = 36. Except that Sam was a bit rusty with his mental arithmetic and had to scribble it all down in his notebook, and give his biro a chew, and stare at the dahlias again, for solace.

Then, 'Thirty-six, is it?' he said. As I'd expected.

'Thirty-six, Sam? So a man loses his best just as quickly as he finds it? Is that what you mean, Sam?' Sam didn't know what he meant. Sam was doing sums. He shrugged. He shook his head.

'Sixty-five,' I said. 'That's when a runner becomes eighteen again. Sixty-five. About the time you're retiring.'

And if they ever got to run against each other, the young lad and the pensioner, it would be neck-and-neck right to the end, and perhaps they'd both break the tape together. I drew him a diagram so he could see how time takes a breather as a man goes back downhill. How it becomes less steep as the years accumulate. 'As they accumulate,' I said. I liked that. Better than getting old.

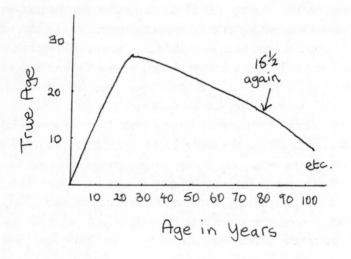

'Which means that I'm fifteen and a half again,' I said. And pointed to the diagram, to prove it. And fifteen and a half's a pretty good age, too, for somebody knocking on eighty. 'I've got the figures to prove it,' I said. 'Dr Bramble. University of Idaho.' I even went to the study and dug out the article for him.

'Everybody stops somewhere,' Sam said.

But where's somewhere? Can someone show it me on the map? It doesn't make sense. If you have to stop on the way down, why don't you have to stop on the way up as well? If you tell me it's time to call it a day, why don't you tell the boy who's celebrating his fifteen and a half for the first time? Why is the youngster's fifteen and a half better than the old man's?

So I've no idea where Sam's 'somewhere' is. All I know is that I haven't got there yet. I said, 'You don't stop running because you grow old, Sam. You grow old because you stop running.'

But he didn't write that down. He wanted a number. A year. An age. So I gave him one. I said, 'Tell them this, Sam. Tell them that Harry Selwyn's fifteen and a half again, just like he was back in 1948, when he was running for his school, when you could buy a Sherbert Dip for a halfpenny. Fifteen and a half and no thoughts of retiring for a good while yet!'

51

Friday, 21 May, 9.18 pm

'Got any more Kenny G, Harry?'

'Best keep it down, Raymond. Neighbours, you know. Thin walls.'

'Something quiet, then. Mellow.'

While Raymond takes another look at the CDs, Harry washes the dishes. He does so quietly and with a studied deliberation, making the most of this brief opportunity to recompose himself. The evening will shortly be over, he thinks. Washing the dishes is the last of its obligations, then all will begin to settle into a soothing familiarity. Even Beti's extraordinary sleep will, as evening gives way to night, become mundane and unremarkable. Harry allows himself to enjoy the warmth of the washing-up water, the cleaning power of the suds, his ordered stacking of the plates, the sense that, beneath its surface turbulence, life is essentially calm and predictable.

'Simon and Garfunkel?'

Harry, still standing at the sink, pauses to consider his brother's suggestion. *Sounds of Silence* – or, to be precise, its slightly shorter vinyl predecessor – is an old favourite of Beti's. Although, as far as he remembers, it is a mellow enough album, he fears its familiarity will somehow make it more audible to Beti. All the more so because it hasn't been played for some time, perhaps for several years: this will surely give it an extra potency, will amplify its impact upon the sleeping ear.

'Didn't know you were a fan of Paul and Art,' Harry says.

Raymond carries on looking through the CDs, at the Nana Miskouri again, and the James Galway, and now, seeking some more palatable compromise, a compilation of Dionne Warwick's greatest hits.

'I'm not,' says Raymond. 'Not especially. But ...'

'But nothing else to your taste, eh?'

So Raymond puts on the Simon and Garfunkel. Harry says 'Keep it down, though,' and leaves it at that, unable to think of a plausible reason for doing otherwise.

52

Harry Selwyn v. The Mau Mau

Fifteen and a half. I knew it rang a bell. And there it was, in the little grey book. *Infantry Platoon Weapons.* On the top shelf in the study, between the *Drill* and the *Recreational Training.*

> *.22 rifle firing is a useful introduction to shooting, in that a recruit can concentrate on aiming and trigger pressing without noise and kick to worry him. But, when he goes on to fire .303, it is important to see that he has not got into bad holding habits, for the kick may make him gun-shy. Boys may not fire .303 until they are 15 ½ years old.*

I thought, how sad. I'd reached fifteen and a half again – heading back to fifteen by now – and I wouldn't get to fire the .303 any more, I'd just have to make do with the little boys' guns. Daft, because I've never fired a gun in my life. Carried a gun, of course, when I was guarding the compound, but never used it. Walked around the fence, kept an eye on things, let people in and out. But never fired a gun in my life. Except for target practice, which doesn't count.

I thought that's what Sam would turn to next. So, Harry, you guarded the fence. What kind of fence would that have been, then? How high, would you say? What colour? A barbed wire fence, was it? But he didn't. No matter. He might get round to it again. Maybe he's just biding his time, waiting until my guard's down. It's possible. So that's why I'm telling you now, in case Sam gets the better of me, like he did before, and everything gets pulled out of shape. You'll have the facts to hand.

I was guarding the fence. No more. No less. Checking the passes. The COs, the doctors, the padrés, the men bringing supplies from town, the lorries from Mombasa. Had to check every one, too, didn't matter who they were, how many stripes or pips. Didn't matter if I saw them every day, knew some of them better than my own mother. Had to look twice when it was a black man. Which is only to be expected, when you come to think of it. You spend twenty years looking at nothing but white faces and then ... In any case, you couldn't be certain which side he was on, the black man, not in those days. Or even where he'd got his pass. *Kipandes*. That's what they called them, the passes. Wore them round their necks. I'd look at the *Kipande* and think, Jesus, is it him? Are those his eyes? Is that his nose? His hair? I'm not a racist. I'm just telling you how it was, what I was up against.

And the patrols. I had to check them in, too. And I'm glad I was just letting them in and not going on patrol myself, out to Naivasha and the Aberdares and the Badlands. Naivasha was the worst, that's what everybody said. Nothing but swamps there, up to their waists in mud when they came back. The worst and the best, though. Good for hunting down the Micks, they said. That's what they called the Mau Mau. Micks. Hippos, too, in Naivasha. Suited hippos better than humans, from what I heard. But no elephants. The elephants were all up in the north, on the savannah. Didn't see a single elephant when I was out there. No lions either.

Two hour shifts I worked. Too hot to do any more. Too hot by day and too cold by night. And that's the top and the bottom of it. Those are the facts.

'Got any pictures?' Sam said.

'Pictures of what?' I said.

'Pictures of Harry Selwyn running against those Kalenjin people, ' Sam said.

'Running *with* the Kalenjin, Sam,' I said. 'With them, not against them.'

It's a pity, all the same. I'd have liked that, a shot of me and the Kalenjin, in Eldoret or Kisumu or Kapsabet. But I don't have one. Maybe you weren't allowed to take pictures in those days: Security risk, probably. Get into the wrong hands. I found a photo of Henry Rono, though, and that was better than nothing. 'He was from Kapsabet,' I said. And talked a bit about Bernard Lagat and Augustine Choge. They came from Kapsabet, too. Which is quite something. As though the best runners in the world all came from Caerphilly. 'They all run there,' I said. 'In Kapsabet. In the land of the Kalenjin.'

Sam was none the wiser.

Fifteen and a half, though, that's what it said. *Boys may not fire .303 until they are 15 ½ years old.* Sounds odd now. Everything's sixteen or eighteen these days. No twenty-one either. But fifteen and a half? Who put the half in? And why? It's there, though, in my *Infantry Training, Volume I, Pamphlet No. 3, Rifle and Bayonet (All Arms), 1948 (War Office Code No. 8368).* I'm looking at it now. Pity I couldn't show it to Sam, as evidence. But it isn't permitted.

> *The information given in this document is not to be communicated either directly or indirectly to the Press or to any person not authorised to receive it.*

That's what it says. I've got it in front of me now. Good job I looked. I'd forgotten about that. Security risk, probably. Get into the wrong hands.

53

Friday, 21 May, 9.32 pm

'Hearts, you said?'

'Hearts.'

'Hearts it is then.'

Harry tries to remember. He had a banana at one. And what's the time now? He looks at his watch. Half past nine. Nine and a half take away one. Eight and a half. So, eight and a half hours sleep. Or, at least, eight and a half hours in bed. Which might be a different matter. But still a long time. Unreasonably long. Even for Beti.

'Worried about the time are you, Harry?'

'No, no, just ...'

On the CD player, Simon and Garfunkel have started singing 'Somewhere they can't find me'. Its insistent beat surprises Harry, who has forgotten that this, too, is a voice from the past, not mellow at all, but anxious and harried.

'Best turn that down, Raymond. This time of night.' He taps his watch, shows it to his brother. Raymond gets up and turns down the volume, fast-forwards to the next track.

'Hearts, then.'

'Hearts it is.'

Unless she got up. To have a bite to eat, a cup of tea. Then went back to bed. It's possible. Provided she did it when he wasn't there, of course: when he'd gone to town the second time, perhaps. An unfortunate coincidence, right enough, but it's possible. Harry tries to recall whether or not he went to the bedroom after returning from his jog.

'This OK?'

'You what?'

Simon and Garfunkel are playing 'Anji'. At the reduced volume, it is only a gentle background pulse.

'This ...' Raymond nods towards the CD player. 'Quiet enough?'

'Nice,' says Harry. 'Acoustic guitar ... Nice.'

He trumps Raymond's Queen.

'No clubs?'

'No.'

'Sure?'

'I've only got three cards left, Raymond. Of course I'm sure.'

And that would settle matters once and for all. If he went to the bedroom to get clean clothes, socks, a hanky, something, opened the door and saw her lying there. But saw without actually *seeing*. Is such a thing possible? That his eyes are like a camera: the picture is taken but it doesn't become visible until it's been developed. Harry tries to develop this picture in his mind. He sees the red curtains and the dressing table. Then the wardrobe. Then the bed. Is it empty? Have the sheets been turned to one side? No, Beti's there. By now, Harry cannot imagine the bed without Beti lying in it, her hair on the pillow, her hand on the coverlet.

'Where did all the clubs go?'

'It's different.'

'Eh?'

'Just two playing. It's different with two.'

54

'Get going you nigs and catch me half a dozen of those fish.'
The Wizard, May 25 1946

'Two hours every day,' I said, 'Then two at night.'

And Sam said, 'Four hours, Harry? *Four hours*? What kind of army's that? Are we safe in our beds?'

I should have shown him the door there and then. But what would that have achieved? What cheap headline would he have thrown back at me? So I said, 'And inventories, Sam. That's what I did the rest of the time. I kept inventories. Listed the supplies, the deliveries.'

It was a good word, inventories, it had the whiff of the army about it. And it wasn't far wide of the mark. I did keep inventories, for a while, towards the end of my posting.

'You can spell, Selwyn?' 'Yes, sir.' 'You got tidy writing?' 'Yes, sir.' And my kit in good order, too. Folded. Neat piles. Knew how to use the Green Blanco. That counted as well. Because there's more to inventories than just good handwriting.

'Supplies?' Sam said, still looking for guns.

'Bedclothes, pots and pans, washing powder, that sort of thing,' I said. 'Checked them as they came in to the depot. Ticked them off in the Order Book.'

Which, now I come to think of it, wasn't that different from checking passes. I checked people. I checked deliveries. I made sure everything was in order. That was my job. People. Things.

'Eight blankets, grey. Six overalls, denim, medium. That sort of thing.' And that's something else they had in common, the people and the things. They were all back-to-front. No Harry Selwyn, not in the army. Selwyn, Harry every time. Dixon, Arthur. Williams, Horace. Same with the goods. 'Inventories, Sam,' I said. 'Wrote it all down back-to-front.'

He didn't know that.

But here's another thing. I had to keep an Inventory of Deficiencies, too. That's what it said at the top of the sheet. *Deficiencies*. Kept a list of the things that were there, and another list of the things that *weren't* there. Which was easy enough if something had just got used up. There'd be an empty box then, with *Soap Flakes* on the side, or *Bootlaces*. Harder, though, if it had gone for a walk, got filched. There was nothing to see then. You just had to go by what people told you, what they remembered, what was on the list the previous chap gave you, and no guarantee it was right, that somebody wasn't pulling a stunt, taking the mick.

I've got a story about the Inventory of Deficiencies. Not my story, not as such. I had it from a Valleys boy who was out there with me, in the Aberdares. Don't remember his name. Dewey. Dowey. Something like that. From Pontypool way. Went to Devonport to do his Basic Training. And that was the job they gave him, keeping the Inventory of Deficiencies. Platoon Sergeant says to him, 'Go and see where those have got to, will you?' Dewey looks at the list. His first inventory.

1 ashtray, glass
2 beakers, plastic
1 boat, gravy
1 boat, tug

'Boat, tug?' he says.

'Boat, tug,' says the Platoon Sergeant. 'Is there a problem?'

And maybe that was right, down there in Devonport, by the sea. Got caught by the tide. Or lads messing about. Who knows? Or there again, maybe the Platoon Sergeant was pulling his leg. Pulled the legs of all the new lads, I dare say. Don't see how you can you lose a tug boat, tide or no tide. Bigger than a bloody gravy boat.

I was good at the inventories. Safe pair of hands, that's what they thought. Harry Selwyn? Safe pair of hands there. Gets on with the job, no whining.

Talking of hands. Another story. My own this time. A platoon came back from the Aberdares. Went straight to the mess. Thirst on them as big as a desert, after the heat, after marching all day. No sweat left. So straight to the mess. Sergeant comes up, drops a sack on the table in front of me, then a bottle of Tusker. That was the beer in Kenya. Picture of an elephant on the label. Tusker. Because of the tusks. 'Extra little job for you, Harry,' he says. Sits down and starts on his own Tusker. 'There's a dozen of the fuckers there. Initials on every one.' His fingers all dust. Fingerprints on the bottle.

So I drew up the inventory, same as the others, because a list is a list. Although a bit more important this time, since there was money riding on it. Five bob the boys got for them, back then. For each hand, I mean. 5/-. That's how you wrote it in those days. Five shillings. Which isn't a lot when you think of it, the risks, the unpleasantness. Worst the first time, I dare say. Got easier after that. Not a nice job for me either, mind you. Carrying a sackful of hands back to the depot, taking them out, putting them in order. But you had a job to do, and you were best getting on with it, things like that don't keep for long out there, not in the heat.

So back to the depot and took them out of the sack. By the

thumbs, too. After the first one, anyway. Gave in to temptation with the first one. What I mean is, the temptation is always there, isn't it? Somebody offers you his hand, you want to reciprocate, you want to take hold of it, say howdy-do. It's only polite. So that's what I did, with the first one. Took hold of the hand as though it were still a *real* hand, and for a second I swear I thought I was going to pull the chap out of the sack, raise him from the dead, body and all. Till I felt how light he was. More of a glove than a hand. Not often you get hold of a hand and there's no body on the other end.

Lifted them out by the thumbs after that. Like taking a cup by its handle. Put them out on the bench, palms down, knuckles pointing away so I could read the letters on the back. They were in a tidy row then. Awaiting inspection, you could say. Read AD on the back of the first hand and wrote down:

Dixon, Arthur, 1 Hand, right.

BF on the next two. Wrote:

Foulkes, Byron, 2 Hands, right.

And so on. All right hands, mind you. That was the protocol. Only the right hands. Drew up the list then, put in the totals, so everybody got paid fair and square. Five bob each.

Not that the boys *wrote* their initials. Not as such. They wouldn't have got the nib to work, not on skin. Black or white, makes no difference. Try it yourself, you'll see. So they cut their initials instead. Just a little cut. Got the clasp knife out, pulled the skin tight, quick little cuts, one, two, three. And the skin peeled back, showed the pink underneath. *AD*.

Not nice, you might say. But a hand was easier to carry than a body. That's how you've got to look at it. Drew enough flies just by itself, too. And where would we have put them, all those bodies, to make the inventory? I'd have wanted more than a bottle of Tusker for that, I can tell you. So it was only right, whatever they said.

And that was that. I put them back in the sack and carried them over to the police hut so they could take fingerprints. I'm not sure how they took the prints, mind you. The fingers had all seized up by then, curled right back into the palm, just like they were all holding sticks. Waited until they slackened up again? Or maybe just cut the fingers off. I can't say. They had their own way of doing things, no doubt. I just gave them the sack and let them get on with it. Passed the list on to the CSM so the boys would get paid.

Dyer. That was his name. Not Dewey. The boy from Pontypool, the one with the tug-boat. Jim Dyer. He got hold of the Inventory of Deficiencies when I was out guarding the fence and he wrote:

12 Bastards, no hands, black

Because there weren't any bodies, only the hands. They were the Deficiencies: the bodies. Good job I spotted that, too. The CSM wouldn't have liked it. There's leg-pulling and there's leg-pulling. And it's me would have got the blame.

Five bob they got. Half a dollar for each hand. To show they'd killed one of the Mau Mau. And I'm telling you this now so you can write it down on your piece of paper, just in case Sam Appleby gets hold of that Dyer chap, gets him to say something different. Because that's all Sam wants is a cheap story. A story about Harry Selwyn, standing in the jungle, knife in hand, ready to get to work.

55

Friday, 21 May, 9.35 pm

'Different with two?' Ramond says. 'How come?'

Harry shrugs. 'Fewer cards out, that's all.'

Raymond shakes his head. 'Haven't been shuffled properly. That's what it is. Need more shuffling.'

As he thinks about Beti's hand, Harry realises with a sudden stab of alarm that this image has remained unchanged since a quarter past nine this morning. The fingers curled around the coverlet, drawing it towards her. The hair on the pillow, a dark halo. The silence. For the very first time Harry becomes aware of his wife's silence.

'Got to go to the toilet.'

'We're in the middle of a hand, Harry.'

'Got to go.'

At the top of the stairs Harry turns for the bedroom. Despite the fears that are now gathering into a tight ball in his chest, he still half expects, on opening the door, to see Beti standing there in her slippers and nightdress, ready to come downstairs. She will turn, look at him and explain what has happened. And perhaps the wisest move would be to say, 'Sssh, Beti, sssh. Not now ...' Then tell her how things stand. 'I told Raymond you're over at Emma's ... You can't come down now!' Get her to pretend that she isn't there at all. Just for an hour. Less, perhaps. Until Raymond goes home.

As he opens the door, therefore, Harry has already raised a finger to his lips, is whispering, 'Sssh now, Beti ...' He is relieved when, in the middle of that sentence, he sees that she is still asleep, and sleeping soundly, too. He no longer has to worry that Raymond will hear her voice, her earnest explanations, perhaps her admonishments. Even as he notices the unusual blueness of her lips, he doesn't abandon his plan.

'Beti …? Can you hear me, Beti …?'

He touches her fingers, is surprised at how cold they are.

'Beti?'

Only when he places a hand on her brow and feels the same coldness does he realise that Beti is no longer there. And if she isn't there, where can she be? He turns his head towards the door.

'Beti!'

Harry whispers to the Beti who isn't there, who's gone away. He must tell Beti that Beti's dead, that Raymond is downstairs waiting for him. They're in the middle of a hand, and what is a man supposed to do when he finds his wife dead in bed and he's already run out of explanations? He needs Beti to tell him. Only Beti will know.

56

Friday, 21 May, 10.10pm

'Odd things to put in beer, mind you.'

'What?'

'Peaches. Funny things to put in beer.'

Harry lifts his glass and sniffs. 'They make cider out of apples.'

'But beer, Harry. Beer's not the same.'

'And perry … Perry's made out of pears.'

'Beer, Harry. Beer's different.'

Raymond looks at his watch. 'Beti's late.'

Harry looks at his own watch and nods. 'You can get chocolate beer, too.'

'Get away.'

'It's true. Chocolate beer. Tastes of chocolate.'

'In a bottle?'

'Not sure ... Yes, probably.'

'Probably?'

'Probably.'

'But you haven't seen it, this chocolate beer?'

'Heard about it ... Over in Barry, that's where they brew it.'

Harry deals the cards, picks up his hand and puts it in order. Raymond does the same.

'There you are, then. You haven't seen it. That's all I'm saying. You haven't seen it, not with your own eyes.'

'Haven't seen it with anybody else's eyes, that's for sure.'

Raymond looks at his watch. 'Fancy another?'

'She might stay over, of course.'

'Mm?'

'Tonight ... Beti might sleep at Emma's tonight.'

Raymond is surprised by the sudden peevishness in his brother's voice. He thinks, they've fallen out. That's why she's not here. Harry and Beti have had a row. He looks at Harry's face, searches for clues. But Harry is concentrating on his cards. And if his lips are pursed, if the brow creases a little, that is only what you would expect of a man studying his hand.

Raymond opens the last bottle of beer and starts pouring its contents into the two glasses. 'You'd better phone her, then.' He waits until the froth settles, then pours the remainder. 'You'd better phone her, to find out.'

Harry nods, sips his beer, tries to decide what is for the best. Should he take the four of diamonds from the pile? Or should he chance his luck and hope for something better from the pack? He chooses the four of diamonds. The five might turn up later.

'I'll phone her if you like.'

'No need, Raymond. No need.'

'It's no bother.'

'Best not. Not this time of night. Cati'll be asleep. You'll wake her up.'

Harry doesn't wish to speak abruptly to his brother. He knows he must treat him delicately. In a short while he will receive bad news, news that will shake his world to its foundations. More specifically, it is Harry himself who will have to impart this news, so it behoves him to prepare the ground carefully. Whatever else he does, he must avoid a quarrel, he must suppress any irritation or impatience. This would only make his task harder. That's why Harry says, 'She'll ring shortly. That's what she said when she went out. She'd phone later. Let me know what's happening.' And says it in a conciliatory, sunny sort of voice. 'No need to worry.' But a voice that also makes clear, with a calm finality, that he is not to be contradicted. Beti is Harry's responsibility. It is the husband's prerogative to look after his wife and no one else's.

Harry is certain now that he will have to wait until tomorrow to break the news to Raymond, for how can he possibly tell him tonight, in the middle of the cards and the beer, that his first love lies dead in the room above his head? He takes a card from the pack, deliberates a moment, then sets a trick down on the table.

'Three kings.'

'Three kings.' Raymond repeats the words in a soft, ruminative voice, rubs his chin, counts the cards left in his brother's hand and takes another card from the pack.

So tomorrow it is. And Emma, of course. He'll have to tell Emma, too. Then he realises, no, he must tell Emma first. Emma must come before Raymond. Of course she must. He must tell Emma before he tells anyone else. Harry feels the ball tightening in his chest. Jesus, he thinks, almost made a mess of that. Emma first. Of course. There are feelings to be considered here, a protocol to be followed. A daughter takes precedence over a brother.

But tell her what? Whatever misfortune is to befall Beti, in the new story that Harry must devise to satisfy the world and its curiosity, it has not yet happened. Beti has not yet had a chance to die. Tonight, she still lives. 'Died, you say, Harry? And you didn't notice?'

No, it's impossible. Quite impossible.

57

Harry Selwyn v. Vertical Displacement

'Wheels.' I said. 'That's the secret. Wheels.'

'What, instead of running?'

'No, Sam. To run properly. If you want to become a real runner, you've got to run like a wheel.'

'What kind of a wheel?'

'A car wheel, Sam. A bicycle wheel. A pram wheel. Any kind of bloody wheel, so long as it goes round.'

I showed him then. Shifted the chairs out of the way, set my heels against the passage door, cocked my arms, then 'Ready ... Steady ...' And ran the length of the kitchen.

But there wasn't enough room, even though it's a long kitchen and I ran as slowly as I could. Five steps and I was banging up against the French windows, and five steps isn't enough to show how a man can turn his body into a wheel. So out we went, through the doors, through the garden and into the back lane and I set-to again, ran the length of the whole lane.

'See what I mean? Keep your head still. Keep your feet low.'

Then ran it again, the whole lane, but not like a wheel this time, like a … Like I'm not sure what, but the opposite of a wheel. Ran like lots of people run when they don't know any better, bouncing up and down, so you'd think they were trying to dig a trench. 'Vertical displacement,' I said. 'You've got to get rid of the vertical displacement.' Which is only common sense really. The more you bounce up and down the less strength you've got to move forward. 'That's the secret, Sam,' I told him. 'You don't see a wheel bouncing up and down, do you? That's what you've got to do if you want to run properly. If you want to keep on running. Run like a wheel.'

58

Friday, 21 May 10.30pm

Raymond drinks the last of his beer. A minute later he places the nine, ten and Jack of hearts on the table and the game is over. He gathers the cards together and squares them up. For a moment Harry fears that his brother means to start a new game. This is why he looks at his watch and says, 'Early to bed for me tonight, Raymond … Race tomorrow.' Raymond nods, puts the cards back in their box, says he just has to go to the toilet, then he'll be off.

Harry winces. He's forgotten about this final, mundane, inevitable part of the Friday ritual. He'd like to say, 'Can't you wait, Raymond? Can't you see I need to get to bed?' But the beer has been drunk, it must take its course. Raymond goes upstairs. Harry stands in the kitchen, motionless. He hears the bathroom door open and close. A minute later, he hears the flush. For a while, the hiss of water through the pipes masks all other noises. Then silence. The silence continues for longer than Harry expects, for longer than is usual, he's sure of it. Perhaps this is merely because Raymond, after drying his hands on the towel, stops to look in the mirror, to give his hair a quick comb, to straighten his collar. But Harry has no time for such innocent explanations. For Harry, the extended silence can have only one meaning. His brother has sensed that all is not as it ought to be. Of course he has. How can a man stand there, in the bathroom, insensible to the presence of a woman's dead body not ten feet away from him? How can Raymond, of all people, stand there, drying his hands, and fail to be aware that his first love has left him for ever?

Harry hears the rattle of the bathroom doorknob. He knows that Raymond has no cause to go to the bedroom. He knows that he has never done so before on a Friday evening, as he comes out of the bathroom and prepares to go home. Nevertheless, he knows also that this Friday is different from all other Fridays and he cannot accept that the knowledge which weighs so heavily upon him has not somehow infiltrated his brother's consciousness. This is why he stands there, in the kitchen, looking up at the ceiling, waiting for the tell-tale squeak in the floorboards.

When Raymond comes downstairs, Harry is waiting for him in the passage. And perhaps his anxieties betray him after all because, as he reaches for his coat, Raymond says, 'Jesus, Harry, you're not looking too clever. You sure you're alright to run tomorrow?'

59

Saturday, 22 May 4am

But if it hasn't happened yet, when *will* it happen?

This is the question that occupies Harry as he tosses and turns in the spare bedroom. The duvet is too hot for such a mild night and the mattress too soft: he will have a backache by morning. He could, of course, fetch the lighter duvet from his own bed, but he doubts whether this would be possible without catching sight of Beti's hand. So he lies where he is, pulling the duvet this way and that, thinking, If it hasn't happened yet, when *will* it happen?

At four o'clock, last night's beer begins to weigh on his bladder. He lies as still as he can, tries to put his thoughts in order.

He'll say, 'She went out with friends.'

They'll say, 'Friends? What friends?'

'What friends? Oh, I'm not sure … She came back from town about five, went for a nap then … Had a headache … A migraine …' Harry turns on his side, pulls the duvet over his shoulder, tries to go back to sleep. 'She had a migraine. Went for a nap … I didn't want to tell Raymond …'

'Oh, why's that, then, Harry? Why didn't you want to tell Raymond?'

'Because … Because …'

But lying like this, on his side, the pressure on his bladder only increases, turns from discomfort into pain. He hears the seagulls screeching outside and thinks, Ah! That time again. As though the seagulls and his bladder were somehow connected. And he wonders, if this is the same bladder, the same pain, are these then the same seagulls?

He gets up and goes to the toilet.

As he bends over and puts his hands under the tap, Harry becomes aware of the blood coursing through his carotid arteries, circling his ears and eyes. He feels his heart's pounding. It is quicker than usual, and more insistent. At first he ascribes this to the alcohol. He has a slight headache: he isn't accustomed to drinking strong ale, and unusual ale at that. He is somewhat shaky on his feet, too: after drying his hands he must hold the edge of the wash-basin for a while to steady himself. He takes a long breath. One ... Two ... Three ... And another. One ... Two ... Three ... He looks at himself in the mirror, sticks out his tongue, examines the whites of his eyes. He hears Raymond's voice inside his head. 'Not too clever, Harry. Not too clever.'

Harry bends down, splashes cold water over his brow and cheeks and feels the blood coursing again. He decides it isn't the alcohol's fault after all. To his surprise, he concludes that his giddiness more closely resembles the little frisson he feels in the middle of a race, just as he gets his second wind. He draws comfort from this unanticipated revelation. The giddiness of the second wind is a purely chemical phenomenon: the interplay of adrenaline and cortisol, the familiar wash of endorphins. It is an involuntary response to circumstances, a knee-jerk, a feeling only in the sense that the lower animals have feelings. For a while, Harry derives comfort from this thought, too, that he is merely an animal, his discomfort the product of blind forces beyond his control.

And if it hasn't happened yet, when?

Only after returning to bed does Harry realise that adrenaline has nothing to with it either. It is a slow, halting realisation: inevitably so, as he has never before followed this particular train of thought, this circuit of unfamiliar sensations. But there's no doubt about it. What Harry Selwyn feels coursing through his veins at five o'clock on this fine May morning is neither alcohol nor adrenaline. It is time. Time itself. He is reluctant to acknowledge this new understanding. He tries breathing again. One ... Two ... Three ... But his heart still races. His head still throbs. One ... Two ... Three ... Because it isn't any old time that is making Harry's heart race, it is Beti's time, and the time of the newly deceased is the fastest time of all.

If it hasn't happened yet.

But it has happened.

At half past five on Saturday morning, lying sleepless in the spare bedroom, Harry considers how his wife might look as she embarks on this, the second day of her eternity. He conjures up once more the hand on the coverlet, the hair on the pillow, the hair that was never cut. That is clear now, merely from studying the picture in his mind: Beti didn't go anywhere near a hairdresser's yesterday.

And if it has happened?

'She's gone,' he'll say. 'Yes, in her sleep ... Early this morning ...'

They'll come, then, to pay their respects, offer their condolences, see to the formalities. Who will come first? Harry doesn't know. But whoever it is, they'd better come quick, because the dead don't hang about.

'Early this morning, you say ...? Mm ... Are you sure, Harry?'

'Am I sure? What do you mean, am I sure? Of course I'm sure. What man would make a mistake about something like that?'

'But Harry, what about the ...?'

Harry tries again. He considers Beti's fingers, their grip on the coverlet, feels the coldness of her hand. Are the fingers still stiff?

'And what about the...?'

Sometime, come what may, the fingers will loosen. Of course they will. Then they will blacken. The slow dissolution will begin.

'This morning, Mr Selwyn? Are you sure?'

No, the dissolution has already begun. Seen or unseen, it is taking its course. It cannot be reversed.

'Yes, this morning. Don't know when, though ... Not exactly.'

Someone else will have to finish the story. That someone will say, 'Don't worry yourself, Mr Selwyn, we can measure things like that these days. Yes, right down to the last breath. We'll have the exact time for you by the end of the week. Why the concern, if I may ask? You don't have anything to hide, do you?'

Because a dead body is a clock, too, and its hands don't stop just because you're not looking at them.

Harry hears more seagulls. He gets out of bed and goes downstairs, walking on tiptoes as though he were afraid of waking someone. He closes the kitchen door, fills the kettle. When he has made his tea, he tears a sheet of paper from the notepad by the telephone and takes it over to the table. He starts writing. After a minute or two he decides that the paper is too small. He goes to the study and brings back an A4 pad. He sits down again and draws himself closer to the table, taking care not to scrape the chair legs against the tiled floor.

Time of Beti's death	~~Friday~~ 4am (?)
Time realised B. was dead	~~Saturday~~ 6am
DIFFERENCE	~~26~~ HRS
Explanation	~~Didn't realise B. still in bed~~

Harry looks at his watch and thinks, Why would he be awake at six on a Saturday morning? And even if awake, how would he know *that*? How would Beti tell him she was dead? He changes the 6am to 7am, the 26 hours to 27. That's when he found Beti. Tried to rouse her for breakfast, but she was gone. Fact. Or as close to a fact as it is possible for Harry to achieve. Apart, perhaps, from that 4am, which is pure speculation. Less than that, even. Is little more than a random number. Who's to say Beti didn't die earlier in the night, perhaps immediately after going to bed? Yes, that would be plausible enough: she fell into a deep sleep, so deep that she couldn't climb out again. So, 2am. Harry tries to remember his return home from the pub on Thursday night. Did he, on going to bed, hear Beti breathing? Would he have heard her not-breathing? He sits back, closes his eyes and tries to recreate those few seconds of nothing-in-particular. But it is last night's Beti that he sees still – hand on the coverlet, hair on the pillow – and he cannot move that picture to one side in order to make room for another. He opens his eyes and looks through the window. A blackbird is pecking for worms. The upper branches of the rowan are quivering: a breeze has got up this morning. He remembers nothing. Despite this, he changes the 4am to 2am, just in case. 2am is safer than 4am. Then changes the 27 hrs to 29 hrs, to keep the sums right. So, twenty-nine hours since his wife died.

'Are you sure, Harry? How can that be?'

Harry looks at the sheet of paper, shakes his head and thinks, No, too much crossing out, and the columns aren't straight. Who could make head or tail of such scribbles? Worse than school. And no excuse, either. Like spiders' legs. He folds the sheet in two and puts it to one side. He tears another sheet from the pad and starts afresh.

Time of Beti's death	Friday 2am
Time realised B. was dead	saturday 7am
DIFFERENCE	29 HRS
Explanation	Didn't realise B. still in bed

Harry sits back and looks through the French windows. The sun is now lighting up the wall at the bottom of the garden, the pink and purple dahlias are leaning into its warmth. It bodes well. 'Except for that breeze.' Harry says this out loud and tries to calculate, from the movement in the tops of the trees, from which direction the wind is blowing. Yes, he thinks, that will be a nuisance, at least on the way out, running against the breeze. He looks at the paper. Twenty-nine hours. Or thereabouts. A little less, perhaps. Or a touch more.

Then Harry realises, with a sudden flash of intuition, that this is all beside the point. It isn't *what* he says that counts, but rather *who* he says it to. Matching the right words with the right ears. Twenty-nine hours will do just fine when he rings up Dr Gibson and the undertaker and whoever else is required to deal with matters of this kind. Indeed, it is only right and proper. The authorities must hear the truth, whole and unvarnished. 'She was in bed when I returned home, you see … Yes, yes, the night before last … And I was out all day then, and the evening, too … When did she go to bed? Well, quite early. Told her not to wait up for me. Can't say when, exactly …' A little uncertainty is no bad thing, is only natural under the circumstances. Too much certainty: now then, that *would* be suspicious. They will understand. They are accustomed to all kinds of dereliction and infirmity. And they must get on with the job.

As for the others – Raymond and Emma – they will be furnished with their own explanations in due course. These will, Harry realises, differ from Dr Gibson's version of events, will need to be tailored to the recipients' requirements. But that's fine. They will not be privy to the paperwork. They will certainly not be chatting with undertakers and doctors about the whys and wherefores. And in any case, who would be so insensitive as to challenge the word of a poor widower in the very depths of his grief?

Fortified by his new understanding, Harry folds this piece of paper, too, and puts it to one side. He tears three new sheets from the pad, gives a title to each, then sets to work.

EMMA

Time of
Beti's death   Friday
                      10 pm

Time informed   Saturday
Emma   8·30 am

DIFFERENCE   10½ HRS

Explanation: B. went to hairdressers, did some shopping. Missed the bus and arrived home late. (Just after you and Cati left.) Went to bed early, worn out.

DR GIBSON

Time of
Beti's death

Friday
2 am

Time informed
Dr. Gibson

Saturday
8 am

DIFFERENCE

30 HRS

Explanation: got up very
early and went out for the
day. Returned very late.
Thought B. was asleep. Didn't
realise she'd been in bed
all the time.

RAYMOND

Time of
Beti's death

Saturday
2am

Time informed
Raymond

Saturday
9am

DIFFERENCE

7HRS

Explanation: B. returned at
11, just after you left. Had
been with Emma after all.
Went to see (name?) instead.
Missed the bus home and
had to get a taxi. Went
straight to bed.

As soon as he's finished writing, Harry places the three sheets of paper next to each other, in chronological order: that is, in the order he intends informing the individuals concerned. He leaves a gap of an inch or so between them, to emphasise their autonomy, and as a visual reminder that he must not get them mixed up. He straightens one sheet, blows a hair off another and thinks, Fine, things are starting to come together. A pity about that slip on the last line but he's certainly not going to start all over again, not now, not on account of one tiny glitch. Then he picks up each sheet in turn and reads it aloud, improvising as he does so, experimenting with different formulations and tones of voice. 'I was out all day, you see, and there she was when I got back, still in bed ...' He stumbles a little as he rehearses Raymond's message, is troubled by the unanswered question mark. 'Went to see who, Harry? Who did Beti go and see?' 'It's on the tip of my tongue, Raymond ... 'P' something. Pam? Pauline?' Then decides that not even Raymond will require him to remember a detail of that kind. This is what would be expected on a day such as today: a little confusion, some lapses of memory. Slips of the pen.

Harry straightens the sheets of paper. He keeps Dr Gibson's message in the middle, moves Emma's further over to the left and Raymond's to the right. Fine, he thinks. There's little risk that Dr Gibson will bump into Emma, even if she falls ill. Her surgery is elsewhere. He's unlikely to see Raymond, either. Raymond has no time for doctors and hospitals and he would have to be very ill indeed before he availed himself of either. Harry scarcely considers the possibility that Raymond and Emma might meet. He is an uncle in name only. Their paths never cross. Except at Christmas, perhaps. And Christmas is far away. The odd wedding. And funerals, of course.

Yes.

Which is fine.

Then Harry realises that this is very far from being fine. No, this will not do at all, it is utterly, utterly unacceptable.

There will be a funeral. Of course there will. And then, how can you stop the tongues? It's one thing to draw a *cordon sanitaire* around sheets of paper on the kitchen table. They will sit there for ever, given the chance, mute and inert. But in real life, when the words become flesh, mix with the spit and the speculation? How to keep them apart then?

'Got home at eleven? But Dad said ...'

'I was there, Emma. Playing cards with him. No sign of your mother.'

'She'd just been to town. That's what he said. Went to town to have her hair cut, do a bit of shopping. So where did she go then, Raymond? What happened to her then?'

Failing to calm the voices in his head, Harry starts to cry. He does so, for a while, without noise. The shoulders shake, then the head, then the lips. And if a stranger were to come into the kitchen at this moment and witness his silent trembling, they might be unsure whether he was crying or laughing. But then, seconds later, a groan emerges from deep inside his diaphragm. The tears follow, but reluctantly. And even as they fall on the table, wet the corner of one of the sheets of paper, the same stranger would not be able to say for certain what had provoked them, whether some traumatic loss or else merely Harry's frustration at failing to get his papers in order.

He looks at each in turn. Dr Gibson. Emma. Raymond. And again. Emma. Raymond. Dr Gibson. He shakes his head. Wipes the tears from his eyes.

60

Saturday, 22 May, 7 am

It is seven o'clock. The sun is already casting the shadows of leaves and twigs on the wall behind him. Harry picks up the phone and listens to the recorded message. The surgery will open at nine: for urgent cases only, please hold the line and you will be transferred ... Harry replaces the phone and considers the implications of these words. Is his an urgent case? Yes and no. It is a case of considerable gravity, of that there can be no doubt: but it can hardly be termed urgent, at least not in any medical sense. Who will be the worse for an other two hours' delay? And even if it were urgent, Harry does not wish to discuss the matter with a stranger, a locum, perhaps only an assistant. He will ring back at nine and speak with Dr Gibson.

At a quarter to eight Harry switches on the kettle, places two slices of toast under the grill and lights the gas. He takes a banana from the fruit bowl, cuts it into small, neat circles and places these on the side of a plate. He returns to the grill and waits, bending down every now and again to check on progress. The corner of one slice, slightly thicker than its partner, has blackened already, creating a little tail of smoke. 'Damn!' He turns it over, placing the blackened corner on the outside, where the heat is less intense. The kitchen is now full of the smell of burned toast. The kettle boils. Harry makes his tea, then goes back to the grill.

As he scrapes the toast over the sink, Harry realises that the implications of the surgery's recorded message are more serious than he had supposed. If Dr Gibson can't be told until

9 o'clock, when will he phone Emma? He needs to be at Bryn Coch by ten. Emma and Cati will be on their way, too. So how can he possibly ...?

Harry is cross with Beti for not being on hand to answer this question. He's cross, too, that she wasn't here earlier to make a better job of the toast, to cut the bread more evenly, and to tell him not to over-do it in the race today. There's a dinner to follow and he won't get much of a chance to recuperate between the running and the eating. And Harry would have said, 'But that's the point, Beti. That's why I've got to do my best. Everyone expects ...' These are the words he needs to speak. But there is no one present to hear them.

He distributes the banana circles evenly across the two slices and mashes them with the side of a knife.

At twenty past eight Harry returns to the spare bedroom and puts on yesterday's clothes: his Adidas shirt, his grey shorts and his blue tracksuit. He comes back downstairs, makes his way to the lean-to and takes the New Balance RX Terrain running shoes down from the shelf. He pushes his fingers into the toes of the one, then the other, to make sure there are no stones or thorns. He puts on the right shoe, pushes his heel back as far as he can, and pulls on both ends of the lace. He adjusts two of the loops, pulls again, wiggles his foot. When he is satisfied that he cannot feel any unequal pressure, he ties a double knot, then goes through the same procedure with the left shoe. He stands up and rocks back and forward a few times, heel-toe, heel-toe, heel-toe. Everything is fine. Everything is as it should be.

Harry goes to the kitchen and fills a mug from the tap, takes a gulp and puts the mug on the counter. Then, leaning against the doorframe, he extends his right leg behind him and counts to ten. One … Two … Three … Then the left leg. One … Two … Three … He drinks more water, just a sip this time, and moves to the middle of the floor, where he runs on the spot for two minutes: small, skipping steps to begin with, the knees getting gradually higher, until both legs and arms are pumping vigorously, the breath marking the pulse. Then a short break. More water. Just a little sip. And starts again.

Harry reaches Bryn Coch at a quarter to ten and leaves his car in the car park behind the leisure centre. A small crowd has gathered here already, near the entrance, to pay their registration fees and collect their numbers. Harry sees several Harriers amongst them, as well as familiar faces from other clubs. Most, however, belong to a category which Harry and his friends would call 'leisure runners'. The Bryn Coch 10k has been a charity run for some years now and a good proportion of these 'leisure runners' will run for half a mile or so and walk the rest. Raising money and having a good time are their chief objectives. One wears a giant bottle of Lucozade, with holes for arms, legs and face. Two others are getting used to sharing a camel outfit, taking their first stumbling steps. Harry goes to the end of the queue. In front of him a woman in an ostrich costume raises and lowers her wings, to the embarrassment of the two children at her side. He takes a drink from his water bottle and eyes them anxiously. People such as these, he is quite sure, do not fully appreciate the dangers of dehydration. The sun is strong, high in the sky, and even though there is a breeze even the fittest runner will sweat a good two pints today. Fact. And in an ostrich suit?

'Is here OK, Harry?'

Harry is about to have a quiet word with the ostrich woman

when the *Gazette* photographer comes up to him, camera in hand.

'Picture here, Harry? You and the wife?'

Thinking he is referring to the ostrich, Harry shakes his head and says, 'No, no, I ... She ...' Then becomes tongue-tied, as he hasn't thought of Beti for several minutes. The ostrich and her children look on, half-posing in case they are caught in the picture. 'Wait here,' says Harry. 'Wait till I've got my number.'

Harry pays his ten pounds and takes the number 50 that has been kept especially for him, to mark his achievement. He walks back to where the photographer is waiting and shakes his head. 'The wife didn't feel too good this morning ...' He pats his chest with his fist. 'Bout of asthma ... Having trouble with her breathing ...' He wants to say more. This is the first chance he's had to talk to anyone about his wife's condition since she died and he feels honour-bound to do her justice. 'She might come later on ... If she's feeling...' But then stops: this explanation is very different from those he left on the kitchen table and he hasn't had the opportunity to think it through properly, let alone rehearse it. Whatever the upshot of this new story, the story that will replace all the others, it must be constructed with care.

'Sounds nasty,' says the photographer, who knows from experience that caution and a certain amount of indulgence are required when dealing with this man.

'Yes,' says Harry. 'Nasty.' He is tempted again to embellish his account, to demonstrate to the photographer and whoever else might be listening that he is a loving and conscientious husband. But the same question spins around in his head. If Beti is still alive, when will she die?

Following the photographer's directions, Harry takes his number 50 in both hands and holds it up in front of him. Behind him the ostrich escorts her children to the toilet, a queue forms at the burger stall, two minibuses unload more runners into the car park. All of these things will appear in the photograph. One of the Harriers jogs by, shouts 'Fifty not out today, Harry!' Harry shouts back, 'Don't count your chickens, Pete! I haven't run yet!' The photographer thinks, Yes, that would be a good caption. *Fifty not out.*

Standing by Harry's side now are his daughter, Emma, and granddaughter, Cati. They will be in the photograph, too. Emma asks where her mother is. Harry pats his chest again. 'Bit wheezy this morning …' It is a rather bald explanation, so he adds. 'Pollen gets to her this time of year, I think …' This is what comes to mind. And pollen sounds innocuous. 'Irritates her chest.'

'Shall I pop down … Check she's alright?'

'Best not, Emma. Not yet. She'll be sleeping now, I dare say,' Harry pins the number 50 to his vest.

'Pity,' says Emma.

Then the photographer turns to Cati. 'Do you like running, too? Are you going to take after your grandpa?' Although *Fifty not out* is a good caption it would be a shame not to make something of the three generations. *Harry passes on the baton* … Or *Following in Grandpa's footsteps*. Something like that. But Cati shakes her head. 'And your Mam …?' Emma laughs. 'Dad does enough running for the lot of us.' The photographer is disappointed, but he takes the photograph anyway: perhaps he'll think of something later.

While Cati asks her mother why Grandma spends so much time in bed, Harry jogs to the side wall of the leisure centre to do his final exercises. He bends over, wraps his hands around his right foot, feels the tendons tighten in the back of his leg. He straightens up, bends over again and does the same with his right foot. Then he jogs on the spot, loosens his limbs. A woman passes, carrying a video camera on her shoulder. Harry raises a hand and offers a smile, but she's following someone else. The Bryn Coch Benefit Run attracts celebrities from many walks of life: Katherine Jenkins once took part, and Rob Brydon too. She's after one of them, Harry thinks. No interest in the real runners, just the celebrities. He lets his gaze follow her for a while, scans the faces on the far side of the car park, recognises no one.

Jogging on the spot again, Harry ponders how he will explain to Dr Gibson why he has left his wife in bed for the second morning in succession. 'Mm ... Have you been feeling yourself recently, Mr Selwyn? A touch confused, perhaps?' 'Well, now you mention it, Doctor, I haven't felt a hundred per cent, no ...' Will that do? Pretend to be confused? Scratch his head, mumble a little, say sorry, he just can't remember when he went to town, when he came back, when he saw Beti last, what day it is ... Can he possibly affect such extreme bafflement? Can he be certain his tongue will not trip him up, pull him back into impossible quagmires of mitigation?

'And yet, Mr Selwyn, you were in sufficient possession of your faculties to travel to Bryn Coch, to take part in the race, to complete it, too ...'

'Yes, Doctor, but it was a very special race, I couldn't possibly...'

Harry must stand for a further quarter of an hour before the race starts. Although he has competed in the Bryn Coch 10k (formerly the Bryn Coch 7 miles) more often than anyone else, and his picture will be in the newspaper on Monday morning, he is not granted special dispensations or privileges.

His finishing position in last year's race means that he is placed in the fifth and last of the designated groups, although he will still set off ahead of the unclassified participants. Most members of this group are veterans, including two others over seventy years of age, but it also contains a number of teenage boys and girls, all huddled together, uncomfortable and self-conscious amongst the bald heads and knotted legs.

As he stands here, watching the first group depart, then the second, moving gradually closer to the starting line, Harry listens to Bill Seymour's deep bass holding forth on the superiority of the Mizuno Ascend 4 over the New Balance RX Terrain for today's dry conditions. He affects surprise that Harry, with his intimate knowledge of the course, should have opted for the latter. Bill is the Harriers' Secretary and he is being especially bumptious because this is his first race as a V70. He walks over to the younger members of the group and reminds them how important it is to maintain a steady speed, to keep up a firm pumping action with the arms, to do this and that, until Harry shouts out, 'Jesus, Bill, you'll be out of breath before you start!' Everyone is in good spirits then, when they reach the starting line, glad to be out in the sun, part of such a good-humoured crowd. They're glad, too, of the chance to prove they can still do what they did in the last Bryn Coch Benefit Run, and perhaps do even better, because only a year has elapsed and you can always improve on last year, whatever your age. Harry waves to Emma and Cati, who are now standing on top of the small bank at the side of the playing fields. They wave back. Cati smiles coyly.

'Three ... two ... one ...'

Once they start running, Harry's group quickly disperses. The boys and girls hurry on to join their friends in the other groups. Harry shakes his head at seeing this folly unfold once more, knowing they will regret their impatience long before the end, and why doesn't someone tell them? Their place is taken by leisure runners from the main pack: they, too, to Harry's dismay, are running faster than they ought. Within another mile they will cross the river and hit the steep incline of Allt y Big where they will pay for their imprudent haste. So easy does it. Keep plenty in the tank. Eke out the fuel, a thimbleful at a time. That's the secret.

After a hundred yards or so, Harry fixes his gaze on Bill Seymour's yellow shirt. And that's another secret. Whenever he races, Harry always sets his sights on someone running a little ahead of him, someone neither too far nor too near, neither too fast nor too slow. And all the better if he's wearing a brightly coloured shirt or unusual shoes: he's easier to spot, to hold in view, especially in a crowd where one runner looks much like another. Bill will be Harry's first pacemaker today, his first 'rabbit', as they say. Focusing on his yellow shirt helps in other ways, too. It makes it easier for Harry to coordinate his feet and his breathing and thereby establish the rhythm that will keep him going throughout the race. Out, out, out, in, in, out, out, out ... It also allows him to disregard the niggling discomforts that mark the start of any race: the slight tightening in his lungs, the hot little needles in his Achilles' tendon, the knees' protest against the earth's unyielding resistance. It helps him, for a while, to forget about Beti.

Half way up Allt y Big, Harry overtakes Bill Seymour. This begs the question, of course, on whom Bill Seymour has been fixing his gaze all this while. Surely Bill, too, after so many years, and in his first race as a V70, is doing his best to coordinate feet and lungs, to look out for the bright shirt up ahead, or the unusual shoes, and let himself be pulled along by their invisible thread. And if such a technique works for

Harry, why then does it not also work for Bill and for all the others who will be overtaken in this race? But there it is: not everyone can be at the front.

After passing Bill Seymour, Harry must find another rabbit. He considers everyone – perhaps twenty or so – within fifty yards. He swiftly dismisses the younger runners. The young, in Harry's experience, are too unpredictable to entrust with such a role. Many, he knows, will burn themselves out before they reach the top of the Allt: he already recognises the symptoms of their prodigality – the flushed cheeks, the leaning forward, the laboured breathing. Some will take a break at the quarry, where the hill suddenly gets steeper. Others will walk for a while, drinking water, pinching the stitches in their sides. Harry's seen it all before.

On reaching the sign, *Bryn Coch Limestone Company 100 metres on left,* Harry sets his sights on two women. Neither wears bright clothes or unusual shoes. What is remarkable about them is that their feet move in perfect unison, step by step, with the result that everything else – their arms, their legs, even their heads – observe the same, precisely synchronised oscillation, as though they were dancing in a ballet. Even after reaching the top of the Allt and starting the descent, a point at which runners inevitably pick up speed, where rhythm and discipline tend to unravel, the two women keep their equilibrium, their poise. Left, right. Left, right. Which is enough to sustain Harry for the next two kilometres. And by then the second wind is safe in his fist, he needs no rabbit or anything else, and he's homeward bound.

61

Harry Selwyn v. The Mouse (2)

I saw the mouse again. In the kitchen. Tea-time, just after I got back from Bryn Coch. Went looking for the trap then but couldn't find it. Looked under the stairs, in the cupboards, in the dresser. Thought maybe we'd lent it to somebody. Emma. Amy. No, probably not Emma, not with Cati there. So probably Amy. Or Raymond. Should have asked Raymond.

Lost him then. No sign anywhere. Front room. Upstairs. Nowhere. Far as I can tell. Went back to the kitchen and shut the cupboards, just in case. Made sure there were no crumbs on the counter. Can't take chances. Kitchen's worst, too. Going after your food. Leaving his dirt.

'If you see one mouse, there's ten more of the buggers out of sight. If you see ten …' That's what they say.

Stood there a while, waiting, watching.

62

Saturday, 22 May, 5.30 pm

Harry stands by the kitchen table, shuts his right eye, then his left. He moves them up and down, side to side, centres them again and waits. The mouse is in the right eye, he's sure of it. He's shifting too, but more slowly than the eye itself, as though swimming in oil. Thinking of swimming, Harry decides the speck in his eye is more like a tadpole than a mouse. He tries to move this tadpole towards the centre of his pupil, so he can see its tail, check whether it's grown legs. But it slides the other way, to the outer edges, and he can't get it back again.

'Bloody floaters.'

Harry takes a banana from the fruit bowl and slices it onto a plate. Then he goes to the food cupboard and adds two oat biscuits and a handful of hazelnuts. He fancies something more substantial after his exertions but the Harriers' dinner starts at seven thirty and to eat a proper meal now would ruin his appetite later on. Even this little snack makes him feel guilty, awakes a small but sharp voice of chastisement inside his head. 'Don't snack now, Harry *bach*, or you won't want your supper.' He will have a shower presently. Shave. Put on clean clothes. His new trousers. Harry knows that going to the dinner tonight is out of the question. On the other hand, he doesn't know how not to go.

He looks at the sheet of paper on which he's written the explanation he will offer the doctor. He's written a bold number **1** on the top to distinguish it from the others and to emphasise that it is this explanation that must, he has now decided, be conveyed first. He has also crossed out 'Dr Gibson' and written 'Doctor' instead. Harry is now ready to release his wife's body even to a stranger, so long as that stranger possesses the authority to take his burden from him and deal with it appropriately. 'Something awful's happened, Doctor ...' Doctors are acquainted with all manner of dreadful events, and all manner of confusion, too. 'I wasn't thinking straight ... Don't think as clearly as I used to ...'

And then Emma. 'She's gone, Emma *fach*.' It will be a relief to lean on his daughter, to let her share his distress, do some of the coping. 'Seems she had a nasty turn when I was out... I couldn't do a thing ... No, they've taken her from here, Emma.' That may not be quite so easy. Emma will perhaps want to see her Mam just one more time, to make her last farewell. He'll have to tell a little fib: that the hospital people had to take her right away, before the Saturday crowds came out, and the ambulances got busy. Something like that. 'But how will I see her now, Dad?' Yes, it will be difficult. Maybe she'll ring the Harriers for him then, to explain why he can't come to the dinner. And he'll say, 'And Auntie Amy. We'll have to let Auntie Amy know, too … Do you think …?' But she'll probably offer first, without prompting. 'Shall I ring her, Dad?' And that's one more thing he won't have to worry about.

Which leaves Raymond. And by now, having gone some way to taming his other fears, Harry no longer balks at the prospect of telling his brother. 'I'm so sorry, Raymond. Beti died this afternoon.' And leave it at that. 'I can't speak now, Raymond … I'll phone again, once the arrangements have been made.' He'll listen to the silence at the other end of the phone, then draw the conversation to a polite but swift close. He is not required to elaborate any further, not for Raymond's benefit.

The piece of paper that bore Raymond's name has already been folded in four and deposited in the recycling bin, along with the pizza flyer and old copies of the *Gazette*.

63

Saturday, 22 May, 7.30 pm

Harry shaves, takes a shower, then stands in front of the bathroom mirror to examine the stiff little hair that is sprouting under his nose. He is puzzled at how this has resisted the blade of his razor. He tries to grip it between thumb and forefinger, but fails. His nails are too short. The hair, too, is short: only its incongruous hardness makes it feel big. Harry turns and looks at Beti's toilet bag, where the tweezers live. He used the tweezers last time, with success, but the pinching and poking left a big red blotch on his skin which was more unsightly than the hair. 'What the hell have you done to your face, Harry? Been in a fight?' And what man confesses to having had an accident with the tweezers? He turns back to the mirror and has another go, pulls the skin tight, grabs and plucks in one swift action, as though trying to take the hair by surprise. And fails.

Harry is rummaging for the tweezers when he hears the telephone. He counts the rings. Three ... Four ... Five ... It stops, then starts up again. 'Emma.' The ringing continues as Harry descends the stairs and sees, through the glass in the front door, a police car pulling up outside the house. The ringing stops and starts once more as the policeman knocks on the door. And although Harry is not yet at liberty to speak to Emma – he must phone the doctor first – he is glad that his daughter has a stubborn streak, is prepared to stand by the phone for a good long time, waiting for someone to pick up. The persistent but unanswered ringing is a sure sign to the policeman that no one is at home. There's another knock. The policeman looks through the letter box. But by now Harry is standing in the study, amongst his books and papers, invisible to all.

Ten minutes pass. The telephone rings. It may be Emma again. Harry looks at his watch. It's a quarter past eight. So he thinks, No, it's not Emma. They're missing me at the dinner. It's Bill Seymour. The dinner started three quarters of an hour ago, the guests have all taken their seats, they've noticed the two gaps at the table. 'Where's Harry and Beti, then? Haven't they arrived yet?' So, it's Bill on the phone, trying to find out what's happened to them. He'll be cursing that blasted Harry Selwyn for being so unreliable. Who else will he get tonight, to entertain the guests? Damn and blast him.

The telephone stops ringing.

Had he the time, Harry thinks, he might well sit down at the kitchen table and write out the explanation – the apology – that he will, in due course, be obliged to offer Bill Seymour, when matters are clarified. But he doesn't have the time.

At nine o'clock Harry pokes his head around the study door. It's already quite dark in the passage but he dare not put the light on in case the policeman returns, or else – and the thought makes him shiver – he is still there, outside, in the shadows, waiting for him to make a false move. He steals another glance but sees only the familiar things: the green of the hedge, the street lamp, the red bricks of the houses opposite. He creeps out of the study, crouching low, and climbs the stairs.

Harry opens his bedroom door. He's glad that the curtains are already drawn and that their material is heavy and thick, an effective barrier against the world's prurience. As he takes the trousers from the back of the chair, he holds his left hand up against the side of his face. By now, even a glimpse of his wife's form would be intolerable. He hangs the trousers over his left arm and turns to leave, now using his right hand to shield his eyes. He shuts the door behind him, then must pause for a while because, without realising it, he has done all of these things without taking breath. He goes to the spare bedroom and puts on his running clothes, the same clothes he took off less than two hours ago to have a shower. He does so reluctantly: his legs are tired and sore after running in the Bryn Coch Benefit Run, and his newly washed body has an instinctive aversion to wearing clothes that carry the smell of his sweat, the residue of the day's dust. He picks up his trousers again, makes his way downstairs and out into the lean-to. He scans the two rows of running shoes. This time, instead of the New Balance RX Terrain, he chooses the Asics GT. These are black, except for two grey stripes on the side, and, to Harry's mind, are less likely to draw attention. He goes to the kitchen, takes a packet of Ibuprofen 400 from the cupboard and swallows two tablets with a glass of water.

It's half past nine. Harry's kitchen is dimly illuminated by the light from next door, where Bob and Brenda Isles are having a late supper with friends. Harry sees Bob bend over the stove, stir the food with a spoon, then turn, smile and say something to his guests. Harry lets his gaze linger long enough to envy the inconsequential banter. He opens the drawer by the sink and takes out a handful of bags. He discards the plastic David Lewis bag, then considers the others: an assortment of supermarket carriers and plain brown paper bags from the farmers' market. He chooses one of the latter, makes sure it is clean inside, then puts in the trousers. He stuffs the other bags back into the drawer, then glances through the kitchen window. Bob is discussing something with his wife. They are immersed in their own affairs. They have no interest in their neighbour or his movements. Harry draws comfort from this knowledge. Nevertheless, before he opens the French windows, he grabs a rubbish bag, to demonstrate to anyone who might be watching that this is his true purpose. He is disposing of the household refuse. And what if he is wearing a tracksuit? Wasn't he running over in Bryn Coch today? Isn't that what you'd expect of Harry Selwyn?

Harry is standing next to the wooden door at the bottom of

the garden, looking at the dahlias and the roses. The roses have blossomed early this year, in the mild spring: the highest of them, which have already grown some two feet above the fence, are silhouetted against the dim glow of the night sky. Virginia Creeper covers half of the back wall. The green leaves of some shrub whose name Harry can't remember spill over the border onto the path by his feet. He wonders whether he should attend to these. Tie them back, perhaps. Or thin them out. He's sure that the foxgloves will shortly need canes because they, too, are beginning to bend under the weight of their blooms.

Harry does not normally concern himself with the garden, safe in the knowledge that Beti will adjudicate such matters, take the necessary steps. But Beti isn't here and he will, sooner or later, have to consult someone else. Who? Bob and Brenda next door? Emma? Amy? Raymond? Raymond would certainly be best. He's the only real gardener amongst them. And if he asks Raymond he'll need to write the answers down, every word, so he doesn't have to ask again.

Harry shuts the garden door behind him and leans the rubbish bag against the wall in the back lane. Then, holding the brown paper bag in his right hand, he starts running.

The moon has waned almost to its last quarter. It rides high over to Harry's left. Venus shimmers dimly below.

Running by the light of the moon and the stars has been part of Harry's routine since he first worked as a teacher. In the dead of winter, when darkness fell at four or five o'clock, he would return home, change into his kit and set off, without pause, into the chill night air. His freedom was somewhat constrained: he had to keep to the main paths, for fear of tripping over a root or some other unseen obstacle, and the experience was a more solitary one than he would normally have sought. Nevertheless, he derived intense pleasure from these evening excursions. He enjoyed in particular the feeling – the conviction – that he could run faster in the dark. On occasion, he ran so fast that his feet scarcely seemed to touch the ground, and he would have to rein himself in, certain that if he ran any faster he would rise straight up into the air and find himself flying with the birds. He had no idea how this could be. Nor did he care. The thrill was sufficient.

Harry enters the park. He knows now, of course, that this feeling is merely a trick of the darkness, and that the trick has a name: motion parallax. In daylight, when a runner sees things both near and far – the summit of the Wenallt, for example, the roof of the church beyond the trees, the new houses on the far side of the river – every step is slow, heavy, infinitesimally small. At night, when he can see little but the path, coursing under his feet, he becomes a shooting star. It is a trick of the dark. But only in his mind does Harry acknowledge this fact. In his body, nothing has changed. The thrill is the same.

On reaching the flower borders where he saw the men working yesterday, Harry transfers the bag from his right hand to his left. He makes a mental picture of the front entrance to the David Lewis store, and more particularly the letter box which must, he's certain, be close by, on one side or the other. But he fails. He can see, in the mind's mirror, an outline of the exit he came through yesterday, but this is a view from inside only. He tries to piece together a picture of the adjacent shops and their own letter boxes, but in vain. In the end, he must remain content in the knowledge that, whether he can visualise them or not, such letterboxes must exist: otherwise, how would these shops receive their mail? They must be quite substantial, too, to accommodate the catalogues and books and other bulky items that companies – as Harry imagines – must be constantly sending each other. David Lewis's letter box must be especially capacious because it's the biggest shop in town. And that is all to the good. It will, he's certain, be quite adequate to receive his modest package. He takes the bag in both hands, pats down the bulge at one end, where the paper has been stiffened, feels how thin and pliable are the trousers within. Good God, he thinks, it's small enough to go through the letter box at home. And he's content.

Harry reaches the footbridge over the river. That's a mile done, he thinks. Another mile and I'll be in town. Part of him regrets running quite so fast. This means the pleasure will cease all the sooner. He also regrets not wearing his watch before leaving the house: despite everything he knows about motion parallax, about the effect on a man's eyes of things far and near, he is convinced that he has run that first mile between the house and the footbridge more quickly than the last time. When was the last time? Well, yesterday, of course. He went for a jog in the park. He's sure he's run much faster than yesterday. On further reflection he's fairly certain, too, that he's run faster than this morning, up at Bryn Coch, even though that was a race, and time was of the essence. It can't be proved, but that's what his legs tell him.

Harry reminds himself that this isn't a race. There's no one else running, so how can it be? And he isn't in a hurry. On the contrary. He might take a whole hour to run the second mile and it would count for nothing: he needs only to reach the middle of town before the pubs and clubs close. Putting a package through the door of one of the big stores might be regarded with suspicion, at that time of night, amongst the drunks and the revellers, when the police are on the look-out, eyes peeled for miscreants.

So, not a race. But more than a jog. He's run the first mile faster than he did yesterday, and feels none the worse for it. Now he wants to see if he can do as well over the second mile. And perhaps, by now, he isn't sure how to slow down. That's the effect of running under the moon: the feet barely touch the path, and it's a hell of a job putting on the brake once the feet have lost contact with the ground.

In fact, by now, Harry isn't certain where his feet are: somewhere near his head, must be, because he can see the GT, big and bold, on the side of his Asics running shoes. And isn't it odd, Harry thinks, that the lightness in the head should come so early, before he's even got his second wind? Odd, too, that this lightness has such an unpleasant taste, a bitterness that fills the nose and the mouth and the throat, and then the whole head, as though that bitterness *is* the whole head. For a few seconds, Harry could swear that he's tripped and fallen, that the fall somehow continues, has no bottom to it, no up nor down, his hands reaching for his feet, his feet off somewhere else, he's no idea where. He knows none of this is likely. Whatever else might be said of him, Harry Selwyn always keeps his feet. Whether in the mud, or on icy paths, or on steep, shifting screes, his balance is never compromised.

After a while, the bitter taste recedes and Harry is content to accept this new sensation as merely a variant on the slight vertigo he has always felt when running at night. After all, what is falling but flying in reverse? Like a swallow catching midges, swooping, soaring, diving. This is how Harry sees himself.

Then, as he crosses the footbridge and hears the flow of water beneath him, Harry notices a man running on the other side of the river. The man hasn't crossed the bridge, of that he's certain: he would have seen the white shirt, heard the feet stamping the timbers. No, he must have come from another direction: from town, perhaps, or the new houses, or somewhere down the Bay. Come for a jog, and here he is, on his way back home.

At first, Harry is surprised at this – that someone else should choose to run in the dark at the same time as himself – and thinks, What are you about, my friend? What is your true purpose here? But then he is forced to acknowledge that he knows nothing about what happens in these parts at this hour. Perhaps running in the dead of night is all the rage, is the very badge of the dedicated athlete.

And there's no doubt about it, this man is a dedicated athlete. That much is clear from his technique, the way he keeps his feet close to the ground, takes short, swift steps, his body and head remaining steady all the while, as steady as though the runner himself were merely a spectator, standing motionless in the crowd, watching his own performance, so steady that you might think the body and the head were mounted, not on legs, but on wheels.

A youngster, too. Although Harry can see little of the runner but his shirt and shoes, his youth is self-evident. This young man, whoever he may be, is still ascending life's incline: a man is more abstemious with his energy, his breath, once he hits the downward slope. A paradox this – that the down should be more demanding than the up – but the metaphor is an imperfect one. In any case, Harry must accelerate a little to keep him in sight. This becomes difficult, however, because the path twists and turns and the shirt disappears repeatedly behind some hedge or clump of trees. And there are so many paths in this part of the park, more than he has ever realised, and there's no telling which he will take.

Then, without warning, the young man gathers speed and Harry, trying to keep up, loses his rhythm. And if some other runner were to hand – someone less impetuous, certainly someone older – he would be quite happy to leave this new companion to his own devices, for what is the point of a pacemaker who constantly changes speed? And a man cannot afford to be profligate with his breath, not at this time of night, at this stage in the proceedings. There is, after all, only so much breath to go around. But there is no one else. This rabbit will have to do. Harry must breathe harder. He must open his mouth wide, steal the air from the trees.

The young runner has heard Harry coming up behind him. There's no other explanation. He's had a shock, too, perhaps, just like Harry, at seeing someone else out running at such a late hour. Who are you? he's thinking. What is your business? And that, no doubt, is why he turns his head and looks over his shoulder: he needs to see what kind of fellow this is, dogging his footsteps. Harry isn't sure whether it's the stamp of his feet that has caught the young man's attention, or else the sound of his breath. One way or another, he's heard something, so he turns his head. Then, in a friendly but mischievous voice, he says, 'You can't beat me.' And turns away before Harry can get a closer look. The voice is familiar. If only he could see the face, he's sure he would remember the name. One of the Harriers, most likely. Young, but seasoned. And even in the park's half-light, the shadows closing in on all sides, he would surely see enough to recognise him, and then to say, 'Ah! Fancy that ...'

The young runner is now only a few yards ahead of Harry. Is it Harry who's had his second wind? Or has his new companion slowed down? It's difficult to say. The yards change to feet, the feet to inches, until they are shoulder-to-shoulder. The young man turns again and smiles. Yes, it is a familiar face. Harry knows him well, although at the moment he can't quite remember how or where. He isn't one of the Harriers after all. Might he belong to another club? It's possible. 'Don't stare, Harry! Don't stare!' Staring at people is rude, even when you know them, even when it's your Mam or your Dad.

Harry's pleasantly surprised when he hears the man start to whistle. It's difficult to whistle and run at the same time. To do it properly you need to whistle on both the exhalation and the inhalation, otherwise the line fractures, becomes a cheap parody of itself. And how can such a thing be possible? Yet that is exactly what he is doing. The tune flows seamlessly, melifluously, as though the young runner were not breathing at all. Harry recognises the song. *In the Still of the Night.* It is a strikingly apt song, too, given the tranquillity of the park, without a sound from town, even though its Saturday tumult is less than half a mile away. No cars. No sirens. Not even any birds. They must all be asleep in their nests by now, Harry thinks. And he's no idea how he can possibly win against someone who runs and whistles at the same time. But that's what he's doing, there's no doubt about it. The young man is now far, far behind so that when Harry turns and looks over his shoulder he is only a white speck on the horizon, his whistle beyond hearing.

Harry slows down, breathes more gently, regains his composure. Anxious that he mustn't lose concentration again at this, the eleventh hour, he tightens his grip on the bag. He's surprised then that the material of the trousers inside feels harder, that the bag is bigger than it was and much, much heavier, so heavy that Harry must stop in his tracks there and then and put it on the ground. And this is highly irregular: Harry never needs to take a break in the middle of a race, let alone a leisurely evening jog in the park.

He looks over his shoulder. There's no sign of the white shirt. The young runner must have taken a different path. Gone home, perhaps. To the new houses, or down the Bay. This is what Harry thinks. He looks at the bag on the ground and remembers, with a jolt, that this isn't a leisurely jog. How can it be? Who would go for a jog weighed down by such a heavy burden? He regrets not bringing his rucksack. He could have slung this on his back, like he used to. Tighten the straps. Get the balance right. Wait for the second wind. The second wind never lets you down.

'This what you're looking for, Harry?'

And how nice that man is, the one in the white shirt, he's gone all the way home to fetch a rucksack, a big one too, just like Harry used to have, with the two stripes and the brass buckles and none of the frills and fripperies you get nowadays.

'There you are, Harry. Put your things in here.'

And that's all I had to do was take my trousers out of the brown paper bag and put them in the rucksack. Job done, I thought, because it wasn't far now. And it would be a lot easier on the way back, without all that weight. That's what you've got to remember. It's always harder on the way out. You need your second wind, and that takes time. Easier coming back, then. Guaranteed. Everything's in step on the home run.

So that's all I had to do. Take my trousers out of the paper bag and put them in the rucksack. Job done. That's what I thought. But I couldn't understand why the bag was so heavy.

How could trousers be so heavy? And so hard? Is that why they call them herringbone? Because that's how they go after you've worn them? Like fish bones? Can't abide bones. Get stuck in your teeth. Beti, too. She's the same. Can't abide them.

I bent down and opened the bag. Trousers nowhere to be seen. So thrust my hand in, felt about. Had the shock of my life then when somebody grabbed it, took a hold, like he wanted to say a quick howdy-do. Or maybe pull me into the bag with him. And another chap then, just the same. Grabbed my hand, quick howdy-do. And another. I could see his fingers sticking out of the bag, waiting his turn. Like little twigs. But that's what was odd, they were all white. Pink, I mean, not white. But odd, anyway. I was sure they'd be black. Can a black hand turn white? Is that what happens when a hand grows old? Does it lose its colour? Now there's a question for you. I need to think a bit more about that one. I was at it for a good while then, pulling them out, popping them into the rucksack, thinking, When's this going to end? Pulling them out one by one as well, by the thumbs, realising too late it would have been better to get hold of the bottom of the bag and just tip them all out, the whole job lot, get it over and done with.

The rucksack was full then, which was a bugger, because there were still hands left in the brown paper bag. And even though it was only an ordinary bag from the farmers' market it didn't have any bottom to it. So I had to go home then and sit down by the kitchen table and wait for the man to come back. Do you remember him? The man in the white shirt? He'll have finished his race by now. And I thought, maybe he'll bring a bigger rucksack next time. Hope so, anyway.

And Sam Appleby said, 'Do you think he'll come back,

Harry?' Sam was there too, sitting at the kitchen table. Made himself a cup of tea while I was out running.

'Who?' I said.

'The man in the white shirt, of course. The one who was whistling.'

Sam Appleby, of all people. Came when I was out running and made himself at home. How he got in I haven't a clue. He's got no right. Raymond and Beti were there as well, at the other end of the table. Sam had made them a cuppa. Odd I hadn't noticed. The eyes, probably. Took time to get accustomed. I was glad Beti had got up. Pretty chipper, too. And eyeing Raymond in that way she has, looking down and looking up at the same time. But Raymond just shook his head. Folded his arms and shook his head. Like a sulky child. That was odd as well. Raymond was always such a good-natured child.

'Yes, Sam,' I said. 'He'll bring a bigger rucksack next time. You see if he doesn't.'

And I sat there for a while. By the kitchen table. Counting the beats. Waiting for the second wind.